Readers love *Haffling*!

"I thoroughly enjoyed this dark and colorful adventure. *Haffling* really captured the essence of a modern fairy-tale, but it was so much more than that."
—Fabulous Fictions

"*Haffling* is a truly fantastic story that captures the age category very well on top of a wicked story."
—Rarely Dusty Books

"I was really enthralled by this novel... aside from being fast paced and full of turn of events, it was also really funny, not a 'light' funny, but more a subtle irony which was probably the author's voice, clever and loud."
—Elisa Rolle's Reviews and Ramblings

"...I think [Alex's] life situation emphasizes the precarious lives of a lot of LGBTQ youth, who often are not served well by an uncaring bureaucracy, and thus more likely to be homeless, and therefore living under the poverty line."
—Lambda Literary

"Readers who enjoy young adult urban fantasy will have a ball with this action story and ride a pooka horse along with the adventurers. Caleb James has combined a lot of imagery into quite a scary full-length story."
—Fresh Fiction

"I had a blast!! ...if you are looking for fantasy, action, with a side of romance which features a gay protagonist, I'd say give this one a try."
—Boys in Our Books

By CALEB JAMES

Dark Blood

THE HAFFLING
Haffling
Exile

Published by DSP PUBLICATIONS
www.dsppublications.com

Exile

CALEB JAMES

DSP PUBLICATIONS

Published by
DSP Publications

5032 Capital Circle SW, Suite 2, PMB# 279, Tallahassee, FL 32305-7886 USA
www.dsppublications.com

Exile

Cover Art
www.alanmclark.com
Cover Design
http://www.paulrichmondstudio.com
Cover content is for illustrative purposes only and any person depicted on the cover is a model.
Author Photo by Bobby Miller.

ISBN: 978-1-63533-260-5
Digital ISBN: 978-1-63533-261-2
Library of Congress Control Number: 2016914515
Published January 2017
v. 1.0

Printed in the United States of America
(∞)
This paper meets the requirements of
ANSI/NISO Z39.48-1992 (Permanence of Paper).

"A terrible beauty is born."

W.B. Yeats

Exile

Prologue

Spring 2016

TETHERED BY a magic collar and trapped in the suffocating Mist, the great white salamander raged. Her thoughts, a jumble of midnight-blue taffeta gowns, an adoring audience, a black-haired boy with green eyes, and an enchanted frog, caused the serpent's fury to spark… literally. In its prison of swirling blue and gray lay piles of charred bones and scorched remnants of winged creatures, unfortunate gnomes, trolls, and meaty ogres drawn by the fragrant lure of her fairy fire.

Words formed in the beast's head, single syllables: *eat, kill, mine, mine, mine*. A spark turned to a flame in the worm's gut. Her powerful jaws chomped through the femur of a fresh-killed troll and the blood-slick humerus of an ogre. Like cracking lobster tails, her tongue scooped out marrow and slurped down the tender morsels.

She growled and chewed. Bones shattered. Ogre and troll shards tumbled down throat and gullet and landed in her belly. She thrashed, mixing the fire in her gut with magic, both that which was hers and that which she stole. *More, more, more. Satin, hunger, party dress, more, more, more.*

As the troll's and the ogre's meager magic separated from bone and blood, an idea sparked in her tortured brain. An image, a girl with blonde hair and blue eyes. Haffling. One of three.

She reared back, balancing on tail and hind limbs too small for her body. She sniffed the poisonous Mist, her mind fixed on the image. The girl, not so little anymore, nearly a woman, nearly ready. The vision cleared, a child of the human realm. *Mine, mine, mine.* She bounced up and down, feeling the bones, the meat, and the marrow meld with fire. Like pebbles in a tumbler, she mixed them well. Chants from her childhood, snippets of songs, skittered through her thoughts.

Grind them into paste,
Mix your magic well,
Come and taste, come and taste,
Fairy fire from my magic well.

She convulsed and coughed, once… twice. She drew up to her full height. Then like a cat hacking a fur ball, she spat out a missile of white-hot flame. The murderous projectile, which smelled of caramel and gooey troll house cookies fresh from the oven, arced high. Her ruby-red eyes watched as it sparked and burned through the Mist. Hope blossomed as it flew. *Please, please, please. Come and taste my fairy fire.* The Mist crackled as the projectile pierced the membrane that separated worlds and vanished from sight.

She smelled fear, death, and cookies. She purred and settled back. Exhausted, she hummed and drifted into a dream. *Come and taste my fairy fire, come and taste it soon.*

One

LIAM SUMMER awoke naked in a strange room filled with smoke and heat. "No!" The smell, like poison cookies fresh from the oven, filled his mouth with saliva and his gut with fear. *Fairy fire!* He coughed as it burned his lungs. "No." He cowered on the hot floor. *She found me. She knows. She knows what I did.... I'm going to die. I am not sorry.*

Smoke hissed up from the slatted wood floor as he scrambled on hands and bare knees in the dark. Through tearing eyes he caught pulsing red and white lights against the walls. They lit the strange space and revealed bare walls, stacked lumber, and tools scattered across a counter.

He crawled toward a blackened window. His hands brushed splintered wood and nails. *Where am I? Why am I naked? I am going to die.*

His head bumped against a wall. He braced against its solid surface and crawled toward the flashes of light. The smoke, so thick, made it hard to breathe. *Not a dream. I don't know this place, a dungeon... a place of death.* The sweet reek of fairy fire was everywhere. *It's her. She's come to kill me.* He knew the uses of his queen's double-edged poison.

Fairy fire and what came after—fairy dust—were both cheese for the mouse and the deathtrap. *She's here. She'll kill me.*

HE STOOD on shaking legs, his hands against the wall. Through a crack in a window painted black, he stared at a strange world. Yet he knew its name. *The See. How did I get here?*

On the ground, stories below, giant metal dragons flashed with red, white, yellow, and blue lights. They screamed like banshees in the night.

The floor burned his naked feet. *How did I get here?* Unable to remember. One moment asleep in the cave he'd called home since.... *She is here... she will kill me... is killing me. This is an oven; she will cook me and eat me....* He pictured his mother and father, Ileana and Cullen, who'd given their lives to save his. *All for nothing. Mother... Father... I am sorry.*

Questions that no longer mattered had been answered. Queen May, who had stolen a haffling boy—Alex Nevus—and vanished from the Unsee to the See with deranged plans of multiworld domination, was alive. *She's killing me. She knows.... She knows I helped him.*

Those last days in Fey had been a frightening blur. The Mist had gone rampant, swallowing villages in a single breeze. He, like so many others, had sought escape as families and fields disappeared beneath its foggy terror.

While life under tyrannical Queen May had been perilous, her disappearance had triggered the worst incursions of the Mist in memory. If he wasn't about to die in a burning building in a strange land, he would have wondered at the connection. Her magic held it back.

His feet blistered, and he choked on the smell of his burning flesh. He pressed against the wall, wondering when she'd appear. Would she roast him to death and then pick at his bones or have a royal chef dress him in a sauce of honey and cream? Or would she do what he'd been forced to witness as a small child with his parents... slit him open from chin to navel and with dainty hands rip out and eat his heart and his liver?

Once her servant—more a slave, if he were honest—Liam knew Queen May better than most. He knew her secrets and the face she did not show. He'd seen what became of the unfortunate souls she butchered. Her murders were neither random nor capricious. Queen May's magic was fed—literally—by the life force of every fairy, sprite, and elf she murdered. When he'd been her fair-haired boy, he'd watched her gloat, her lovely face flushed with stolen power.

I don't want to die. His betrayal, his aid to the haffling boy she'd ordered him to seduce, had been discovered. It was treason. It would be punished.

Snippets from the last days in Fey flew through his mind. Her disappearance, the ravaging Mist... something exploded.

Backed against the wall, he braced one foot on the burning floor and shifted his weight to the other. There'd been a sound, like a tree limb cracking only thousands of times louder. It had ripped the Mist, or more exactly torn a hole, maybe more than one. Like a tunnel, like something he'd seen before.

The tunnel. I fell... was pulled... into this house on fire. Well done, Liam. Out of May's frying pan and into her fairy fire. I have to get out! There has to be a way.

Choking on the delicious smoke, his heart raced. He searched for escape. He climbed into a tub in front of the blackened window. The inside was littered with tools; his feet slipped on sawdust and porcelain. He grabbed something half wood and half metal. He smashed the window.

It was a mistake. The influx of oxygen fueled the fire, and where before it had just been smoke, red and blue flames pierced the floor. Through shattered glass he looked out on the human world, with its flashing lights, sirens, streets of liquid black, and buildings far taller than anything in the Unsee.

The cool night air, like a cruel joke, tickled his face as he sought for his own magic. It would not come. He tried to quiet the terror in his heart, to steady his pulse. *I have no magic!* Since before he could walk, Liam could ride the wind. He felt for the rhythm of this strange world, for the moment when air would mix into the fabric of his flesh and carry him aloft, carry him from this prison on fire. He panicked. *I have no magic. I cannot fly.*

The porcelain of the cast-iron tub grew hot, like a pot set to boil. He felt the air and the smoke, but his body would not obey his will. *It's gone! My magic is gone.* "Stay calm." *Try harder.* But he knew, as all creatures of the fey are taught, travel between the worlds comes at a cost. *I have no magic here.*

He startled as someone banged on the door. An inhuman voice growled, "FDNY. I'm here to get you out. Please, open the door."

Frozen with fear, Liam thought to jump out the sixth-story window. It would be certain death.

A crash came against the door that stood between him and whatever terror May had sent to kill him.

An ax ripped through the wood, once, twice. Liam stared across the floor on fire as steel tore away the door. With each blow, more of the murderous weapon slashed through.

He had but seconds. No magic. He looked out the window at a world of metal dragons and humans who gaped up at him. They pointed and held small black rectangles in front of their faces, all trained on him. Liam clutched the tool with which he'd smashed the window. It was puny compared to the ax that any moment now would reveal its wielder and Queen May's assassin. *It's too far to jump. Certain death… but a death of your choosing, not of hers. I don't want to die.* He spoke aloud. "Then fight, Liam. For once in your life, fight. For once in your pathetic life… fight!"

The hinges of the door ripped. Liam turned from the window to face his death. A clarity washed over him. He stood firm as the door's upper hinge separated from the frame by a powerful blow. It hung for an instant and then crashed to the flaming floor.

The impact caused Liam to slip and fall. The tub burned hot, and still clutching his weapon, he spotted the monster sent to kill him. Sweat poured down his legs and back, and he stared at the hulking ax-wielding creature dressed in black with bands of yellow, like a honeybee, around the tops of his boots and on the sleeves of his jacket. The giant, with his single glinting eye and strangely shaped head, straddled the doorway. All pretense of bravery gone, Liam curled up tight and tried to vanish in the depths of the burning tub.

An ogre with an ax… this is how I end. He wanted to stand, to face his death with honor, as his mother and father had faced theirs. But the heat of the tub and the sweat that poured from fear and fire made the porcelain too slick. So clutching knees to chest, he waited for the ax-wielding assassin. He waited for death.

Two

As FDNY firefighter Charlie Fitzgerald straddled the burned-out hole in front of the sixth-floor walk-up, he was all business. This was no time to stop and think what a bad and weird call this had been, from pulling up to the smell of a burning bakery to basketball-size holes burned through the floors. He knew someone was trapped in this north-facing unit, and when a portion of the hall two stories below had caved over the stairwell, he also knew that he, and God willing whoever was in here, would not leave the way he'd come in. He banged his gloved hand on the door, and with a voice like Darth Vader through the respirator of his self-contained breathing device, he shouted, "FDNY. I'm here to get you out. Please open the door."

No answer.

He unbuckled his ax and whaled at the door. He cursed the old construction and dense oak, at least not as bad as the solid steel security doors where you had to separate the frame from the wall to get through. He swung the four-pound steel-head ax in smooth, looping blows. Sweat from the heat and exertion trickled from the hair on his head to his insulated rubber boots. Condensation fogged his mask, only to be pulled away by the negative pressure of his respirator.

They'd spotted someone in the window of this unit, an apartment that didn't currently have a fire escape. The guy... maybe more than one, might already be dead, based on what Charlie heard through the wireless feed in his helmet. This was the hot side of the fire. He readjusted his stance to avoid the weird crater, like something had burned through this floor and the floors above and the floors below.

What the hell caused that? Worse still, the holes acted like a chimney for whatever had burned through.

A fire marshal—possibly his friend Finn—would figure that out later.

He flipped the ax to the pick side and, with three blows, tore a melon-size opening in the wood. He felt the inrush of air against his back and knew he had seconds to get through, get the guy and whoever else was in there, and get the fuck out of Dodge. Oxygen fueled the fire, and between the hole in the door and the shattered window in the apartment, he'd just created another chimney.

As the pick ripped at the opening, the hinges started to tear from the frame. *Great.* Holstering the ax, he stared down at the hole, big enough to swallow a child or catch his boot. *What the fuck caused that?*

Careful to avoid a fall—*A dead hero is no hero at all*—he kicked at the bottom hinge once, twice, and on the third smash, the hinge popped free. The door, pulled by the inrush of heat and air, hung for a second and then crashed onto the floor, spiked with blue-and-orange flames like jets on a gas grill.

Charlie stepped onto the door. He felt sick inside, knowing the chances of finding someone alive in here were bad. *Don't let it be a kid.* His voice growled through the respirator. "Anyone in here? I'm here to get you out."

No answer. He took in the open room, probably a kitchen, but like a lot of the old tenements, the bathtub was in the kitchen, with a bedroom on either side. Only this was a construction site, with bare studs, Sheetrock stacked against a wall, a table made of planks, two metal horses, and a table saw. It looked deserted. *Is this the wrong fucking apartment?* "Crap!" He wondered how much time he had before the floor would give out and how many more doors he'd have to get through. He was about to head to the unit next door, trying not to be pissed at Kyle Schmidt, his station mate and friend from probie school, who'd guided him over the wireless to this apartment.

He heard a noise, stopped, and turned to the shattered window. "Who's there? I'm here to help. I'm here to get you out of here." It had come from the bathtub.

Praying the fire hadn't charcoaled the floor joists, he stepped off the door and crossed to the tub in front of the shattered window. His boots crunched on piles of sawdust, which sparked and ignited with a pumpkin glow.

As his sightlines cleared the tub's edge, he caught the sight of bare skin. A man huddled in on himself, clutching his knees, his face obscured, just a head of long blond hair tucked to his chest.

Charlie froze. He'd seen death come in this shape, a last desperate effort to hide from the heat and flame, people curled up, animals curled up, and that's how they died. *Don't let me be too late.*

"Guy, I'm here to get you out of here." He reached a thickly gloved hand to the man's shoulder. "You okay?"

The man startled and backed to the far edge of the tub. "Stay away! Stay away!" He brandished a screwdriver. "Don't come near…." He choked on the smoke and coughed. "Stay…." He doubled over.

"It's okay," Charlie said, holding up his hands. "Calm down. I'm here to help. We got to get you out of here." Charlie had seen this before, usually with kids and, sadly, with pets, who would run terrified from the firefighters and later be found dead in the attic, having succumbed to smoke inhalation. *He's freaking out…. He's fucking beautiful.* "Guy—" He lifted the face shield of his helmet. That sometimes helped with kids, made him look less like a nightmare. "We've got to get out of here."

The man, who had to be about his age, in his early twenties, with matted blond hair that glinted gold from the reflected flashers on the streets and the shoots of fire that surrounded them, met Charlie's gaze.

Even in the dim light, Charlie marveled at the color of his eyes— purple. *Guy's naked in an abandoned apartment, wearing colored contacts. Stop staring at him, Charlie.* "Come on. Can you stand?" *Is he totally naked? Shit!* He averted his eyes. *Don't be a perv.*

The blond shook his head and pressed back against the now burning-hot porcelain. Tears streamed down his face. "I'm going to die here."

"The hell you are." Charlie tore his gaze from the beautiful man to the task ahead. "Cover your face." And using the ax, he smashed the remaining shards of the window. He raised a hand to guide the cherry picker from his station's hook and ladder that was headed toward them.

"What's your name?" he asked and looked down at the blond, who instead of hiding his face was staring at him. His voice caught and his throat tightened as he looked into violet eyes. *Don't stare at him, Charlie.*

Look away. It didn't help that, even covered in soot and sawdust, *He's perfect.* Like someone out of an underwear ad, only… no underwear. "I'm Charlie, Charlie Fitzgerald, and there's a ladder coming. If you can't stand, I can carry you."

"I can try."

Charlie reached a hand toward Naked Guy. He saw terror in those beautiful eyes. "I'm not going to hurt you. You got to believe that."

Naked Guy nodded, but the fear remained. He edged back against the tub, in obvious pain from the heat. As his bare feet found purchase, he winced.

"It's too hot," Charlie said. "I got you." Not waiting for a response, he lowered his shoulder, wrapped an arm around Naked Guy's middle, and hoisted him over his back. "I got you. Just stay loose." And like he'd do with kids and old folk and even the occasional full-grown man, he talked nonsense. "I've never dropped anyone. We've got a cherry picker coming for us. They're kind of fun, like a carnival ride but safe. I'm not letting go. You know, you never told me your name." He paused. *Please tell me your name.* There was silence. *Please.*

"Liam."

"Okay, Liam." *Even his name is beautiful.* He felt his arm tighten, but not too tight, around Liam's naked body. His throat and mouth were dry, and not from the heat—at least, not from the heat of the fire. The cherry picker's broad basket bumped against the building. Inside, Gerry Callahan tossed out window anchors attached to bright yellow webbing.

"Charlie boy, can you clear the frame?"

Charlie gauged the opening. He heard a crash floors below. It would take little more than a minute or two to rip the window frame from the building. He wasn't going to risk it. He also calculated the other piece—that with ninety pounds of gear and a guy who looked a hair under six feet and weighed about 160, one tiny misstep and…. "We're good."

"How many you got?"

"Just one," Charlie yelled back, and then to Liam, "Was anyone else in here with you?" He knew if there was, they were no longer among the living.

"No." Liam's voice trembled.

"Okay, then. We're going out the window."

"I can't fly here."

"Neither can I," Charlie replied, wondering if Liam had made a joke, in which case it was the most deadpan one he'd ever heard. "It's called a cherry picker." And he turned enough so Liam could see the metal basket that could safely hold four. He felt Liam's body tense. Which, considering they were about to step out of a sixth-floor window, wasn't abnormal. "Liam, I do this all the time. All I need you to do is stay loose and hang on to me. Can you do that?"

"I can, Charlie Fitzgerald. Wait!"

"What?"

"Something's in the door."

Charlie turned and looked back into the burning apartment. At first he didn't see it, and then a terrified little short-haired Chihuahua, its eyes wide, stared at them from the wrong side of the flaming hole.

"Wait!" Liam shouted from over Charlie's back.

"Liam, you got to leave him," Charlie said, wondering if this were the guy's dog. But animals spooked, and no way was that little thing about to jump over a hole twice its size and run through a room on fire.

Liam squirmed on Charlie's back.

"Guy…. Liam, you got to stay still. We got to get out of here now!" He tried to see what Liam was doing, but the helmet and thick protective collar of his turnout coat limited his range of motion. What he did see reflected in the helmet's plastic visor…. *What the hell?* Liam was staring at the frightened dog, his purple eyes intent and focused. And then the Chihuahua did the unbelievable. It backed up and then shot straight ahead. Its tiny legs leaped over the fiery hole, darted across the burning floor, and scrambled to get up into the tub.

Liam squirmed lower down Charlie's back as the firefighter did all he could to not lose hold of the sweat-slicked man and tried not to think about how hot—in the total perv way—the guy's naked body felt in his gloved hands and against his well-padded back.

"This is crazy."

"I got him," Liam said. "I got him!"

What just happened? And without words Charlie repositioned Liam so his weight was balanced over his shoulder. "Are we ready now?" he asked, blown away by what he'd just seen.

"Yes, Charlie Fitzgerald."

"Okay, then." Charlie felt his chest tighten at the sound of his name out of Liam's mouth. With his free hand, he gripped the edge of the window frame, then hoisted first one booted foot and then the other up onto the sill.

Callahan nodded from inside the basket. "We're good on my side."

"Hang tight, Liam."

And feeling every inch of Liam's naked body, plus a four-pound dog, against his, Charlie held tight and bridged the distance from a building on fire to safety.

Three

LIAM CLUTCHED the panting dog in the folds of the rough wool blanket he'd been given by the smiling woman seated before him. Dressed in her shiny red jacket with white crosses over her chest and on her back, she was filled with questions. Just like Charlie Fitzgerald, who'd left him with her and the others in red. Clearly they were a clan, but no obvious physical distinction defined them other than the red costumes, many of which included a matching cap. *Possibly an army.*

"What's your name?" She smiled at him, her hand poised over a paper clipped to a board.

"Is this where you live?"

He and the dog shivered despite the thick, scratchy wool. These were tricks and traps. That's what questions were. It was something every sentient fey child, regardless of species, was taught. The lesson was usually couched in the cautionary tale of the Questling, a creature purported to have once existed but was now extinct. *Curiosity killed the Questling. All these questions, and I have more than a few of my own.* But habit, fear, and the chaos of the building attacked by fairy fire made him hold his tongue.

"Do you have family… friends, you can stay with?"

Her smile stayed fixed, her expression expectant, as if he were fool enough to fall for her trap. *But Charlie Fitzgerald asked me questions, and he saved me from death. He asked for nothing in return… and he left me.* Liam shifted in the flimsy folding chair and looked across the street at the building, which no longer burned red but filled the street with dark smoke and the mouthwatering reek of fairy fire. The sirens had stopped, and behind bright orange plastic barriers, crowds flocked to gaze and drink in the smoke. *Perhaps it's like a bonfire to them.* Would they break into song and dance? Was this a ritual? It's one May would enjoy, burn a building, see who dies, and dance among the ashes… or worse. *I know what comes after fairy fire…. Do they?* The little dog peeked from the folds of the blanket and licked his chin. Its liquid round eyes fixed on his.

"I don't mean to be rude," Red Jacket Lady said, "but can you hear me?"

Liam turned his back to her, not able to tell which one of the men in black with bright yellow bands on their boots, jackets, helmets, and gloves was Charlie Fitzgerald. His eyes welled. *What kind of man goes into a burning building to save a stranger? Please be safe, Charlie Fitzgerald.* He looked back at Red Jacket Lady. Her face was pleasant and held no malice. There was a string around her neck that ended in a small plastic-covered rectangle with her picture on it… and words—Jenn Trainer.

"You are Jenn Trainer," he said.

She nodded. "Yes."

He felt the question about to leave her mouth and rushed in before she could speak. "I am Liam Summer. I have no family here." Although where exactly *here* might be, he did not know. Bits reminded him of the Unsee. Clearly this was a great city, the streets not covered with meadow grass but hard and black. Buildings were far taller here. He tried to think of what to say, and unlike the Questling, which prattled itself into the jaws of death, he chose silence.

"So, Liam Summer, I'm assuming this was your home. And your dog, he's cute. What's his name?"

And you'd assume wrong. This is not my home. This is not my dog.

He did not correct her, as a woman in a tight gray skirt suit and perfectly applied makeup pointed a metal wand at him. "That one there. The guy with the dog," she said to a man shouldering a large black metal box. At her command, he pointed the box's glass eye at Liam. With the wand in front of her and the glass eye trained on Liam, they approached.

"You poor thing," Makeup Lady said. "Was this your home? And what a cute dog."

Liam shivered as the Chihuahua ducked back into the blanket. Its tiny heart beat fast against his chest. Unlike red-jacket Jenn, this one had no name tag, and her face was perfect, like a mask without pores and too-red lips, like May's.

"What's your name, darling?" Makeup Lady turned to Jenn. "Is he deaf?"

"You might want to find someone else," Jenn said. "I think he's in shock."

Makeup Lady nodded and thrust her metal wand in front of Liam's face. "Do you know how the fire started?"

Liam shook his head, but the question was a good one. He wondered at the coincidence of his travel from the Unsee to the See and how he landed in a building on fire. He tried to remember—the tunnel, the mist… coming through—like a sliver of his memory had been ripped out.

Makeup Lady turned to the guy with the glass-eyed box. "Get some close-ups on his face. A guy who looks like that doesn't need to talk." She chuckled. "Probably better that way." She spoke to Jenn. "Did you at least get his name?"

Jenn looked at Liam.

"No," he said. "Don't give it to her."

"Okay, then," Makeup Lady said, displeased with the response. "Guess young, blond, and gorgeous wants to keep his mystery. Sal, did you get your shots?"

Liam realized that just as May constantly broadcast her image and her rapidly changing entertainment shows, the man with the box was recording this.

Makeup Lady asked red-jacket Jenn, "Do they know how many have been hurt? Any fatalities?"

Jenn shook her head. "No clue, but if you want to do us a favor"— she pulled a card from inside her jacket—"please post the information for donations. We're looking at three dozen families we're going to have to feed, clothe, and shelter."

"Got it," Makeup Lady said as she and her cameraman headed toward another woman in red, this one seated in front of a woman holding a baby, with a cat carrier at her feet. Beside her, an anxious dark-haired boy of four or five looked back at the fire, his face wet with tears.

"Sorry about that," Jenn said. She looked at her clipboard and then back at Liam. "You really have no place to go, do you?"

Liam's gaze caught on the little boy. He felt the dog against his chest, and he knew. "Wait a minute." He stood. His feet were raw and blistered from the fire, but he knew. Not caring how the blanket exposed his nakedness, he walked to the little boy. The dog peeked out.

"*Maxie!*" the boy shrieked and broke free from his mother as the dog wiggled out of Liam's arms and sprinted toward his family.

The woman with the baby and the cat carrier looked back as Makeup Lady with cameraman recorded it all.

Liam felt the loss of the little animal's beating heart. He nodded and wrapped his blanket tight. He looked at the little boy, the dog lapping at his tears. *So that's one good thing, Liam Summer. If anyone anywhere keeps track, that's one good thing.*

He shook his head and turned. His thoughts felt thick, from the smoke or the chaos. He needed to remember things, important details. *An explosion, a tunnel in the mist… a giant white lizard…. It looked at me. Something about it… its eyes, red, but blue for an instant… like hers, like May's. Not possible but connected. And fairy fire. This is her doing.*

A man and a woman in navy uniforms wheeled a stretcher toward him.

The man spoke. "We're making it down to the walking wounded. How you doing, guy?"

Liam looked into the man's kind face. His partner, clearly part of the same navy blue clan, had lustrous black hair. He wondered if she might be part pixie. Between them was a metal bed on wheels with a bright orange mattress and a shiny red metal box. Tucked beneath was a canister like the one Charlie had on his back. Only that one, which he'd clung to as Charlie carried him into the cherry picker, was gray and had the word SCOT. This one was small and green. *The colors mean things. Jenn in red and white, these two in dark blue, Charlie and his band of bumblebee men with funny hats who save people from fire… from fairy fire.*

"I think he's in shock," the woman said.

"How bad you hurt?" Navy Guy asked.

Liam felt the itch of the wool on his skin. Here and there, dried blood stuck the fabric to his back. He wiggled his toes… still five of them, and his fingers, also five on each hand. "Not bad," he said, wondering who in this world kept track of so many questions.

"Still. Why don't you have a seat up here." Navy Guy wheeled the bed closer and lowered the red metal box to the ground.

His partner spread a sheet across the mattress and encouraged Liam to sit, which he did. She wrapped an inflatable cuff around his bicep. It beeped and squeezed. Alarmed, *My arm! They're trying to cut it off!* With his free hand he tried to rip it off, when it hissed and deflated.

"It's okay," she said as she unfastened the arm balloon with a loud rip. "I'm going to give you some oxygen." And she strapped a clear plastic mask over his face.

Cautiously he sipped in the air that hissed through the tubing. He expected a smell, but no, just cool, clean air.

They too started with the questions, but other than his name, he had no answers. "Liam Summer."

"Where do you live, Liam? Where do you work? Do you have relatives you can stay with? What insurance do you have? Do you have any allergies? Are you on medication? Have you taken any drugs? Do you smoke cigarettes?"

The navy woman encouraged him to lie down. He winced from the pain but did as instructed.

"You're going to be fine," she said as she wrapped him, blanket and all, in the white sheet and strapped and buckled a webbed belt across his middle.

Swaddled in cloth, he panicked. "No. Please don't." *This is a trap!*

"Shh," she tried to gentle him.

He bucked against the restraint. His fingers grabbed at the metal buckle. "Get it off! Please get it off!" He tore at the mask as Navy Guy helped his partner wrap Liam's hands tighter into the swaddle formed by the blanket and sheet.

"Get the restraints," she said.

"*No!*" He had to break free. "Let me go! Get off of me!" he screamed into the night, his cries barely registered over the sirens, the smoke, the crowds, and the flashing lights.

Undeterred by his frenzy, the two members of the navy clan wheeled him toward the gaping mouth of a giant metal beast.

Liam strained to see. Nothing made sense. *I have to get away. They're going to feed me to that.* He sought for the magic that would take him away from this place, from these strangers wheeling him toward the belly of a beast. *I am food. I have been baked, and now they're going to feed me to that creature. Fly… fly.* "Let me go!" he screamed with all he had.

He heard a man's voice and the sound of heavy boots running from behind him. "Whoa!" A hand landed on Liam's shoulder. "It's okay. They're not going to hurt you."

Liam twisted in the sheet and restraints. For an instant he couldn't recognize the tall man, but he knew those blue eyes, the dark hair matted to his scalp from the helmet Liam had originally taken to be an ogre's head. "Charlie Fitzgerald, help me. Please."

"You need to get checked out," Charlie said, his hand on Liam's shoulder.

"Don't make me go with them. You can check me out."

The medics paused. The woman asked, "You know this guy?"

"Just met him tonight. He was up there." Charlie pointed to the smashed sixth-floor window.

"Don't make me go," Liam pleaded, even as he realized the white-and-red metal beast on wheels was not meant to kill but to transport. *But why tie me down?* He bucked against the belts across his middle, legs, and chest. He freed his hands and searched for a way to undo the strap.

The medic asked, "Is it because you don't have your insurance cards? Is that it? Because if it's about the money, emergency rooms are obliged to treat you by law."

"No more questions!" Liam shrieked. "I don't want to go! Please." He stared at Charlie, the big man with kind deep blue eyes—not an ogre at all—who got him out of the burning building. *You saved my life, Charlie Fitzgerald.* "Don't make me go."

The medics looked to Charlie. "He doesn't have to," the woman said. "He seems pretty traumatized. Did he lose everything?"

Charlie met Liam's gaze. The two men seemed frozen. "Yes."

"Does he have any place else to go?"

Charlie felt the world shrink as he stared into Liam's violet eyes. His chest tightened as he crouched beside him and whispered, "You should go with them, Liam. They just want to help."

Liam shook his head. "Charlie, I don't know this place. I have no power here and nowhere to go. Please don't make me go with them. Please."

Charlie thought of lots of reasons this was a bad idea. He could hear the things they'd say at the station—*If they find out…. They always find out.* But looking into Liam's eyes, he saw raw fear but something more. *Fuck it!* "My gran rents out a room in Gramercy. She needs help around her apartment, and her last tenant graduated from CUNY and moved away. Interested?"

Liam flinched at the inflected question. "Yes."

Charlie, still kneeling with his hand on Liam's shoulder, asked, "You're not some old-lady serial killer are you?"

Liam heard the question, but having survived so many this night, he answered in seriousness. "I've never killed an old lady."

"Good to know. It's going to be a long night, Liam." Without asking permission, he unbuckled the straps and helped him to sit. "You see that truck over there?"

"Yes, with the red cross like Jenn Trainer."

"They'll give you something to eat and some clothes. I'll find you when I'm done."

"You put out fires," Liam stated.

"I do."

"And save people from burning houses."

"Sometimes."

Liam pondered. "Putting out fires and saving people." Swaddled in his blanket and the sheet from the navy people, he stared at Charlie, with his soot-streaked face and bright blue eyes. "And invite a stranger into a loved one's home." He shook his head. "You're a saint or a fool."

His statement floored Charlie. "I hope neither." He stood, but it was difficult to move. His work was far from over, but he didn't want to leave Liam, who should go to the hospital, who was confused and in shock, and who made Charlie feel like he was filled with light. "Eat something. I'll find you. So wait for me, okay?"

Liam nodded.

Charlie stepped back, not wanting to break the connection. "I'll find you." And with a force of will, he returned to the smoldering building and the smell of cookies.

Four

WHEN HER bedside phone rang at 3:00 a.m., eighty-three-year-old Flora Fitzgerald braced for badness. She pushed aside the bound doctoral dissertation she'd fallen asleep reading, entitled *On the Trail of Maeve and the Hound*, and reached for the illuminated handset. Acid churned in her stomach as she picked up. Aldo, one of her five cats, repositioned himself, brushing his lush tabby tail against her cheek.

"Gran?"

"Charlie." She heard smoke in his voice. "What's wrong?" She pressed against the headboard as Aldo pounced on her blanket-covered legs. "What's happened?" *Don't be hurt, Charlie.*

Flora was no stranger to bad news in the night. Born outside Limerick in 1933, she'd lost her father, Michael, to Hitler when she was eight. Always poor but never before desperate, her dad's death had pushed her iron-willed mother, Rose, to pack up her five children, and with the sponsorship of relatives, they'd made the voyage to New York in 1947.

She gripped the receiver and saw the faces of her dead—two of her own children, three of her NYPD and FDNY grandsons on 9/11, her no-good but loved-him-madly husband, Rory, to lung cancer and drink. "What's happened, Charlie?" *Why isn't he answering?*

"Nothing bad, Gran. It's just… I have a favor to ask."

While Flora knew it was wrong to have favorites—everyone from Oprah to Doctor Oz said so—there was no denying that of the entire brood, Charlie was hers. From that moment in the delivery room with her daughter-in-law Kate, when she'd first locked eyes on him, she'd known. As they'd pulled off the membrane that covered his head and one of the young resident doctors had quipped, "Isn't that called being born with the caul?" she'd known. *This one is mine.* "Not another cat, Charlie."

He paused. "Not a cat, Gran… but since Derrick graduated and moved out…."

She sighed. *No, not another cat.* "Why are you bringing up my boarder… and my empty bedroom, Charlie?" The weirdness of their bond kicked in. *He's up to something.* "Where are you?"

"In the lobby."

"Of course you are. And you've brought someone."

"Yes."

Aldo had now been joined by his white-faced brother, Andre. The two of them, like furry sharks, circled her feet as she sought for her slippers and grabbed her fleece robe from the end of the bed. "Then you'd best bring him up, hadn't you?"

"Thanks, Gran…. How did you know it was a him?"

She paused, wiggled her toes, and Aldo jumped on her foot. She looked at the sweet creature and remembered something her ma had said about cats. *Don't be the toy.* "I just did, Charlie." *Is that what this is about?* When he was sixteen, Charlie had told Flora he was gay. He'd been frightened of her response. In truth, she'd suspected, and they'd spent the afternoon talking about how he'd break it to his family, his pa—her son Mike, never Michael—in particular. She'd told him that everything would work out, that his family, including his pa, loved him, and they always would. She'd not been certain, but she had been right.

She hung up, and knowing the rhythm of her building, where it took three minutes to get from the lobby to her twelfth-floor three-bedroom apartment where she'd lived for over fifty years, she did the only thing one does in these situations. She put on the kettle and loaded the counter with eggs, link sausage, and the grainy wheat bread that Charlie liked.

Aldo and Andre followed underfoot, now joined by the more senior black-and-white long-haired sisters, Lulu and Lily, and the psychologically disturbed Siamese, Daisy. All rescue cats, all brought to her by Charlie. To them, Flora in the kitchen signaled the possibility of snacks. While pulling mugs from a glass-fronted cabinet, she let herself be swayed by their meows and purring passes against her bare ankles. "This is not snack time." As the *S* word left her mouth, their excitement grew. Aldo swatted at Daisy's snakelike tail and tried to bite it. She growled and hissed at him. "Stop it! Be good."

She flipped the top of a can of Salmon Feast and divided it onto two flat saucers. She bent down, feeling the familiar sciatica pain in her right hip, which ached like an infected tooth. She placed the dishes by the oversized water bowl and stroked Aldo's still kittenish fur as Daisy whined with envy.

Suddenly the oddest thing happened, because nothing kept her fuzzy brood from the delights of canned food—especially the fishy varieties. Their heads turned in unison to the hall. Two seconds later, the doorbell rang.

Flora stared as they galloped from the kitchen to her bookshelf-lined foyer. She shivered. Yes, her cats were fond of Charlie, but even he couldn't compete with Salmon Feast. *What have you brought, Charlie? What are you bringing into my house?*

"Coming," she yelled. The stove clock read three fifteen. *Something is wrong.* She paused and for an instant wondered what would happen if she didn't open the door. It was an odd thought as she imagined leaving Charlie—her beloved boy—in the hall with whomever he'd brought. Another thought intruded as five cats howled from the hall. *What if it's not a who but a what?*

"Shh." She waded through the cats, not liking the way their backs arched and their fur hackled. "I'm coming." With one hand on the doorknob, she unlocked first the top and then the second dead bolt. She exhaled and opened the door.

The smell hit her first—cookies fresh from the oven. Her gaze landed on Charlie, her tall and handsome grandson, still in his navy workpants and FDNY T-shirt. She scanned for injuries with practiced eyes. That all the men—and now a good portion of the women—in her family felt the need to chase criminals or run into burning buildings was a painful reality. *He's not hurt, just filthy.* His face, hands, and arms were smudged with soot, and his thick wavy hair clung matted to his scalp from the Kevlar hood of his respirator. *This part feels familiar. A late-night visit with a cat or two.* He'd grab a shower and a change of clothes before heading home to Staten Island. But this was no new furry friend. *What have you brought me?* She took in the young man dressed in gray sweats and an oversized Red Cross tee. He was fixated on the howling cats, his face obscured by shoulder-length hair the color of ripened wheat.

"I don't know what's wrong with them." She needed to see the stranger's face.

"They don't like me," the blond said, edging to where he was half-hidden by Charlie's taller frame. He glanced up at Flora.

Even in the dim light, the color of his eyes gave her pause. She squinted and didn't hide her scrutiny. *What is this feeling... and that smell?* She looked to Charlie, who held his breath, as if awaiting her verdict.

Oh no, she thought. "Tell me your name, young man."

"I am Liam, Liam Summer."

He appeared dazed, and like Charlie was filthy with whatever tragedy he'd gone through. But there was more, as memories of her childhood intruded. Ancient bits, before the voyage across the sea. *I have smelled this before.* Her mother's scolding tone. *"It's just stories, Flora. You mustn't tell lies."*

The five cats grew silent, arranged like sentinels on either side of her feet, their gazes fixed on Liam.

Still in the door, wondering why Gran was acting so odd, Charlie spoke. "He's nowhere to go, Gran. I don't know if you saw it on TV. It was a bad one."

Flora let his words wash across. She heard them but wasn't listening, at least not to what lay on their surface. *He's nervous, talking too fast.... How he looks at this Liam. Charlie, no, no, not this.* Clear as a bell, she heard the shuffle of her across-the-hall neighbor's feet. She pictured the blousy thrice-divorced actress, still a regular on a popular daytime soap, spying through the fish-eye.

"You'd best come in."

The chorus of cats growled as Charlie and then Liam crossed the threshold.

"Odd." Her gaze lingered on Liam. In the brighter light of her hall, made narrow by crammed floor-to-ceiling bookshelves, his attractiveness was undeniable. *A handsome face can hide the devil.* She tried to glimpse his ears, concealed by his hair, and the shape of his teeth, but those were perfectly white and straight. *"You're imagining things, Flora,"* her mother would say. *"It's all fairy tales.*

Don't tell lies, and don't talk about the things you thought you saw. Just a child's imagination. You don't want people to think you're queer."

"Come." She led them into her spacious kitchen with its black-and-white-checkered floor, which Charlie had crawled across as a babe and where he'd taken his first steps. The hiss of the kettle turned to a whistle, and even with hunks of Salmon Feast still on the plates, none of the cats followed. *Stranger still. You are not imagining things, Flora. Nor did you as a child, no matter what Ma said.* She watched the men reflected in the cupboard glass as she pulled down mugs and poured boiling water into a cat-shaped teapot—a gift from Charlie. This Liam was too quiet and far too handsome, with his high cheekbones, strong jaw, straight nose, and eyes like Elizabeth Taylor's. *And Charlie, I know that look. This one is not for you.*

With practiced efficiency, she scrambled eggs, browned the sausage, and made toast. She placed the steaming plates before them and sat. She watched as Liam pushed the food from one edge of the plate to the other. "It's not to your liking," she stated.

"I'm sorry. I have no appetite."

"Of course." She looked at Charlie. "Shouldn't you have brought him to the hospital?"

Charlie, who had no trouble plowing through his eggs and sausage, gave a weak smile. "I tried. He wouldn't go."

Liam sniffed the tea. He sipped. "This is bitter."

Flora edged the sugar bowl and creamer across the table. "Try this." *No, his ears are normal. Not like theirs.* A memory, worn faint by time—she'd been no more than three or four that first time—played in her head. Twinkly lights in the woods out back of their thatched-roof hut. She'd been playing with her doll. *It's the smell. He carries the smell. His face, perfectly formed. Those eyes... what person has purple eyes?*

She watched as he tentatively scooped in three spoons of sugar and a dollop of cream.

He sipped. "Better. Sweeter." He drained the mug.

"Good." She poured him a fresh cup. "Charlie, we need to get you both cleaned up. Help me find some clothes for the two of you."

"Sure, Gran." He stood and looked at Liam, his plate untouched. "You need anything? The bathroom's the first door on the right.... Try to eat something."

Liam tensed at the question. "No, Charlie, the tea is enough. It's good. It's sweet."

"Okay, I'll be right back." Charlie wondered if maybe the guy was a model and the way he maintained his zero body fat and rippling abs was by only drinking tea.

He followed Gran to the back bedroom, the one where he, often with other siblings or cousins, would crash after a visit to the city. The instant he was through the door, Gran shut it.

"Okay, Charles Michael Fitzgerald, what possessed you to bring him here?"

"He had nowhere, Gran."

"Doesn't he have family?"

"I don't know. He's in shock. I think he lost everything." As the words left his mouth, he couldn't help but think of that bare apartment where he'd found Liam. No one was living there. It was being renovated. *What was he doing there? Why was he naked? There were no clothes, no suitcases....*

"People have insurance for that," Gran said as she opened a closet filled with an assortment of mostly men's clothes. She grabbed clean tees, sweatshirts, a pair of Charlie's jeans, and another from one of his shorter cousins.

"Gran, he was renting… I think, maybe subletting. I don't know." *Why am I lying to her?*

"And you brought him here? Why not back to Staten Island? You and your folks have more space than I do. What's going on, Charlie? What aren't you telling me?"

"I don't know."

She looked him in the eyes. *I think you do.* "Fine, he can stay a day or two till he gets sorted. I'm not promising more."

A caterwaul of cats interrupted.

"What the hell?" Charlie raced to the kitchen and found Liam cowering in a corner, surrounded by the cats, who'd arranged themselves at perfectly spaced intervals.

"Get them away from me!"

Flora entered the kitchen. The smell of cookies had faded, but that, combined with her cats' odd behavior, made the memory stronger. *She'd followed the dancing lights into the woods.... So pretty, and she'd seen them... and they'd seen her. Fairies, mostly naked, with butterfly wings and beautiful faces but pointy ears, and as she got closer, close enough to smell their bonfire, she saw their teeth, sharp as needles.* She shook her head, grabbed another can of cat food even though they'd not finished the first, and popped the lid. It distracted the two older cats, but Daisy and the near-grown tabbies stayed fixed, their eyes on Liam. *Don't be the toy*, Flora thought.

With the two black-and-whites following her, she set the food down outside the kitchen and closed the door. Charlie grabbed the kittens and gently tossed them out after them and returned for blue-eyed Daisy, who hissed and clawed as he pulled her away and dropped her in the hall.

Liam let go of the counter. "They don't like me. If I were small enough, they'd eat me."

Gran smiled. "Yes, there's something about you, Liam. But there's a door on your room. Close it and they won't bother you." She looked to Charlie. "Best you get home, and call me later."

The kittens clawed at the door, trying to get back in.

She looked at Liam's untouched food, next to Charlie's ketchup-smeared plate. She watched the blond's hand tremble as he poured a fourth cup of tea and loaded in scoop after scoop of sugar. She tapped the table to get his attention. *This is not my imagination.*

He looked up.

"Liam Summer, you will do no harm here."

He met her gaze. "No, ma'am. I am your guest. I will do no harm to you or to those you love."

"Yes, the rules of courtesy must be obeyed. I shall hold you to your word." Flora sensed her grandson's confusion. How to explain the inexplicable or how she knew that danger had entered her home? If her ma still lived, she'd tell Flora it was all her imagination. The good people—the fey, the sidhe—were folklore and legend. They didn't come into your home and gulp tea. But that was her ma, who had not friended the fairies in the woods, gazed into their fire, and listened to their high-pitched gossip. And while Ma and the housewives of their little town would say it was stuff and nonsense, they'd still toss the heel of a fresh-baked loaf into the backyard and leave a saucer of milk on the windowsill as offerings. It's why they kept a cat or two, to sound the alarm should the good people try to steal a baby and leave a changeling in its crib. *Yes, Liam Summer, with your beautiful face and witches' eyes. You shall do no harm here.* But as she looked at Charlie and the way he gazed at Liam, she knew. *The harm is already done.*

Five

LIAM WANTED Charlie Fitzgerald to stay. Or to take him to the Staten Island. The old woman with her devil cats frightened him, but she also carried the whiff of something familiar.

He watched as she kissed tall Charlie good-bye and extracted a promise that he would call in the morning.

Emboldened, Liam approached the man who'd pulled him from death. He would not beg him to stay, much as he wanted to. "Thank you, Charlie." He reached up and kissed him on his darkly stubbled cheek.

Charlie pulled back. "What was that for?"

Liam saw the blacks of Charlie's eyes widen. He heard the catch in his throat and saw the artery in his neck quicken. *No!* In his short time in the human realm, Liam had faced the loss of his magic. But seeing… sensing Charlie's response, he knew that was not entirely true. *No.* Of all his abilities, this was the one he would gladly lose, the thing May had used him for—his glamour. It's why she murdered his parents, who would not be her whores.

Charlie appeared dazed, and Liam felt the connection. *I should not have kissed him. I promised to do no harm. I did not know. I thought my magic was gone.* In the court of Queen May, it's what he and his family were raised for, the queen's courtesans, her cat's-paws. "I'm sorry."

"Don't be," Charlie said.

"You saved my life, Charlie. I.…"

"It's my job." Charlie smiled, unable to pull his gaze off Liam.

I should not have kissed him. At least it wasn't on the lips. Just a partial glamour. He's strong. He'll shake it off. I will never do that again. He sensed the old woman's eyes on them. *I must do no harm.* "You did not have to help me. You did not have to save me from the fire or from the people with the bed on wheels. You did not have to bring me to the home of your Flora." He felt tall Charlie's struggle and knew it was the glamour. *Get away from me, Charlie. Distance will help. Go to your Staten Island. Water eases a glamour's hold. I'm so sorry.*

"You're welcome."

The space between the two was electric, and if Flora hadn't been present, Liam knew Charlie would have pressed for the kiss that would have completed the glamour and bound him body and soul. He edged back, needing to make distance and not wanting to. *I'm sorry, brave Charlie. I will do you no more harm.* "Go home, Charlie." And Liam attempted something he'd heard was possible for fey in the human realm.... He lied. "We'll talk tomorrow."

"Good."

"Go home."

"Right." Charlie looked down at his feet and then back to Liam. "Right." Awkwardly he backed toward the elevators. "I'll call tomorrow." He paused and looked from Liam to his gran. His expression brightened. "I've got two days off. I'll take you to Mass on Sunday if you'd like."

"That would be lovely." Flora's gaze narrowed. "You've not done that in a while. Can you even remember your last confession?"

"I know. I'm sorry." He struggled not to look at Liam. "I'll come by early, maybe take you both to breakfast." His thoughts were scrambled by the kiss on the cheek, the need to look into Liam's eyes, and a hunger to do much more.

"Go home, Charlie," Liam urged. "You need rest."

"And we'll have breakfast in the morning," Charlie said. "The three of us."

"Yes, Charlie," said Liam with a second lie, as he and Flora watched him make it to the elevator.

"He is a good man, my Charlie." She turned to Liam. "You will not do him harm."

"I won't," he said with lie number three. *And I have.*

"Good." To the background noise of cats howling from their living room exile, she led him back to the kitchen. "We have much to discuss."

He settled at the table as Flora put the kettle on.

"I will tell you what I can." *I will make amends.*

She turned to him as the water heated. "Show me your ears."

He grabbed his hair and pulled it back.

"And your teeth."

He smiled.

"You look human."

Liam's fingers played over the tops of his ears, and he ran a finger against the tips of his teeth. "I need a looking glass."

Flora opened a drawer, pushed aside unpaid bills, and retrieved a small compact. She clicked it open and slid it across the table. She watched as he studied his reflection.

He startled. *This is not me.* The reflection was of a man with gold, not silver, hair and dark lashes rimming eyes…. *Those are still mine. I should have known.* The tips of his fingers played across human teeth and ears shaped like the curve of a clam. *It's not just my magic that's changed.* Liam knew that for both human and fey, travel between realms came with cost. Yet predicting what it would be was impossible. For many it was their sanity, for others, their magic. For him, it was not only the loss of fairy flight, but his image was changed. His hair, his teeth, his ears, even his skin had darkened from pale white to a golden human tan. He stared back at himself through the looking glass. *Only my eyes remain. I am still in here. And I don't think I'm mad. Although….*

The kettle whistled, and Flora brought a fresh pot of tea to the table. She poured mugs and spooned in four sugars and cream for Liam. "Yes, you are a handsome man, Liam. I see the effect you have on my Charlie."

"I did not mean—"

"Shh. We both know you are not suited. But there's more."

Stunned by his reflection, he put down the mirror and looked at Flora.

"It's time," she said. "Tell me what you are, Liam Summer. Tell me everything."

Six

DEEP IN her misty prison, May slumbered and dreamed. Her senses traced the arc of her fairy fire projectile. She purred, curling in on herself, as the missile pierced through worlds and landed on its target. She smelled chaos, blood, and cookies as the fireball ripped into the roof of the home where the haffling children once lived and where magic lingered. She hoped, like one hoped when placing a worm on a hook, that something, something good, would take the bait.

She dreamed of a little girl, nearly a woman, with straight blonde hair, china-blue eyes, and skin smooth as cream. *Fairy fire, fairy fire, come and taste my fairy fire.*

May's dream traveled miles north in the human city of Manhattan. She drifted up the side of a building and into the window of the sleeping girl, her head lost in its own dreams. May watched the child, her body with the shape of a young woman, her breasts nearly full, her lips like petals of a rose. A body like that would be lovely in satin and lace. She envisioned a strapless midnight-blue gown and jewels. *Shoes, shoes, pretty shoes.* May hummed in her sleep. Her tongue flicked a bit of ogre from between her teeth. *Dresses, pretty dresses, twirl and dance. She's ripe enough, ripe enough. Tap, tap, tap.*

May's magic seeped into the sleeping girl—*Alice, her name is Alice. Hello, Alice. Show me your dream.*

May growled at the image of the girl's brother—Alex—now a full-grown man. *I will eat you and grind your bones to a paste.* The thought calmed her. He'd bested her once and likely thought her dead. *I'm not. Show me, Alice. Show me more.* Images tumbled—sitting in class, a small room with men and women dressed in ugly clothes fighting one another, sometimes with bare hands, sometimes with wooden sticks. A boy with auburn hair, younger than Alice, but his image caused the girl to stir. *Tell me his name, Alice. Tell me of this boy who quickens your pulse.*

The girl resisted. May pushed, and the dream shifted to a building filled with books, and inside, Alice, with her nasty brother and his nasty boyfriend.

May squirmed. *I will grind your bones into paste. Tasty, tasty, tasty paste.* She watched them with their books. *This smells familiar.* Before she could make the connection, the dream morphed. Alice grabbed a book as her brother and his beau faded. She was on the street. *Yes, yes, yes.* And May let her magic dream, like a directional arrow, pull the girl down block after block. *Fairy fire, fairy fire, come and taste my fairy fire.*

Alice dreamed of her old apartment, the tiny one where she'd slept side by side with her brother Alex, in a room so small she could reach her hand from her bed to his. *That's right, child. Such a happy place for you, protected and loved by your brother. Your mother locked safely in her room. Now smell. So delicious. Fairy fire, fairy fire, come and taste my fairy fire.*

FOURTEEN-YEAR-OLD ALICE Nevus woke from a dream. For an instant she wondered—hoped—that she was back in their pathetic old place on East Third. But no, this was her light-filled bedroom with attached bath. Her brother Alex, now in his second year of premed at NYU, no longer lived with them. A strand of hair caught in her mouth. She chewed it and tried to clear her head. It was six thirty, and morning sun streamed through the sheers. *Not a school day.* Though her book bag and tablet were loaded with many hours of weekend homework. As a freshman at Stuyvesant High School, staying on top of her studies was not an option and was not easy.

She grabbed her phone and read through the texts she'd exchanged last night with Clay. *He was in your dream.* He wanted to know if she'd make it to kung fu. She'd texted back she would, knowing it was one of the only places in her life—in that tiny Chinatown basement studio—where she could relax with people who knew her and her secrets. That they'd also be trying to clobber one another, often with wooden swords, didn't seem to ruin that.

It's too early to call Alex, who'd be snuggled in bed with Jerod. Besides, his life was filled with his own crazy goals and the need to get straight As so he could get into medical school, preferably NYU or Columbia so he could stay in the city.

She scanned her room, with its creamy lemon walls, a tribal rug she'd bought at the Twenty-Fifth Street flea market, bookcases, all the stuff she'd never had before when they were dirt poor. And it wasn't just Alex she missed but his impossible little fairy—Nimby. This was so much nicer, and so empty.

Her phone's message notification chirped; it was Clay.

"You up?"

"Duh."

"Check out Channel Eight. NOW!!!!!!!!!!!!!!!!!!"

"K."

Still holding the phone, she grabbed the remote from the side table and clicked on the TV. At first, she didn't get it.

"Holy shit!"

"Yeah… good thing U don't live there anymore."

She stared at the screen and the female reporter in front of their old building, who was trying to interview a long-haired blond guy wrapped in a Red Cross blanket. Alice perched on the edge of her bed and searched for the windows that would have been theirs. Her breath caught as she saw the glass had been smashed out in the kitchen. Something twisted inside. The place had sucked, it stank of garbage in the heat, and by the time you made it up the six flights of stairs, you'd be winded and drenched with sweat. There was no air-conditioning. *I miss it.* Even the bathtub in front of the kitchen window, where Alex had cut and painted a piece of plywood so it doubled as a counter. *I miss Alex.* Yes, she was glad he and Jerod were together, but she was jealous too.

The reporter moved on to a Hispanic woman holding a baby, who Alice remembered from the building. She was with her kids, and one of them held a cat carrier. Beneath the picture were instructions on how to get donations of food, clothing, and money to the fire victims through the Red Cross.

A message dinged. She glanced at the screen.

"You okay?"

Not needing to look, her thumbs whipped back, *"Weirded out."* The news shifted to sports, and Alice caught the smell, the one from the dream. Something baking… and something burning. Her mouth watered.

"You want company?"

She pictured Clay, two years younger than she was. He looked a lot like his older brother, Jerod, and if the genetic gods held true, the cute tween would break hearts. Alex had already pulled her aside and told her to be careful with him, that Clay had a crush on her. She wished he'd never told her. It complicated things. Clay was her best friend and one of the few people she trusted. Years back he'd even tried to save her, when the Office of Children and Family Services had carted her off. He didn't succeed, but still…. How many people would break the law for you? She looked at the screen. *Yes, I want company,* she thought. But she texted back, *"No, but thanks. I'll see you at Sifu's."*

"Kewl."

She ended the conversation with an eye-rolling animated emoticon. The smell grew. She opened the window to let in the spring air and the sounds of Lexington Avenue, nineteen floors below. She inhaled. *It's stronger. Where is it coming from?*

Phone in hand, she glanced at her emoticon and thought of texting Clay to see if he wanted to go with her. *No, don't lead him on. And you have way too much work to get through. That smell… so delicious.*

She grabbed jeans, a tee, and one of Alex's Stuyvesant hoodies. *Just a quick walk.* It wouldn't be the first time, either. Sometimes she needed to go down the old block and remember. They weren't good times… but they kind of were. She stared through the open window. It was a beautiful day in New York City, and it smelled of cookies.

Seven

CHARLIE GOT off the Staten Island ferry operating on no sleep, Red Cross coffee, and Gran's tea…. *Why did he kiss me?* He couldn't shake the feeling that he'd let a moment, possibly the most important of his life, slip by. *He kissed me…. On the cheek, man. Pull it together.* He couldn't. The half-mile walk from the train was a tangled medley of Liam, starting with the feel of his skin and Charlie's attempts to not ogle the guy who'd nearly died. *You got him out of there. So he kissed you—on the cheek. You saved the guy's life.* The feel of his weight against his back as he'd carried him into the cherry picker. Even more, the look on Liam's face as he'd coaxed the little dog to jump through fire. *And it wasn't even his dog. Those seconds could have cost both of us our lives—for a dog that wasn't his.*

Out of your league. The guy probably has someone—boyfriend, girlfriend, one of each, several. Shut up! Those eyes. The way he looked at me. He stopped at the bottom of a bifurcated driveway. To the right stood his parents' waterfront home—still a construction site years after the near-total devastation of Hurricane Sandy—and to the left, the two-story garage and apartment where he'd lived since he was seventeen.

Gran's question rang in his head as he walked up the stairs to his place. *"Why not bring him back to Staten Island?"* He keyed in, pulled out his cell, and scrolled through long lists of texts and voice mails. "And that's why," he said.

The texts started with his brother Michael's reminder about dinner with the family on Sunday, followed by his sister-in-law asking him to pick up a bottle of her favorite wine in the city, which he'd not done. He clicked from there to his mother's voice mail telling him she saw him on the morning news at the fire in the East Village, followed by his father—Mike, not Michael—asking to borrow his truck to pick up tile in Jersey. Then a message from Dad saying he went ahead anyway and took the truck, and that he'd fill the tank.

Exhausted, wired, and ripe from the fire, he needed a shower and sleep. But his mind would not shut up. *Liam.* He sank to the couch and stared through the window at an unobstructed view of the water and the rocky beach where the Murphys' house once stood. *So he's handsome… beautiful, is that it? You don't go to bars, you don't hook up because you want something real, and the first naked guy you pull from a burning building….* He smiled and replayed Liam's voice, his halting responses, as if testing each word before it left his mouth. The trace of an accent, maybe Irish but faint, like someone born there but here for many years.

His back against the cushions, he pictured Liam at Gran's kitchen table and then when he'd first met him, so frightened, *so naked.* Self-consciously Charlie thought of his own physique—strong, sure, but not since high school football and his days as a running back had his stomach been as flat and ripped as Liam's. *Probably a gym rat or circuit guy. Why else would he be naked in an abandoned apartment… but then, wouldn't there be someone else or a whole orgy?* He pulled his mind from the disturbing and arousing thoughts that too little sleep and a kiss on the cheek were leading to.

The rest of the fire blurred in his mind—the weird smells, expecting to find an illegal bakery somewhere in that building, but no. And every chance he got, searching the crowds to see if Liam was still there. The first break he'd gotten, telling himself he was just checking on the guy he'd saved—*Yeah, right*—his pulse quickened at the memory. Wondering, worried that he was gone, vanished into the night, and the moment he spotted him with the Red Cross lady and the medics. *He should have gone to the hospital.* The fear in Liam's eyes and how that changed. *Stop it. You helped the guy out. He was grateful. He kissed me—on the cheek.*

The arousal he'd been fighting since first locking eyes on Liam would not let go. *Just do it.* And feeling like a perv, he replayed stolen images of Liam's perfect body—*He's got to be a model*—broad shoulders tapering to an impossibly slender waist, a light trail of golden hair down rippled abs, leading to…. Charlie barely had to touch himself as he pictured Liam's ass. While he'd done everything possible to not cop a feel, it couldn't be helped. *Firm.* But it was the memory of his beautiful face and violet eyes looking into his that pushed him into the most intense orgasm of his life.

Flushed and drained, he sent a message from his brain to his body. *Get up and take a shower.* The message never made it, and with thoughts of Liam curled in his bed and in his arms, he fell asleep.

He dreamed. It was like he'd never left work. It started with the station-house alarm. He looked around for the rest of his crew. *I'm the only one here.* He shouted, "Patrick! Kyle! Bill! Gerry! Steve! Sarge!" *There's no one. What the fuck?* He knew, as one does in dreams, that he couldn't wait. There was no time to call for backup. He suited up, climbed into the Number 25 engine, and with sirens wailing, tore out.

You've got to be kidding me. The navigation system on the truck was blacked out, and he tried to remember the address. *Where's the fire?*

He turned; Liam was beside him.

"You don't need that," the beautiful man said.

"I do. I don't know where the fire is."

"You saved me. That's enough for one day."

"It's my job."

"I understand, Charlie. But turn around. Please. Don't do this."

Charlie spotted a billowing wall of smoke in front of them, only more like fog, blue, swirling, and strange. It obscured all behind it, like half of Manhattan was submerged in an impenetrable fog.

Liam pleaded, "Turn around, Charlie. You can't stop it."

"It's my job."

"Charlie, no! You can't stop it. Please listen."

Charlie aimed the truck into the mist. He grabbed ventilator masks and passed one to Liam. "Put this on."

The truck barreled into the fog.

"What the hell?" Blanketed in fog, Charlie saw moving shadows and lights. Something lunged at the truck. "What was that?"

Liam clutched the mask and pressed back. His eyes went wide as something clawed at his window.

Charlie leaned forward, as though that might give him some visibility. It didn't. He was torn between speeding up and crashing into a building or God knows what was out there, or stopping to face.... *What is that?* A massive white snake, its wide jaws lined with flat razor-sharp teeth, big enough to swallow a man, pressed against Liam's window. Its claws—*Snakes don't have claws*—tore at the metal door.

"Charlie, she found me! She's going to eat me!"

"Tell me what to do."

"I don't know…. I'm sorry, Charlie. I promised your gran I would not harm you. I'm sorry."

Charlie knew they were about to crash. You couldn't drive blind in Manhattan without hitting something or someone. And this thing at Liam's door wanted in. Its tongue sparked fire and poked the window. The glass blossomed with one, two, and three spiderweb cracks.

"Hell *no!*" Charlie slammed on the brakes. Whatever this thing was, it would not get Liam. He braced in the seat. His right arm shot out to protect Liam as the truck fishtailed and screeched to a halt.

Before them, the mist parted and fell away from the truck.

Charlie's heart raced. He was ready to grab his ax and do battle with whatever that thing was, but he couldn't wrap his mind around the bizarre scene through the windshield.

They were downtown. *This ain't downtown. Too green.* He pictured all the parks in the city.

He ripped off his mask.

Not even Central Park had this much green, as far as he could see, and flowers, not just in beds but everywhere, purple, yellow, pink… periwinkle forget-me-nots in mounded clumps.

He turned to Liam and to the spiderwebbed window. The lizard was gone. "Where are we?"

Liam shook his head. He turned from Charlie to his ruined window, back to the sun-kissed meadows before them. "I don't understand this. *No!*" He grabbed Charlie's hand. "This was hers."

"What was hers?" he asked.

"Shh! Don't. Not here."

"What?"

"Stop! No questions. Ask no questions, Charlie Fitzgerald. I cannot have done this." Tears streamed down Liam's cheeks. "I was to do you no harm, Charlie, and that is all I have done. You brought me back. You brought me home."

Guilt-stricken, he stared at Charlie, studying him from the top of his head down to his booted foot, still pressed against the brake. He shivered and shook his head. "Perhaps the truck protects you. Please, you must pay heed and do as I say. I will get out now. I see that. This can't be an accident. I've been brought back for a purpose. But you must leave the way you came, and go quickly. Good-bye, brave, kind, handsome Charlie." He opened the engine door and peered out. "She's truly gone. This was hers, and now…. She's a beast in the mist. I mean, truly she was a beast here as well, only one that dressed in silks and diamonds."

Charlie stared at Liam. His words of good-bye felt like someone had stolen all the air from his lungs. "Stay with me."

"No, Charlie. Your gran knows. She will tell you it's for the best. I'm not good." Liam winced at the effect his words had. Now was no time for kindness. If he were ever going to do one right thing, it had to be now, and it would have to hurt. He averted his gaze and spoke. "May killed my parents and raised me a whore. That's what you see. I am a vicious thing, unworthy of your affections. I will leave now and never forget your kindness. But trust me in this. I am not good, Charlie. Not for you… not for anyone."

"No…. Liam. Stop."

With the door open, Liam locked gazes with Charlie. He couldn't stop himself. He wanted a final look at Charlie… his Charlie.

Charlie seized the moment, lunged across the space, grabbed Liam by the shoulders, and kissed him full on the lips.

Like a baby taking its first breath, Charlie was not prepared. His molecules sizzled with the contact, like bacon landing on a hot skillet.

Liam stiffened, but knowing the thing was done, he surrendered to the sweetest kiss of his life. Finally, slowly, he pulled back. With Charlie's hands on either side of his face, his expression was unreadable. "You should not have done that, Charlie Fitzgerald. Go back as you came." He broke from Charlie's grasp and jumped from the truck.

Startled and dazed from the kiss, Charlie stumbled out. He raced around to Liam's side, but he was gone. *Liam!*

Before him, the meadow stretched in all directions. He turned. "*Liam!*"

He glimpsed a broad river to the right and another far off to the left. "*Liam!*" Somehow he must have driven over one of the bridges and…. *That's impossible.* Behind the truck he saw the mist, like a giant wave between the ground, the sky, and whatever lay on the other side. It was thick and alive. "*Liam! Liam!*"

A bell sounded and then another. Desperate, Charlie ran through the meadow. *Liam!* The faster he ran, the less clear things became. The meadow vanished. The bells chimed louder.

"Liam...."

He awoke. His pulse pounded in his ears. His breath came in short gasps, like he'd been running far and fast.

He tapped the Off on his cell's alarm. On the screen was a missed call from Gran. He thought of Liam. *The dream... the kiss... just a dream.* Hope surged. *But maybe I can make it something more than a dream.*

He pressed Redial, and as he did, doubt crept in. It was 11:00 a.m. Gran knew he'd be sleeping till past noon. *So why call?* With a sickening dread, he knew.

"He left without a word," she said. Before he could ask, she added, "No note, nothing. Just gone. I'm sorry, Charlie. But something about Liam Summer was not right."

It felt like he'd been sucker punched. "Gran, he'd just lost everything he had in a fire. Cut the guy some slack."

"Don't you raise your voice to me, Charles Michael Fitzgerald!"

"I'm sorry, Gran. It's just...."

"Yes, you have feelings for him. Best forget those, Charlie. Liam Summer is not the man for you. He's not...."

"He's not what?" And bits of the dream returned. *Ask no questions here.* The odd way Gran spoke to him, ordering him to answer her. "What aren't you saying? Tell me."

"Nothing. It's best we not speak of him... ever. You did a handsome man a favor. He repaid you by leaving before anyone could get hurt. He did the right thing. You should do the same and put him out of your mind. It's what comes from bringing home strays and wild things. You have a crush on a stranger, Charlie. It's nothing more."

"I can't talk right now." He didn't want to speak in anger. So he told her he loved her, and he hung up.

"Crap! Crap, crap, crap." He stared out at the water. *Gone, no note, nothing.* He felt disoriented by Gran's blunt words, Liam's disappearance, and the feel of the kiss. *It was a dream.* First the brush on his cheek and then the one he took in his dream. *I must have known he would run.* He looked out at the driveway and across at his parents' house. He'd share none of this with them. Yes, they knew their youngest boy was gay, and while his sixteen-year-old's declaration had been met with stony silence from his father, Mike, and tears from his mother, Kate, he'd never once brought home a guy for them to meet. Because frankly, the two he'd been with weren't parentworthy. Gran's words echoed. *"Why not bring him to Staten Island?"*

I should have. Yeah, and he'd still have run.

But why didn't I? His gut twisted on the answer. "Because you're chickenshit. They'd take one look at Liam and know I was into the guy… and what's wrong with that?" *I should have brought him here. Maybe he wouldn't have run…. Maybe….*

His cell rang. *Maybe it's him!* His mom's name popped on the caller ID. "Hi, dear. I see you're up. I've got breakfast. You're off today, right?"

He was, and a day off meant working on the nearly completed rehabilitation of their beachfront homestead. Today's project, tile the powder room he and Dad had just Sheetrocked and taped. Normally he'd look forward to the afternoon with Dad and the accomplishment of ticking one more project off the list. But not today. He felt wired and sad. *Why am I so angry?* Maybe slapping on thinset mortar and cutting slate tile with a wet saw was what he needed. Take his mind off…. *It was a dream, for God's sake. Get over it.* But he couldn't. *Liam, why? Crap! Pull it together.*

With his head wrapped around a day with Dad and a bucket of thinset, he headed into the bath and turned on the shower. *God, I smell.*

He took a long look at himself in the mirror, from the thick black stubble on his face, to the tired circles under his blue eyes, to the mess of his black hair, which should have been cut weeks ago. He shucked off his tee and peeled off thick socks that stuck to the bottoms of his feet from sweat and the heat of the fire. His fly was still open, and he remembered how he'd fallen asleep. *Pervert.* Because it had to be on his clothes, he caught a whiff of that delicious bakery smell from the fire. He kicked his pants and boxers into the hamper next to the sink, and standing naked in front of the steaming shower, he grew hard. Maybe it was the smell or the way the steam filled the room, like the dream.

Get a grip.

He stepped into the shower. Hot water cascaded over his skin. It mixed with the layers of sweat and soot. The cookie smell of the fire was everywhere. *Liam!* His erection was so hard it verged on pain. *Just do it.*

He drew up precious memories. The one that brought him over the edge was the chaste kiss Liam had pressed on his cheek.

The orgasm buckled his knees, his toes curled, and he shot a hand against the slick tile wall to keep from falling. He stood motionless, head bowed, water racing down his back. *You've got to find him. No....* Unable to move, his breath hot through his lips, he knew Liam's running off in the night was not a sign of interest. He wasn't one of Gran's cats who'd brush against his leg and then scurry off with tail raised, hoping he'd pursue. The guy left because he probably remembered where he needed to go. *Which isn't with me.* His mood plummeted. He grabbed the soap and washcloth and scrubbed every inch of his body. He rubbed till his skin turned pink. The delicious smell vanished down the drain. *He doesn't want you, man. You can jack off all you want, but he's gone.*

The problem was, the more he thought through the reasons why he had to stop obsessing about Liam, the worse it got. *What the fuck.* He threw on paint-spattered cargo pants, sneaks, a threadbare FDNY tee and crossed the drive to the house where he grew up.

Four years after Hurricane Sandy, the outside was near normal, although in order to get insurance, the house no longer had a basement, just steel-and-cement supports sunk deep into bedrock and meant to withstand a hundred-year flood.

Due to his and Dad's efforts, the kitchen and upstairs bedrooms, the least damaged of all, were better than new. They'd gutted the main level down to the studs and filled Dumpster after Dumpster with ruined Sheetrock and hundred-year-old oak flooring too damaged by salt water to be saved. It was like a new house: clean wiring, new plumbing, the furnace, the ducts, the AC, the twenty-kilowatt propane generator, the roof… all new. The final piece—Mom's dream powder room—was all that remained.

He stopped in the drive and gazed out at the water. Calm today, but there'd be another Sandy, and was living in a place that was so familiar and so beautiful worth the risk? He breathed salt air. The visibility was low, and mist like in his dream hung over gentle waves. *Shake it off, shake it off.*

He tried to block images of Liam as he entered the home, which smelled of bacon and biscuits. As though he were still eight and coming down before school, his place was set with orange juice, eggs, bacon, and two buttermilk biscuits. *And that's why my abs don't look like his.*

"Rough night?" Dad asked as Mom nudged the ketchup across the table.

"Long," Charlie said. He poured his coffee and remembered Liam spooning ridiculous amounts of sugar into his tea.

"Want to talk about it?" Dad asked.

"Not much to say. Old tenement, probably arson. Bad all around."

"We saw," Dad commented. "You were on the news. Lots of people with no place to live."

Charlie avoided Dad's gaze. Living with a retired NYPD detective had its up and downs. This was the latter. Lying to his Dad never went well. Just as Gran would joke about the cats—*Don't be the toy*—he and his brothers and sister, Annie, had a similar one for Dad—*Don't be the perp.* So he clammed up and waited him out.

"I spoke to your Gran...."

And here it comes.

"She said you offered to take her to Mass tomorrow. That's good of you, son. Maybe we should all go."

He looked at Dad, his clothes smeared with light gray thinset. He'd been hard at work all morning. "That's okay. I got this one. But not to curse anything, I've got the whole weekend off. I can't remember the last time that happened. So I figured today with you, Mom, and the dynamic duo and tomorrow with Gran. And back in time for Sunday dinner."

Dad's gaze narrowed as Mom settled in her place at the other end of the table.

"And you, dear?" she asked. "What about you? No plans... no going out? Like you said, you don't often get the weekend...."

"I'm good," he said, used to the double-front interrogation tactics of his parents. But as he sat there, enjoying the warmth and familiarity of his folks and their resurrected home on pilings meant to withstand a hundred-year flood, he couldn't rip his mind from Liam.

He focused on breakfast and turned the conversation to the project before them. As he did, an idea took root. It was all he could do to hold his tongue. He thought back through the night and the dream. The regret in his gut, the awful sense that something... someone who mattered had left. *Why couldn't I kiss him for real? Because I just met the guy. Because it would have been a total perv move. Yeah, like jacking off while thinking about him isn't?*

"Where are you, Charlie?" Mom asked.

"A bit fuzzy," he admitted, knowing what he intended. *I've got to find him.*

"About the fire?"

"Ask no questions." He snorted, and coffee went down the wrong pipe.

"What's so funny?" Dad asked.

"Nothing. It was a long night…. So, anything left for me to do?" And he listened to Dad's DIY update, ate his eggs, and tried not to despair over the millions of places violet-eyed Liam Summer could be.

Eight

WITH HER hood up, Alice Nevus turned onto the familiar block where she'd lived for five years with her brother Alex, her real mother—not the one asleep back in the Murray Hill apartment—and Alex's fairy, Nimby. She stood and stared. Like a war zone, the seven-story redbrick building that had been their home was scorched, its windows either shattered or blackened from the fire. Yellow crime-scene tape stretched across the broad front stoop and stairs, and orange plastic barriers closed off either end of the block, with a double row of them in front of the building. A fire engine stood parked along the sidewalk beside a red-and-white van with a gold Fire Marshal emblem on the back window. Black-and-white police cruisers sat like bookends at the ends of the block.

A woman walking her miniature dachshund stopped next to Alice. "It was awful," she commented.

"You live on this block?" Alice asked.

"No, I'm on Second, but it was scary. They say it was arson… a mother and two kids died."

"I used to live there," Alice said.

"Good thing you don't anymore."

"I guess."

The woman looked at Alice, unable to see her face, just strands of blonde that had escaped the hood. "You okay?"

Alice nodded. "Sure. Guess I'm just curious. Why would someone set a fire where so many people live? What kind of person does that?"

"Hard to know," the woman said as her dog sniffed Alice's sneakers. "This city is filled with nutjobs…. It could be that. Someone who likes to see things burn. Or someone with a grudge, someone who's going to make money from an insurance policy...."

"What is that smell?" Alice asked.

"What smell?"

"Like cookies."

The woman sniffed. "I'm not catching it. But I've got horrible allergies, and the pollen has me totally blocked."

Alice drank the delicious odor, much stronger here than when she'd first caught the whiff outside her bedroom window. She nodded. *How come she can't smell it?* "Cute dog."

"Thanks, and don't think she doesn't know it."

"I've got to get a closer look."

"I'd be careful. I think they're still putting out hot spots."

"Sure." Keeping to the north side of the street, Alice approached her old home. Directly across from the building, she gazed at their shattered sixth-floor kitchen window. To the right was the teeny room she'd shared with Alex, and on the other side, the bigger bedroom, which had been for their crazy mother, Marilyn, who Alex would sometimes lock in at night to prevent her wandering the city. But things in the world of Alice and her brother Alex Nevus were not as they appeared. In truth, her mother, her real mother, did not have schizophrenia but had been driven barking mad by a trip between the human world and the fantastic realm Alice had been dragged to three years prior. Every day her rational mind struggled to make sense of the nonsensical. How she had another brother, Adam, she barely knew, who lived in that other world with her mother, who wasn't crazy there, and her fairy father, Cedric. Not things one shared with schoolmates. Those who knew the truth, the whole truth, and nothing but the truth, she could count on the fingers of one hand.

The smell, like Chinatown cookies thick with almond paste, came from the ravaged building. *Which makes no sense.* Her belly churned, something about this familiar and dangerous. Her lips trembled. *I need to see. I need to go inside.* The woman with her dog had said it was arson. The news said the fire's cause was under investigation. *Something is wrong.* She looked down the cordoned-off street littered with charred wood, shattered glass, a child's blackened stuffed rabbit. People's lives strewn like garbage.

Her fingers played over the cell phone in her pocket. She thought of Alex. As she did, a competing urge told her not to call. *Why does this smell so good?* Fighting with herself, she gripped her phone and pressed his number. Pain blossomed behind her eyes, like the start of a migraine.

"Alice?"

"Hey, bro." *I don't want to talk to him. Then why did I call?*

"What's wrong?"

Hang up. "You don't know. There was a big fire at our place last night." *Just hang up. He's got things to do. He doesn't need you bothering him every minute.*

"What are you talking about?"

"Our old place on Third. People died, a woman and two kids. I wonder if we knew them."

"Where are you?" he asked. He sounded concerned.

Don't answer. Don't tell him. It's none of his business. "In front of the building. Alex… it smells like cookies."

"What are you doing there?"

"I had to see." *The smell. Hang up the phone. Hang up. Follow the smell. So delicious.*

"Alice…. Alice, you need to get away from there. Alice? Alice?"

But the phone was back in her pocket, and she crossed the street. A cop sipping coffee with his partner looked up. "Miss, you can't be here. You need to stay behind the barriers."

Without breaking pace, she pulled back her hood and looked him dead in the eyes. "That's okay, officers."

The cops turned as she gazed from one to the other, her clear blue eyes wide, trusting, and something else. "It's okay, officers. It's okay for me to be here."

They nodded—*Of course you can be here*—as she crossed the barriers and headed up the stairs into the delightful-smelling burned-out shell she'd once called home.

FROM A world away, May tugged at the strings of her magic. Like an angler reeling in a trout, she tickled the line and sought access to the girl's thoughts. She'd nearly lost it at the sound of the horrible boy's voice. *Alex Nevus, you will pay. I will grind your bones to paste.* She snorted, realizing she'd eaten far too much troll and had started to think like one. *We are what we eat.* Which for May, with her ravenous hunger, meant gorging on the slow and easy-to-trap trolls and ogres. Plus, the magic in their bones, blood, meat, and organs was considerable, the fuel to feed her fire.

With more force—*but mustn't scare her away*—she pressed Alice to hang up on her wicked brother. *Breathe deep. So delicious, my pretty girl.* The intoxicating scent of fairy fire was a prelude of what was to come. She marveled as the lovely teen used magic—*She has glamour*—to bypass the soldiers in blue. *Alice, Alice, Alice, I should have waited for you. I was too impatient. Boys are such a bother—no pretty dresses, no midnight-blue satin with diamonds in our hair. But you, pretty, pretty. Breathe deep.*

Every step the girl took into the building ripe with fairy fire and its highly addictive byproduct, fairy dust, heightened May's access to the girl's thoughts. She felt the pores of her skin and how her feet skimmed over the rubble-strewn floor. *Lovely*, like it was her own fingers now delicately touching the charred banister.

May inhaled, fanned the fire in her gut, and blew out a stream of tether magic. It caught fast to Alice, and like a pirate boarding a ship, May was nearly in. *Come, child, let's do what we came for.*

Through Alice's eyes May stared up through the tunneled hole the fiery ball had caused in the building. She glimpsed the sky. *Inconsequential. We must go down... quickly.* She knew the girl had alerted her horrible brother and he'd soon appear. *Quickly.* She found the basement door, its hinges removed, the stairs drenched and dark.

We must go down. Smell it. So wonderful. So delicious. Hurry.

ALICE LOOKED down the stairwell and salivated. She breathed deep. The dark wasn't so bad. Her eyes adjusted and kept her from falling down the slick and rickety stairs. At the bottom she spotted a gentle orange glow, where the smell originated—*Something's still burning*—but not dangerous. It felt warm, delicious, and safe, like Alex's everything-in-the-fridge stew on a February day. She had to see, to feel its glow on her face. The heat and the smell. Without thought she reached a hand toward the glowing basketball-sized orb. Its surface shimmered. Something about it was both beautiful and sad, as its fire faded and it blackened.

She expected it to be hotter than it was. It didn't burn, and as her fingers drew close to its surface, there was no pain. Just a wonderful tingle in the tips of her fingers that traveled up her arms. A sense of security, like nothing bad could ever happen, washed over her. Even more, as her forefinger touched down—*It doesn't burn*—all her pain, all the horrible things that had been done to her as a child, the years of paralyzing fear that she'd be taken from her brother and crazy mother and stuck in yet another dangerous foster home, her self-doubt, her sense of being a freak, of not fitting in—it was gone.

Her fingers splayed over the wonderful sphere, and then her other hand touched down. Holding it in her grasp, so beautiful, so warm….

"Who's down there?" a man's deep voice called from the top of the stairs.

Alice startled and drew her hands back from the orb.

"Who's down there?" Heavy boots descended.

Alice looked back at the dying ball. Her fingers were sticky. The smell was on her hands, and she stuck her fingers in her mouth. *Oh my God!* White light exploded in her head, her eyes widened, and a grin spread across her face. *Oh my God!* All her sadness had been replaced with joy, bliss, euphoria. She threw back her head and gazed up through the hole punched in the building. *This is amazing! I don't want this feeling to ever stop!*

A WORLD away, a giant white salamander hummed and slept and sang.

"*Fairy fire, fairy fire, come and taste my fairy fire.*

After fire comes the dust. Fairy dust, fairy dust, come and try my fairy dust.

Just a taste, just a taste. It starts a lust and becomes a must."

Nine

CHARLIE, DRESSED in his navy go-to-church-weddings-and-funerals suit, white shirt, and tie, arrived in Gramercy. He parked his red 4x4 Ford SuperCab pickup with the FDNY sticker in the front window and rode up the elevator to Gran's.

A day later and his thoughts were still fixed on Liam. His chest ached, like a piece of himself he'd not known existed had been ripped out. *Why did he run? It's something I did. What did I do?*

As Gran opened the door, Aldo streaked for the hall. Charlie was quicker. He scooped up the squirming tabby and, as he stood, caught the force of Gran's scrutiny. While he sometimes got things past Mom and Dad, Flora Fitzgerald could not be fooled.

"No, he did not come back," she said.

He put the cat down. "That's not—"

"Don't even start. Your head is like glass... at least to me."

"You look nice, Gran," he said, taking in her soft-gray dress, green cardigan, and pearls.

"Ah yes, the Fitzgerald bait and switch. Your blue-eyed charm gets you far." She sighed. "You're disappointed. I'm sorry."

"About what?"

"The boy, your Liam."

"He wasn't mine."

"But you'd hoped. I'm not blind." She gathered her hat, gloves, and purse.

"Maybe I did."

"No *maybe* about it. But let me ask you this, Charlie. Did you know a single thing about that man... I mean, other than his pretty package?"

Charlie choked on his laugh.

"What?"

"Nothing, Gran." His cheeks flushed as he thought of how he'd first encountered Liam, stark naked. *A pretty package indeed.* And from there he hurtled into the near-constant erotic free fall he'd been having ever since.

She cuffed him upside the head. "I know what filth runs through your head, Charlie. Now behave, or the good Lord will strike you dead in the middle of Mass." With that she grabbed her gloves and hat, handed him her keys, and they left.

OUTSIDE, THE Uber car he'd ordered—a black SUV—waited. Even on a Sunday, it was too risky to get parking close enough to the Thirty-Fourth Street St. Michael's. Throughout the familiar service, his thoughts ran back to Liam, his face like one of the stained-glass angels, the brush of his lips, his voice.... Beside Gran he dutifully stood, sat, and knelt, his mouth going through the motions. His eyes drank in the morning sun that streamed in colors through the intricate window. He knew this was an obsession. It was unhealthy. He knew it had to be based on physical attraction. *The guy's hot.* What else could it be?

Mindlessly, he mouthed the prayer responses as he replayed his moments with Liam. *What did I miss? His eyes. Who the fuck has purple eyes? Why was he so frightened? What was he doing in that apartment in the first place? With no clothes. How do you get a body like that? What happened to him? Why was he there?* Disturbing questions intruded. *Did he have something to do with the fire?* The fire was obviously arson. Some incendiary device had landed on the roof and burned through the floor in front of the apartment where he'd found Liam. His friend Fire Marshal Finn Hulain, a presence in the Fitzgerald home his entire life, would say *"There are no coincidences."*

Charlie rose up from his knees and helped Gran do the same. His stomach churned. *A woman and two kids, one of them a baby, died in that fire. If Liam had something to do with that... or knew something.... Is that why he ran?*

I have to find him....

You're not a cop or a fire marshal. This is not your job....

I have to find him.
Fine, and how exactly do you plan to do that?

AFTER MASS he asked Gran, "Do you want to go for brunch?"

She turned. "Did I just fall off the turnip truck?"

"What did I say?"

"Charles Michael Fitzgerald, not once have you ever asked if I wanted to go to brunch after Mass. You just take me. Today you ask because you're hoping I'll say no and you can run off to whatever scheme you've concocted to track down Liam."

He was struck silent.

"Cat got your tongue? And don't you think five perfectly sweet cats hissing at a stranger and howling so loud they woke the neighbors was a bit odd?"

"He smelled of fire."

"You smell of fire all the time, as do half your cousins. Not once have they behaved like that. It's the boy, Charlie. Trust me on this. He's not right." She shook her head. "I'm wasting my breath… of which I've a limited amount. No, Charlie, your gran, who lives alone with too many cats and only gets out when her family sees fit to remember she's alive and fetch her for an hour or two, doesn't want to go to brunch. Nothing would make me happier than to know you're off chasing one of the good—" She stopped in midrant.

Charlie's ears perked. "A good what, Gran?"

"It's nothing." She looked up from under the brim of her hat and smiled.

He narrowed his gaze. "Or the kind of thing to be discussed over brunch?"

"Eggs Benedict and boozy Mary has been known to loosen the tongue."

"Fine, we're going to brunch."

"Of course we are. It's what we *always* do after Mass. If you're going to chase a handsome man who will break your heart, you mustn't also break the things that will piece you back together."

"Point taken."

"I hope so, Charlie, because you've not yet felt the pain of heartbreak." She stopped herself. "Not that kind, son.... I know you've had loss. We all have. I'm surrounded by my dead. They crowd me."

Gran's words hit deep as he caught sight of the black Uber Toyota. It never took much to feel his own dead—his oldest brother, Rory, his uncle Michael, and the man he was named after, Uncle Charlie, all killed in 9/11, when Charlie was eight. He could still remember them, how they'd crowd into cabs after Mass and shout over each other at Sunday dinner with the never-ending Fitzgerald family feud of *Was it better to be a cop or a firefighter?* Each faction took Charlie and his brother Michael aside and exacted promises that when they were old enough they'd make the proper choice, which often included bribes of a silver dollar to seal the deal.

"Traditions matter, Charlie," Gran said as they pulled up to Camille's, her favorite brunch place in Gramercy. "And they fade. Your generation doesn't understand, and the past gets tossed like yesterday's paper. Your boy Liam didn't smell of smoke but of something much older, something forgotten... something dangerous. That's what the cats smelled."

Charlie forced a laugh. "You're making stuff up."

"I'm not," she said without humor. "I wouldn't do that to you, Charlie. But I'll tell you this." And she waited as he opened the door and helped her out. "You're about to liquor up your gran... and have two or three yourself. There's things you need to know... and booze will help."

Ten

FROM THE hidden protection of a boulder, Liam stared transfixed as Charlie shouted and searched for him. It took all his strength to not call out *"I'm here, Charlie."*

Something tore inside as Charlie's dream, which had brought Liam home to Fey, unraveled, and he and his great red firefighting dragon vanished.

Paralyzed and broken, he watched. *She was in the Mist.*

Be safe, Charlie. "I should not have brought you here." Though that had not been his intent. He'd been in the old woman's guest bed, the vile cats outside his door, clawing to get in. He'd fallen asleep... and then here he was. *How did this happen? How is it possible for me to ride on Charlie's dream? You kissed me. You should not have.*

He stared at the dense wall of blue-gray that separated worlds. The kiss still lingered. It tore at him. The smell of Charlie... *and of something else.* He struggled to put the connections together. *He smelled of fairy fire. And what comes with fairy fire?*

His tongue played inside his mouth. *What comes after fairy fire is fairy dust.* It didn't add up, riding on the dream of someone he'd just met. Someone brave and strong, who'd rescued him from a burning... *that was caused by fairy fire. She set that fire.*

Not one to pray, he did. *Be okay, Charlie. Don't let her get you.... Don't be broken. Please stay whole.* The thought was too awful to contemplate. But passages between the See and the Unsee exacted a price from the traveler, whether human or fey. For most humans, and many fey, the cost of the voyage was your sanity.

Moments back in the Unsee, he'd gained one vital piece of information—the whereabouts of Queen May. She was in the Mist—*and she's trapped, or she would have followed*—and in the form of a massive white salamander. *But trapped isn't dead.*

He looked to where Charlie had vanished. A tear tracked down his cheek. *Please be safe. Please be whole.*

He shuddered at the memory of the salamander's gaping maw against the window, her tongue like a poker on the glass, wanting to pierce his heart. To devour him and swallow what little magic remained. Charlie hadn't flinched. He'd driven them out of danger... again. *How can someone be so brave? He walks into burning buildings and brings a stranger into his grandmother's house. A foolish man. A beautiful man.*

He batted at his face. Tears fell. *I don't cry. Not since....* Brutal scenes of his childhood played in his mind. The last time he'd shed tears was when she'd ripped his parents open and feasted on their organs. *Why now?* The wet on his cheeks felt strange. He licked the saltwater from his finger, the faint taste of fairy fire... a hint of dust.

He scanned the meadow for signs of life and made another realization. The Mist was both a wall between the worlds... and a potential passage. He thought of another boy, one May had sent him to seduce. He'd come another way, on the back of a puka, a nightmare.... *But I did the same. I rode in on Charlie's dream. Through the Mist, past May, to here. And I'm alone.*

Something skittered over his bare foot. He looked down; there was nothing. *But wait.* He narrowed his gaze. As he did, forms shimmered in the air and on the ground. Like a cat's eye adjusting to the night, creatures of the Unsee were revealed. A family of elves gathering juniper berries, a flock of pixies hovering over the Western Sea, and far to the south, he glimpsed the turrets of May's palaces, the place he'd been raised, the place he'd witnessed and experienced May's sadism, including the murder of his parents and of hundreds, if not thousands, of fey who displeased her. It was there, in her private kitchen, he'd learned her greatest truth. The murders were more than her means of filling her subjects with fear and obedience. They were her source of power, or at least its greatness. From a hiding hole, he'd seen. It hadn't just been his parents. Beautiful Queen May, with her satins and gowns and romantic cotillions beneath fairy light, ate her victims. Her jaw unhooked, and the dainty queen swallowed the little things whole, and the bigger creatures, the ogres and trolls, she'd cut into bite-size chunks and wolf down. It's what became of his parents. It's what she would do to him for his failure to seduce Alex Nevus and his complicity in Uncle Cedric's plot to help Alex and Jerod escape.

He closed his eyes, wondering if back in the Unsee his magic had returned. He opened himself to the air currents. Nothing. He did not move. He tried a second and then a third time.

It's gone. Both here and there. He knew the rules, and he knew the exceptions. It's why May was obsessed with possessing a haffling, a half human and half fey who could travel unbroken between realms. The only other exception, one he would never know, was with the protection of pure, unconditional, and reciprocated love.

"Liam." He turned at the sound of a familiar voice.

"Cedric." At first he was barely able to see his uncle's form, but by holding still and squinting, his shape solidified. His flowing silver-blond hair, a russet jacket with braided green piping, his mouth pursed, his expression perplexed.

"You've changed." Cedric's eyes, violet like his own, took inventory. "Tell me of your whereabouts."

"The human realm, and now I'm back," Liam stated. "I can barely see you. I cannot take to the wind. I am like the three-legged dog."

"They're often the happiest."

"True, and happiness is not my due. I would know what's happened in my absence."

Cedric looked behind them. "The Mist, it stopped growing. There was the great upheaval, when May possessed the haffling and left our realm. I was certain we would be devoured, and then it stopped. In places, it's retreated. Here and there a village that was gone has returned. Inhabitants remember nothing more than a dream."

"And that's how I returned, though I do not understand how… on the back of a dream." He kept his tongue about the rest of it—that the dream was not his and that the dreamer smelled of fairy fire and his stolen kiss tasted of fairy dust. "May lives. She is in the Mist, trapped… as a giant white salamander." Still shaken, Liam wondered at the queen's choice of form. *Perhaps it's not a choice but her inner self.* He remembered how she'd eaten his parents' hearts and other bits she'd ripped from their ruined bodies as he stood frozen and watched.

Cedric nodded. "I had heard, and it won't be forever. She will return. We must prepare, though in truth, I know not how. Her first acts will be to kill us both, which I could bear. But she will kill my Marilyn, and she will again attempt to use one of my haffling children as a bridge. You look like one of them now. Like a human."

"Tell me," Liam said, having but briefly glanced at his changed image in the old woman's looking glass.

"Your ears, your teeth, even the color of your hair. You are still beautiful, but you do not look fey. You look human."

"I would see your family. I would beg their forgiveness."

Cedric wrapped Liam in his arms. "Marilyn has forgiven me. She will forgive you as well. We are family, and we are few. The past cannot be undone. We were vicious puppets, you and I."

Liam, not used to tears, seemed unable to stop. He sobbed. "She made me a whore."

"She gave you no choice. She gave me no choice."

"We had choice, Uncle."

"To die, yes. That's the choice your mother and father took. I wanted to join them."

Liam looked up into his uncle's face. This was indeed a day of revelations. "You stayed for me."

Cedric nodded. "You are my brother's son. You are all I have left of him, and you are mine."

Liam nodded, uncertain of what to say, his thoughts a jumble from his journeys through the realms. Through the tears, he laughed.

"Tell me," Cedric said.

"Questions, Uncle. It would be so much simpler if we could ask and answer questions."

"Perhaps, but not for me to say. Questions cost."

"Right, so I shall tell you what I know, or think I know. She chose to be a salamander, although I believe her hand was forced. I would know the reason," Liam said.

"Simple. She is not done and for some reason was unable to retain her fairy form." Cedric's breath caught. "And my son... I am frightened for Alex, if he even still lives. For May would not have left his body willingly. He was her vessel, her safe passage between worlds. My son...." Cedric straightened his shoulders and shook back his silvery mane. "Yet there is hope. Our Alex is brave. He is clever, and he is loved. I will not think him dead…. The salamander, Liam, is a creature of singular talents. In order to rule, May must be whole. If you cut off a salamander's arm, it grows another. She means to trick our magic, to trick our rules. But all has not gone as she'd planned. Indeed, I wonder at her true object. Yes, she wants power. Yes, she wants to rule the See and the Unsee, but there's a piece we have missed. I know not what it is. And I know it is important."

Eleven

"IT'S CLEAR as the nose on your face, Charlie. You want to find him," Gran stated, well into her second boozy Mary.

"So what?" Charlie said, his second screwdriver drained, along with two cups of black coffee.

"You won't find him."

He stared at Gran. Of his entire family, she'd been the most accepting of his being gay. She'd told him of other relatives, both male and female. *"Times change, Charlie,"* she'd said when he was sixteen. *"No need for you to marry a woman, make the baby or four, and live a second secret life."*

"Gran, what have you got against Liam?"

"He's not for you."

"Yeah, you've said that a couple dozen times and keep hinting at a big secret. So what is it?"

She smiled. "You ask a lot of questions, boy. How did your Liam like those?"

Charlie paused. *She does know something.* "He didn't."

"Odd, don't you think?" Her words were deliberate, and she exaggerated the lift at the end of her sentence. "And his accent.... Did he say exactly where he was from? Or the fact that five cats all agreed something was not right with that man."

Charlie shook his head, not certain if the booze and caffeine were making this easier or worse. "You're saying he's a vampire, which might explain his disappearing act. You know, daylight and all. Did he vaporize or something?"

Gran signaled for the waitress and another round. She turned back, her tone serious. "I don't talk much of my childhood. It was hard, and the best decision Ma made was to leave Limerick and come to the States. The biggest difference between here and there was this—in this country, people shed their histories like a pair of underwear. We're an old family, Charlie. The fact that I started as a Fitzgerald, married a man named Fitzgerald, is not so unusual. And with the old families, there comes history, stories, and some other things…."

"What does this have to do with Liam?" He wondered if, at eighty-three, Gran wasn't slipping into senility.

"The good people, Charlie… I've heard the wail of our banshee." Her pale eyes looked at him dead-on.

"Okay, now you're pulling my leg. Not just any banshee, but *our* banshee?"

"Nah, you're not going to become one of *them*."

"One of the good people?"

"Don't be absurd. You're not going to become someone who tells me that what I see with my own eyes and hear with my own ears is my imagination. I'm done with that. What I'm telling you is truth. When I was twelve, before the telegram and the two soldiers came to the door to tell my ma, I heard the howl. I knew my da was dead." Her eyes misted, and a lilting accent, schooled away years ago, returned. "Growing up, they were just a part of my life. I didn't think much about them, and mostly, I didn't see them… except when I looked for them. But I knew they were there. I knew that cats howled in their presence, and I'd hear the stories of babies left untended by the fire. I watched my ma and all the other women throw bits of food outside the door. Though Ma said she believed in none of it. Yet every loaf she baked, the heel got tossed as an offering to whatever wasn't in our backyard. You don't do things like that if on some level you don't believe. Those were things we did there, but not here. Here it's nonsense and superstition. A circle of mushrooms in the woods is that and nothing more."

Charlie leaned in. "We're talking what? Fairies, leprechauns?"

"Fey, Charlie. Your Liam reeked of it—sweet and unnatural. It was on the both of you."

"The cookie smell was from the fire, Gran. It was strange, and not everyone smelled it. But you did… and cookies make you think of fairies?"

The waitress returned with a fresh screwdriver and Bloody Mary. Gran stirred her drink with its celery garnish.

"Charlie, I do not have Alzheimer's, and I can't make you believe me, but I want to tell you a story I've not shared since I was eight. When I was little, very little, almost my first memory is of seeing dancing lights in the scrub behind our house. I followed them, though I couldn't have been more than four or five... maybe younger. I've seen the little people, fairies no bigger than your hand. So pretty and mostly naked. I've heard their chatter and brought them sweets—they like sweets best. Like your Liam piling sugar into his tea."

"So he likes his tea sweet. And couldn't it have been your imagination... or...." His own dream of Liam was still fresh, the white snake-thing in the mist, his stolen kiss. *But that was a dream.* "Or the fact that you've got a few hundred books on Irish folklore and fairy tales and maybe.... These are the stories you'd read me as a kid. They're not real, Gran."

"It wasn't the one time, Charlie. The day we left for America, I bid the fairies good-bye. They never harmed me, but I knew to ask them no questions, to bring them sweets, and to treat them well. They are playful by nature, but the intended targets of their merriment don't see the humor in barren fields or pretty babies replaced with changelings." She gazed over Charlie's shoulder through the restaurant window. "I've not seen the good people in over seventy years. But I know what I saw, and I hear the cry of our banshee."

Charlie stilled as memories of 9/11 intruded. "I don't get it. What do you mean '*our* banshee'?"

"It's ours, Charlie. It's for our family. It howls when one of us falls. It's not a human cry—it's older."

Charlie shivered and remembered that morning. He'd been eight. As for everyone else, it was a day of terror, in a city and country under attack. He lowered his voice. "I heard it too, like an animal."

She nodded. "I'm not surprised."

"So you think Liam is—what?"

"A trap, Charlie. I was taught be kind to the good people, never cross them, and never trust them. They don't think like us."

Charlie met Gran's gaze. She was serious, which worried him. It was too fantastic, and while he knew she had an obsession with these stories, he'd never considered that she thought they were true. So yes,

Liam had a weird effect on her cats, and liked his tea sweet and had the most beautiful purple eyes, and smelled of cookies, and.... "No, this is crazy, Gran. He's just a guy." *A really hot guy who's way out of my league.*

"Fine, then. But don't say you weren't warned."

He paid the check and took her home.

They rode the elevator in silence, his thoughts on their conversation and on the futility of tracking Liam in a city of millions.

Inside her bookcase-filled hall, she asked him to help her with a couple of chores.

"You're trying to keep me here," he stated.

"Yes… here's the thing, Charlie." She walked back into her living room, which like the hall was crammed with books. "It's not make-believe. Each of the old stories carries two halves of truth, the human half and the fey. Where each starts and ends, no one knows."

Charlie shook his head. "They're stories, Gran, and I've got to go." He walked up to her, gave her a warm hug, and kissed her on the cheek. He felt her age and how thin she'd grown… but still strong.

She squeezed back. "The smell is gone."

Charlie sniffed. *She's right. It's gone.* It made him sad.

HE LEFT Gramercy and drove to the East Village. He parked on the corner of First Avenue and Third. The block of the fire was still barricaded, and he stared at the charred building with yellow crime-scene tape across the front. *This is stupid.* But the instant he opened his door—*cookies.*

With every step it grew stronger, until he was directly across from the weathered brick façade, now blackened, with most of its windows smashed. Something to be said for its late-nineteenth-century construction that it still stood. While he'd not have thought it on Saturday night, as big chunks of the ceiling and walls gave way, the building could probably be saved.

He spotted the fire marshal's red-and-white Ford SUV and wondered who'd gotten the call. He hoped it would be Finn. Having a friend to explain to might go easier.

If you're going to do it, just do it.

He walked past the barriers, ducked the tape, and headed up the litter-strewn stairs and still-damp stoop. The outer security door was closed but not locked. Same with the one inside, past the rows of metal mailboxes and a buzzer system that had been ripped from the wall.

He heard footsteps and hoped it would be someone familiar as he hunted for information, favors… and Liam.

He spotted a marshal in black boots, blazer, and hard hat on the first-floor landing. The red of his short sideburns gave him hope. "Finn."

Marshal Finn Hulain turned at his name. "Charlie, what the hell you doing here?"

He had no clear plan other than to revisit the scene and…. *He's not going to be here, but maybe you'll find out something, like who he is.* He looked at Finn and tried to read his mood. His brown eyes gave away nothing. From under the brim of the hard hat, his flame-red hair had started to gray at the temples. The Hulains lived two blocks away from his family on Staten Island. Twelve years older than Charlie, he'd been his brother Rory's best friend, almost since day one. At Rory's grave he'd stayed with Charlie, the two of them the last to leave.

"I helped get a guy out of here. He left some important papers behind and wondered if I could get them for him." *Why am I lying? Really? You want to tell him the truth, that you're macking over a guy you just met who you kissed in a dream?*

"The guy on the sixth floor?" Finn looked up at the stairwell that had collapsed between the third and fourth stories. "Great picture, by the way. I hear it's gone viral. Naked Chihuahua guy."

Charlie met Finn's good-humored smile and eased up. "Publicity was not my intent."

"And the little doggy too?"

"That was his doing."

"He got a name?" Finn asked.

"The dog?"

"Jesus, Charlie…." Finn stared at the ground. "The guy, the hot-looking bare-assed blond guy."

Finn's response took Charlie aback. While people knew he was gay, he'd never thought Finn Hulain would notice if a guy were hot or not. Then again, at thirty-six Finn wasn't married, no girlfriend…. "It's Liam."

Finn nodded. "You sure go the extra mile, Charlie. Guy's lucky to be alive. From the look of the upper floors, the same's true for you. This one was bad, and it was no accident."

"I know… I was there. Any chance you'll let me up?"

"You know I shouldn't." Finn looked at the floor and then at Charlie, still in the lobby. "This Liam… you like him?"

"I do," Charlie said and wondered at the conversation's direction.

"Three people died in this mess. One was a toddler."

"I know."

"Fuck it. Just don't muck up the scene, and don't fall through the floor. In fact…."

Charlie paused halfway up the first flight. "What?"

"I'll go with you. You need to see something, and because you were here, maybe you can explain it to me."

He joined Finn on the first-floor landing.

"This." Finn walked Charlie over to a charred hole in the floor outside a north-facing apartment.

"I know," Charlie said as they both stared up at the perfectly aligned openings. "You can see the sky."

"So whatever it was started on the roof… and burned its way to the basement."

"What was it?" Charlie asked. "Like a bomb, a missile? Someone get their hands on a Scud?"

"Got me. Whatever it was, it's just a pile of ash in the basement. I'm going to have it analyzed, but it was incredibly hot. Never seen anything like it. So come on."

And they moved up floor by floor, noting the weird series of burned holes. Halfway up the third-floor stairs, the way was blocked by the partially collapsed stairwell and ceiling.

"Stick to the edge," Finn said. "It's passable but barely. And if you get killed… I never saw you."

"Coward."

"Nah, smart. I know your family. They'd come for me."

"Just Gran."

"And she don't take prisoners."

With their backs braced against the rail and focused on their footing, they made it to the fourth floor. "Jesus!" Charlie stared at the devastation, walls little more than char, wood and plaster now no stronger than chalk.

"You're damn lucky that you and Chihuahua Guy made it. This is where they found the two kids and their mother. The smoke got 'em,"

Finn said, his throat choked. "Better that than the fire. Shit!" Finn gritted his teeth and averted his gaze.

Charlie waited for his friend to regain control. It's what you did. Especially 'round guys who'd been through 9/11 or some of the other tragedies they encountered in the bad calls, like dead kids or pets that curled up and died from the smoke and the heat. Don't make a big deal. Seconds dragged by. Hell, they even had psychologists and social workers come in and give mandatory in-services, which all had a rah-rah feel and numbers to call for help, which few used. Charlie waited. "You good?"

"Yeah, just want to make sure whatever fucked-up bastard started this doesn't ever do it again."

"Agreed." They continued up to the sixth-floor apartment where he'd found Liam. They stopped outside the door he'd smashed. It looked like a raft lying on the kitchen floor.

There was the hole in front of the doorframe, like all the others. Charlie shone his light down to the basement. He tilted his head back and looked at blue sky. He inhaled fresh spring air, scented with cookies.

"I got to ask," he said to Finn. "What do you smell?"

"You mean Mrs. Keebler?"

"Yeah. Weird… night of the fire, some of us smelled it and some didn't. The ones who didn't thought it was a gag, that we were making it up. But you smell it?"

"Yeah, and the pile of ash that started out as something hot enough to burn through a seven-story building smells superstrong. So I'm guessing whatever did this comes with fresh-from-the-oven cookie smell."

"Right." And Charlie, his thoughts buzzed from the smell and the three screwdrivers with Gran, could not piece this together. He crossed the threshold into the construction-zone kitchen. Light streamed through the shattered window where he'd carried Liam.

Finn followed. "Charlie, this place wasn't inhabited. It's a gut job."

"Yeah." He walked over to the porcelain tub. There was blood smeared on the surface, and inside was the screwdriver Liam had used as a weapon.

He heard Finn in the tiny bedroom off to the right. "No one's been in here for a while. You know what I think?"

"What?"

"This smells of a rent-stabilized apartment about to become destabilized."

"Explain."

"These old tenements, a lot of times people have been in them for decades, and you can even pass them down through relatives, like a mother to a daughter. End of the day, landlords get a fraction of the market rate, and nothing they can do about it. When and if someone finally moves out, if the place stays empty long enough and they invest a certain dollar amount in rehabbing it, they can rent it for the prevailing rate. So a unit like this, where they were getting four hundred bucks a month, is now two or three grand."

Charlie looked around, one room no bigger than a prison cell, toilet in a closet, a decent-size kitchen with the bathtub next to the sink, and one other okay-size room. "Right... for this little thing, but I get it. Lots of NYU students with lots of money."

"Yeah, pretty much pushed out everyone else. You got to be rich to live in this slum."

Charlie wandered from the kitchen to the bedroom with two windows, both shattered. He wrapped his hand with a tack cloth he found on the floor, looked out to make sure there was no one below, and smashed out the jagged remains of the one on the right. He ran his hand over the building's seared brick and felt the bolt-holes where there should have been a fire escape. By code, any rentable apartment had to have at least two points of egress.

Finn joined him. "Yeah, it's a violation. Probably figured that while they were doing the reno, it was kosher. It's not, and it's not the only problem with this rattrap. The sprinklers didn't function on half the floors, and the alarm didn't sound at all."

Charlie's jaw tightened. Kids died, and Liam.... If he hadn't come when he did, Liam would never have made it. *But what was he doing here? No one lives here.*

"So now my turn," Finn said.

"What?"

"Your man, Naked Chihuahua Guy."

"He's not my man."

Finn cleared his throat. "Fine, we'll play by your rule. Generic naked blond guy. What was he doing here?"

"I don't know."

"You didn't ask?"

"He wasn't big on questions."

"Yeah, suspicious fire… no, screw 'suspicious.' This was set. And your man is on the sixth floor of the building where whatever burned its way down came in just above him. So… let's go with things you can't ever say I said… like a cookie-scented Scud missile hit the building. It came through the roof, so either it landed there or was set there. Either way, your Liam… he was… like a target."

Charlie listened. It was a possibility he'd not considered. He walked to a homemade closet built from sheets of plywood, its garishly painted outer surface bubbled and destroyed by the heat. Whatever images had been there were largely undecipherable. The handleless doors were shut tight. He pulled out his pocketknife and worked the blade into the opening.

"What's in there?" Finn asked, coming to his side.

The doors swung open. The painted scenes inside took their breath. "Holy…." Charlie stared, trying to take in the beauty and madness before him. A painted jungle gone bonkers. Every inch covered with unimaginable creatures, some with wings, some with bodies that were half insect and half human. A giant dull green ogre with an ax. It grabbed Charlie's focus. *That's how I looked to him. Was that why he was so frightened? What the fuck is this?*

Finn pulled back the other door. "I can see why this is still in here. Somebody figured it was worth some money. Pity about the outside of it. You know what it reminds me of?"

Charlie braced, kind of knowing where this was headed.

"The stories your Gran would read us, Rory and me. Look, it's the little people, the toadstool circles. Jesus, it's like memory lane…." Finn shot a hand against the closet. "Oh shit!"

"What's wrong?"

"Nothing." He could barely speak and braced his other hand on the solid wood to steady himself.

"Right." Charlie guessed at the cause of Finn's emotion. He too thought of Rory as he stared at a trio of silver-haired figures in the back of the closet. They looked mostly human but with pointy ears and sharp teeth that made him think there was more than vegetables in their diet. But their eyes made his heart race—purple. Something about the expression of the one in the center…. *Not possible.*

"So no clothes in the closet," Finn said, doing the one thing that helped when his ghosts came to visit—work. He stepped back. "Nothing in the fridge. It wasn't even plugged in. So again, Charlie, what was naked Liam doing here?"

"No clue."

"All right. I don't mean to treat you—or him—like a perp, but we got to figure this shit out. You told me Liam left some papers here. That means you know where the guy is."

"I lied," Charlie stated.

"Okay, then." Finn smiled. "So guess I will treat you like a perp. You lied to get up here. What are you looking for? And do not lie to me again, Charles Michael Fitzgerald."

Charlie turned to his friend. "It's not a what, but a who. I'm looking for him, Finn. I'm looking for Liam."

Twelve

UNABLE TO take to the wind, Liam followed Cedric on foot through the meadow into the bustling ruins of May's royal city. The magic she'd used to maintain her various ventures—Fey TV studios, a movie set—had returned to the white-marble bones of their earlier existence. The ruined colonnades, playing fields, and temples were ancient and beautiful and dated to the days before the See and Unsee were separated by the Mist. And, for the first time in Fey history, no one had stepped forward to take the throne.

"We have no king or queen," Cedric explained as he swiveled to the side to let a mother elf, with her hand-holding brood, pass.

Ruler or no, commerce lived on in the stall-filled open-air market. As Liam's vision acclimated, the Unsee, with its rich diversity of sentient inhabitants, appeared to him: fairies of all colors and sizes, from tiny sprites to gargantuan cyclops, who despite their reputation were the gentlest of souls.

"Anarchy suits us," Liam commented as he took in the bustling market.

"History tells us this will not last," Cedric replied. "One hopes for the best and braces for the worst."

"There are three royal sisters. May is but one."

"True, but Katye is lost to our world, and Lizbeta, if she still exists, does so in the Mist. One wonders if any of them are still whole and fit to rule." Cedric turned to Liam. "I would know how it is you traveled to the See. One day you're here, and then…. Tell me."

Shame colored Liam's cheeks. Like a well-worn pair of pants, the emotion clung. "When May left… when she took the haffling, your son

Alex, I ran. I knew she would kill me. So I went to the one place where her power does not reach."

"The Center."

"Yes. I sought asylum but was not allowed in. I do not blame them. They knew me for what I am and what I've done. I'm sure they thought me May's spy. So I hid in a cave by the Western Sea, waiting for her to come. Or for the Mist. I waited for death."

"I'm surprised any of us are still alive. But let's not forget"—Cedric placed a hand on Liam's shoulders—"you helped Alex in the end."

"Barely. And it did no good. She took him anyway."

"I still don't understand how you left, or how you came back, not exactly broken but not whole… different." Cedric stared at Liam. "Tell me of my son. Tell me that you've seen him. That he is alive."

"I have not seen him, and I'm not clear on either how I left or how I returned, other than the latter was on the back of a hero's dream. This is what I remember…. There was an explosion, and the smell of fairy fire, and a tunnel in the mist. Like something had burned a hole through worlds." He remembered the heat and the reek. "It pulled me in… and then I don't remember. I woke to fire and flashing lights. I was no longer here but there. Cedric, it was fairy fire." A creature at a linen stall, with the lower bits of a praying mantis and the torso and head of a woman, turned. Liam recognized her.

"Hello, Liam," she said.

"Dorothea." The sound of May's closest servant's voice was like stepping back in time. His vision narrowed, and blood-filled memories caused him to freeze.

"You look…."

It was hard to speak. "Different, yes. I'm aware."

"We thought you dead. It's what she would have wanted," Dorothea said, twisting her head on its long green neck. "Tell me—"

"No, he'll tell you nothing," Cedric said. He placed a guiding arm on Liam's and led him to a fruit stall. He whispered, "She may be gone, but her reach remains. Those who were closest speak of her return. They pray for it."

Liam kept his voice low, "May lives. It was her. She has fairy fire. She has power."

Cedric nodded, aware of Dorothea's acute hearing. "No surprise, although it does not make sense. Pieces are missing. If May is in the

Mist, she will not give up. She will not let my children rest. It's not in her nature. She means to rule, not just here but there as well. She will come for them."

Liam felt an ache in his chest, a thing that needed to be voiced. "I was meant to glamour and seduce your son Alex, to trick him in love."

"As I tricked my Marilyn… and she tricked me right back. What confounds me is how she forgives my treachery."

"I would know of that. I would know of forgiveness. Tell me."

Cedric looked back at a graceful dark-haired woman in a flowing floral dress, accompanied by a redheaded boy, no more than seven. The pair were headed toward them.

Liam followed his gaze. "I should go. She will not wish to see me."

"No," Cedric stated.

"She must hate me."

"Perhaps. Cowards run, and heroes face what must be faced."

"I am no hero." He thought of Charlie and of a stolen kiss in his fire-red truck. "I will face your Marilyn."

The woman stopped a ways from Cedric and Liam and stared. With her young son at her back, she approached. "Speak of the devil, and I will appear. What happened to you?"

Her blunt question startled Liam.

"Cat got your tongue?" She motioned her son to stay back. Her deep blue eyes widened. "You've been there, haven't you? Answer me. You've been to the See, to my world."

"Yes," Liam said, frightened by her rapid-fire questions. *She has no fear.*

She closed the space, her face inches from his. "Alex… my son. Have you seen him?"

"No."

She gasped and bent over, her hands on her hips, anguish on her face. "I don't want to know this." She looked up. "Is he alive?"

"I do not know. I know that she no longer possesses him. She is in the Mist."

She nodded. "We'd heard rumors. She's out of my boy. My brave boy." Tears flowed. She looked to her husband. "Could he have survived that? Tell me, husband."

"I do not know, but he is strong, and he is brave. He gets that from you," Cedric said, going to her side. "Shh." He kissed her cheek and wiped her tears with his sleeve. He looked at Liam. "We fey scoff at the humans and think them lesser creatures. My Marilyn is braver than I have ever been or could hope to be." He wrapped her in the folds of his russet jacket, his arms around her waist. "In her love I find the seeds of bravery. Never again will one of our children be placed in jeopardy." He motioned for redheaded Adam to join them. Holding his family, he sighed. "I say these things, but we know that valor is quick to the tongue and tested in battle. Alex, our brave son, put his life after that of his mother, his brother, his sister, and the man he loved. I learn from him and from my Marilyn."

Marilyn stared at Liam. "Alex's Jerod—what of him? He was in the Mist when May devoured Alex."

"I do not know. I was not there long."

"So what can you tell me?" Her frustration seemed at the boil.

"I don't know," he repeated, amazed at how question after dangerous question shot from her lips.

"You look human," she spat at him. "You've lost your pointy sharp bits, and your skin is not so pale as my pasty Cedric. Your hair too, it's more gold than silver. Did you dye it?"

The little boy smiled at Liam from the warmth and safety of his father's long coat. "I'm glad you're back, Liam. We thought you'd been eaten by the Mist."

"No… I was in the See."

Adam's eyes lit. "But you did not see my brother or my sister. Could you go back? Can I? I'm a haffling, you know. I can make the trip… like my brother. I won't break."

Liam glanced from Cedric to the boy. Any other fey child would have received a sharp blow across the mouth and dire warning about the dangers of questions. *Curiosity killed the Questling.*

Marilyn looked from Adam to Liam. "Yes. Smart child. I cannot make the trip. And you're too young. But you…." Her gaze was glued to Liam.

Cedric whispered in her ear, "I'm sorry."

"Yes, I know you are," she said with more anger than she'd intended. "You have been forgiven… though at times I don't know why. You, on the other hand…," she spat at Liam through gritted teeth.

"Sweetness… try to calm yourself. And no more questions," Cedric said.

Marilyn pulled away. She turned on her husband and his nephew. "Why should I? I have more than paid the cost for any questions, past or future. I will not live bounded by your fear and superstition. I will not raise Adam to be afraid. You say you want courage, husband? This is how it's done. Do not hide from things that frighten you. You face them. And if they want a fight, you give it to them." She gave him no chance to respond. "Now tell me, Liam, before you vanished, you begged my forgiveness for the role you played in May's schemes. I called you a whore, for in truth, you were sent to seduce my firstborn son. It didn't work. His heart was taken, and your glamour bounced like an egg off of Teflon." She teared up. "Words are cheap, Liam Summer. But… I am prepared to offer forgiveness. You must earn it! You want my forgiveness, and I want news of my children in the See. I need to know if Alex is alive. I must get word to Alice, to tell her that I am well, that her brother Adam lives, and that we love her. I cannot take the trip, as I'm broken and barking mad on the other side. My place is here with Adam and Cedric. If you want my forgiveness, it is yours… for a price. I would know of my children. Do we have a deal?"

Liam nodded. He looked at redheaded Adam, young and innocent, and at Marilyn, the source of Alex's courage. He thought of Charlie, storming into a house on fire to save a worthless, whorish fey. "It is a fair price, Marilyn."

Cedric interjected. "It is not! Marilyn, there are few enough of us. I will not watch Liam killed for news of our children. See what the trip back and forth has done to him."

"Husband, know that I love you, and know that your sins have been absolved by your love and your actions. Liam has paid no such price, nor need he. He wants forgiveness…. It must be earned," she said through gritted teeth.

Cedric repeated, "The cost is too high. Do not be foolish, Liam. You are needed here."

Liam held Marilyn's gaze and nodded. "The price is fair. All that remains is the means of my passage. I traveled on a dream. It brought me through the Mist."

"There are other means, as I know better than most." She shot Cedric a pointed look. "There are mirrors, though I smashed the one that brought me here."

Liam looked to Cedric, the thought of returning to the See both terrifying and.... *I could see Charlie again. Just to thank him, nothing more.* "Alex rode in on the nightmare," he stated.

"Yes," Cedric admitted. "But the nightmare, the puka, is beyond reason. It's as likely to drown you as it is to carry you across."

Liam weighed his words; they were truth. Marilyn's child had sacrificed himself to save his family, and in the process had set in motion the downfall of despotic Queen May. Yes, he wanted Marilyn's forgiveness, and yes, he wanted to see Charlie, but there was something more. He could not find the words for it. It had something to do with ancient memories of his true parents, his mother, Ileana, and father, Cullen, of their murder, of the role he'd been forced to play in May's court. And it had to do with a stolen kiss.... "Summon the puka, Cedric. I will do this."

Thirteen

STILL IN his navy suit, Charlie left Finn and tracked down the manager of the burned-out building on East Third. As he walked the few blocks to the rental office on Sixth Street, he tried to clear his head. The things Finn had told him about the fire, that he'd seen with his own eyes, reminded him of why he chose to became a firefighter and not a cop like his dad, his brother Michael, and a couple dozen Fitzgerald uncles and cousins.

"It's what our clan does, Charlie," Gran had said over brunch. "It's what we've always done. We serve, protect, and run into buildings on fire."

As he entered the small un-air-conditioned storefront office, the smell hit first—cigarettes, which spilled from a dinner-plate-size ashtray, sweat, and vinegar. The source of it all was a squirrely man with an Eastern European accent, a bad comb-over, and a dingy button-down white shirt soaked under the pits. The man's name—George Slotnik, Property Manager—was etched on a plastic pyramid at the edge of his desk.

Charlie flashed his FDNY ID. "I need the name of the last resident in apartment twenty-four. And if you've got a forwarding address, that would be swell."

"I cannot give that information," Slotnik replied, his attention split between Charlie and a plastic fork with which he was trying to spear something from a tall container, which stank of vinegar and cabbage.

"You can, and you will," Charlie said. "Unless you want to obstruct an arson investigation."

"You have warrant?" Slotnik's tone was disinterested as he popped a forkful of cabbage-wrapped goodness into his mouth.

Charlie stared as a trail of sauce dribbled across lease agreements. "We'll get a warrant. I can have the marshal here in five minutes."

"So? Marshal's not same as cop."

"Yeah, it is."

"I did not know… all fire marshals?"

"Yes, that's how it works. Been that way for decades with the Bureau of Fire Investigation. All the marshals are cops, and they can all issue warrants. So, why hold back something as simple as a prior resident? It makes no sense."

"I am not a rich man, Mr. Fitzgerald. You have bosses. I have bosses. They do not appreciate people doing things that aren't their job. I have wife and children. A son who was brutally assaulted by a neighborhood thug and needs medical care…."

Something in the creep's expression let Charlie know what was needed. He reached for his wallet, pulled out four twenties, a five, and some singles. "I just need the name of the tenant."

Slotnik eyed the bills. "That is not enough."

"Take it or leave it. I will get this information. The fact you've delayed the process won't matter in the end…." And then he did what his dad would do. He squeezed. "In arson it comes down to one of three things—money, revenge, and firebugs. If this is arson, which it looks like, it's also murder. I'm just going to be the first one to ask questions and to wonder just how far you'd go to help your bosses. Someone's going to go down for this. If you haven't figured that out, let me be the first to tell you. Someone, maybe several someones, is going to jail. And that's just the criminal side. Lots of people lost their homes in a building filled with code violations."

Slotnik put down his fork. Sweat beaded under his nose and across his broad forehead. "Fine." He grabbed the money and wheeled his chair to a filing cabinet. "What was the number?"

"Twenty-four."

With his back to Charlie to conceal the drawer's contents, he pulled out a thick manila folder.

Charlie wondered how much illegality and how many scams were buried in those drawers. The fact that half the sprinklers in that building had been nonfunctional and the alarms hadn't gone off made it hard to not leap across the space and pummel the guy. Three people died—two of them kids—and they didn't have to.

Slotnik grunted, as if surprised by the file's contents. He wiped his forehead with the back of his sleeve. "They always paid on time."

"Good to know. What name was on the lease?"

"Nevus, Marilyn Nevus."

"What do you know about her?"

"Nothing. Why should I? We just rent apartments."

Fed up with the evasiveness, Charlie grabbed the folder from his hands.

Slotnik protested. "You need warrant for this."

Charlie ignored him and riffled through the contents. Cancelled checks and neatly filed inspections commenting on the apartment's immaculate condition, all signed by the same housing inspector. Charlie double-checked the address and number, as the reports bore nothing in common with the actual apartment. "They had a voucher. A mother and two children in that tiny place."

"It met code," Slotnik said. "The mother and daughter in one room, the boy in the other. It was legal."

"These checks weren't signed by the same person," Charlie noted.

"Who cares, as long as they clear? We are a management company. We do not oversee the comings and goings of our hundreds of tenants."

"What's this?" Charlie pulled out an official report with the seal of the Office of Children and Family Services. Unlike the other reports, it was less glowing about the apartment's condition. It was signed by a social worker—Lydia Green, OCFS. He scanned the findings. The apartment was poorly maintained. A section of the ceiling had collapsed and been repaired by the tenant's son, Alex Nevus.... *And that name is so... not possible.* "The woman's son, Alex Nevus. He was a contestant on *IT*."

Slotnik glared back. "I don't know what you're talking about."

"You do. Just tell me, is this the same Alex Nevus who nearly won *IT*?"

"I don't have time for TV shows."

Charlie had enough. "Mr. Slotnik, this is your last chance to give me the information I want. Whether or not you're involved with arson will be discovered. But even without that, there's sufficient evidence in this one folder to show you've been defrauding the city with bogus condition reports. I was in that apartment."

"I don't know—"

"Mr. Slotnik, how many similar reports are in those files? More importantly, what you may or may not understand is that housing vouchers, while they come through the city, are funded from three sources—city, state, and federal. If fraud has been committed, it's a federal and criminal offense. Even before we get to the arson investigation… and murder. This is not a slap on the wrist. This is hard time for you and your bosses in federal prison."

"I'm just the manager."

"So maybe you'll be able to cut a deal, and maybe your bosses won't let a family man like you hang out in the breeze and say it was all your doing. After all, you are the manager…."

Slotnik caved. "Yes, it was the same thug boy, Alex Nevus. He was on that show. He…." His face reddened. "He is the one who assaulted my Gregor… for no reason. He broke my boy's kneecap. He still cannot walk right." He pointed to the report in Charlie's hand. "They… the Office of Children and Family Services, pulled them out of that apartment. And no, I do not have a forwarding address, and no, I will not help you."

"Fair enough." In earshot of Slotnik and not letting the man out of his sight, he pulled out his cell. "Finn."

"Charlie, what's up?"

"If I were you, I'd send someone down for the records on that building." He smiled at Slotnik. "I've a feeling there's about to be a shredding party."

"I'm on my way. Do me a favor. Don't leave till I get there."

"Wouldn't dream of it."

"So, did you find what you were looking for? Your Liam?" Finn asked.

Charlie sensed Finn's unasked questions. "Maybe. Not him, exactly. But maybe a lead."

"None of my business, but the guy got to you. What is it about him? I mean, other than he was hot…."

For the second time, Finn caught Charlie by surprise. "Since when do you talk about guys being hot?"

Silence.

"Finn? You there?"

"Yeah."

"Okay, then." *What the hell is going on with Finn?* And then to Slotnik, "I ain't going anywhere, so don't even think about it."

"I call my boss." Slotnik pulled out his cell.

"Good idea. I'm sure the marshal will have questions for him too. Like why half the sprinklers in that building didn't work or that the alarm never went off."

Slotnik hesitated. Charlie lowered his voice. "Finn, get here fast. Bring backup and lots of boxes."

"On my way."

Fourteen

LIAM SUMMER waited in silence with Marilyn. They stared out at the edge of the Western Sea. Cedric had gone to summon the puka.

Liam's knees trembled. He tried to quiet his thoughts. It was impossible. *What would Charlie do?* His one trip to the See had changed his form and cost him most of his magic. *What will happen this time? Will I go mad?* He glanced at Marilyn as she searched the shore for her husband's return. *What would Charlie do?*

Thoughts of the tall firefighter, with his stubbled face and deep blue eyes, made him smile. *He wouldn't hesitate.* His breath caught. *Is he okay? What did the trip cost him?* His smile vanished as he remembered the promise to Charlie's gran—*Do no harm. And I did.*

Liam sat on a rocky outcropping and listened to the waves against the shore. In the distance was the wall of mist, where May waited, *or is trapped, or....*

Beyond the dunes and a vast meadow, he glimpsed the white spires of the Center, built centuries ago by the famous Doctor Redmond Fall. They'd not been cruel when he'd begged asylum, but they'd been clear that May's taint was on him. "You are not welcome," the head guard had told him. Had their places been reversed, Liam would have done the same.

He thought of Queen May and her lust for power and blood. It was her hunger to rule both the humans and the fey that had fueled her plot to steal the body of Alex Nevus, the haffling son of Uncle Cedric and Marilyn.

"It won't be long," Marilyn said, turning back to him. "I feel the puka's approach. Listen...."

Liam quieted his breath and tried to catch the vibrations of the powerful creature. "I have little magic left," he admitted.

Marilyn looked at him. "You're luckier than most. Your travel left you beautiful. Where you're going, magic is not as useful as May would believe. Humans have little need for it and a long tradition of burning witches."

Liam held her gaze. This was Cedric's Marilyn, an odd fixture in the Unsee. Certainly not the only human, as the fey were wont to snatch pretty children and replace them with changelings. "Tell me, Marilyn.... Oh, to hell with it." And through gritted teeth, he asked a question. "Why you?" He glanced behind him, wondering who else might have heard.

"Why me, what?" She chuckled, amused by his discomfort.

"Why did May pick you?"

She nodded. "Got it, and it took me a while to figure out. I'm not all the way there, but it's something like this. There are old families, Liam, both here and in the See. Families who go back to a time before the worlds were split and before the Mist appeared to separate them. Because that is what the Mist is, a barrier to keep the fey on one side and the humans on the other. Only here, you can see the Mist. There's none of that in the human world."

"Right." Liam thought back through his short time in the See, the night of fairy fire, of being carried in Charlie's arms. It had been dark, but there'd been no mist. "Even in the daylight one doesn't see the Mist."

"Correct.... The puka is close. Not long now. So why me, you ask? It's my blood, Liam, and that I'm a seventh daughter of a seventh daughter. And that even in the human world, I possessed a bit of magic. I was a painter, ever since I was a little girl.... Something would come over me when I painted. I saw the Mist, and I pierced its veil. I wasn't more than four or five when I began to see the fey and drew what I'd seen in crayon and then watercolor, acrylics, oils....

"It never stopped. I knew not to talk about what I'd seen, and because the paintings were good, people thought it was my imagination. I told myself it couldn't be real, the things I saw. That it was just a beautiful madness, an artistic psychosis. They say that human children with special abilities often lose them as they grow. For me, it was the opposite. It got to where picking up a paintbrush or staring at a blank canvas was like saying *abracadabra*. I painted you all. It must be how I came to May's attention. Her nose for magic is strong. She saw me look in. Perhaps she even sent me the visions—or some of them. Though I'm not about to pop over into the Mist and ask. Regardless, she saw me, she knew what I was, and she set a trap."

"Uncle Cedric."

"Yes…. Cedric. I had a mirror in a gold frame. Nothing fancy, but sometimes I'd set it up on an easel so I could draw myself into paintings. I had the idea that it would be fun to juxtapose something as mundane as a woman painting against scenes from Fey. Only the first time I did it, what stared back from the mirror wasn't me but Cedric's beautiful face. His eyes. You're lucky to have kept those."

Liam nodded as the ground quaked with the pounding of hooves. His gut churned. "I may not keep them this time." *How will I change? What would Charlie do?*

Marilyn spoke fast, knowing they had little time. "I am the object lesson of what the journey costs. I came here for love of your uncle. I became pregnant and awoke back in the human world. Only what had been the madness of my painting had spread to my every waking moment. I won't bore you with what happens to mad humans. Suffice to say, my life was not easy. And worse still, I was in love, and Cedric was lost to me. My every waking moment, I was obsessed with finding him, of finding a way back."

"You did."

"Yes, and I learned the truth about my love. That he, like you, was a creature of seduction. I had been glamoured."

The thunder of hooves grew as Liam tried to unravel the thread of Marilyn's story. Queen May's plan to glamour Marilyn and have her bear haffling children had been hatched over two decades earlier, longer if Marilyn's childhood visions were not a coincidence. With every answer, a dozen questions appeared. "But Cedric loves you."

"Yes, he does. But not at first, and that's what broke me. My last trip to the human realm is little more than a blur. I can't return… not ever. I am sane here… at least sane enough, but there…. It's just confusion, and voices, and walls dripping with blood. It's where my children are. Liam, I pray this journey does not break you. I wish it with all my heart, and for selfish reasons. I need to know of my children. When you do this thing, I will fully and truly forgive you for every transgression you have ever done to me and the people I love. I will love you for this." Through gritted teeth and tight jaw, she said, "Get me word of my children, tell me they are well, and all is forgiven."

Before he could respond, the sand on the shore started to bounce. Pebbles and bits of sea glass jumped into the air. The waves upon the water flattened, and like a door opening, the slick black puka, in the form of a massive mare, with Cedric upon its back, appeared a few yards from the water's edge.

The creature's eyes blazed red. Its flanks dripped with green-black algae from the depths. It stood upon the sea, the surface smooth as glass.

Cedric, his eyes wide with fear, gasped for air, jumped off the beast, and sank thigh-high into the stilled waters.

Liam glanced from the puka to his reflection in the water. He barely recognized the face that looked back, more human than fey. It was the cost of his first journey. He looked up into the creature's fiery eyes. *And what will this cost? Will I go mad?*

He straightened, and like a mantra, he again thought, *What would Charlie do?*

"Liam, it's not too late. You need not do this." Cedric huffed as he slogged toward the shore, his boots and pants heavy with seawater.

Liam looked to Marilyn. Her request was fair. It was the correct price to undo the wrong he had done. "No, Uncle. I will go."

Expecting to sink below the surface, he stepped into the water. It held his weight, and he approached the monster. Its powerful neck bowed before him. Liam touched its slick hide, grabbed a handful of its matted mane, and mounted.

As he lit upon the creature's back, they sank below the surface.

Unprepared, Liam hung on, unable to breathe, his eyes seeing only darkness and his skin freezing in the depths. Unlike Charlie's dream, the passage was not through the Mist but through water. He knew the puka would carry him from the Unsee to the See. He also knew that delivering him alive was not a given. More than once he'd seen lifeless bodies pried from the creature's flanks. He'd seen young Alex Nevus breathe life back into his boyfriend, Jerod Haynes, who'd sacrificed all for his lover. He'd seen the contempt in Alex's eyes as he'd pressed him to abandon Jerod. Shameful memories flooded him. The creatures Queen May had forced him to seduce. The death of his parents, who would not submit to her demands. Life at the court. The queen's fury at his failure to seduce Alex Nevus. Her rage at Cedric's betrayal.

As his lungs hungered for oxygen, Liam's life—a life he found wanting—flew past.

The puka landed on the bottom and galloped forward. Liam realized that his body, more human than fey, would not survive. Darkness and cold clouded his mind. His heart slowed. *I'm dying.* His final thoughts were of Charlie, brave, kind, Charlie Fitzgerald. His stolen kiss. The feel of his hands on the sides of his face. *He'll think it nothing but a dream. He will not remember me.* He slipped into darkness, and though he was dying, he was not afraid.

AT THE cusp of death, he did not feel the strong hands that pried him from the beast's back. As consciousness returned, he wondered if he were dead. For he was not on dry land, his feet barely visible in the Mist. All around him was fog. And then, with a dazzling display of opalescence, it parted and revealed a raven-haired woman dressed in the swirling sea-foam light of a hundred tiny fairies.

While she had left the Unsee centuries before his birth, Liam knew the creature before him. One of the three sisters. "Lizbeta."

"Yes, Liam Summer, and no, you are not dead. Though you came close. A ride on a puka. There is hope for you yet, my love."

As his thoughts cleared and he gulped misty air, he felt at peace. It emanated from the shimmering woman, whose movements sent ripples and eddies through the Mist.

She threw back an arm, and the Mist retreated. Revealed in its absence was a fearsome white salamander that twisted and writhed, a braided silver yoke around its neck. Its pale blue eyes stared at Liam, its mouth open as its talons clawed at its restraint.

"Behold my sister, May. Her plans for world domination met with a setback."

Liam shook, but something about Lizbeta kept his fear at bay. He stared at the creature with her flat razor-sharp teeth. It was she who had attacked Charlie's great red fire dragon. In the creature's eyes, he glimpsed the mad queen. She had stolen Alex Nevus's body. She had traveled between realms, and now… she was a salamander, a creature of change, a creature of fire. He caught the scent. *A creature of fairy fire. This is her doing. It's all her.*

"Tell me, Lizbeta. The boy she stole, the haffling Alex Nevus. Tell me he still lives."

"I do not know. I cannot see beyond my Mist. Here and there I catch a glimpse, before my love, my Mist, takes his due. And when someone steals a ride on a puka or a dream, yes, I see… for a bit, but not far and not much. Some travelers we let pass. Others.…"

"You saved me."

"I did, Liam Summer, for we are of the same blood, you and I, and you have important work to do. The fate of the Unsee and the balance of our worlds depends on your actions. I cannot hold my sister much longer. Her fury, her rage, and her power grows. She will soon outstrip my strength and that of the Mist. She seeks power and vengeance. They consume her. She hungers for blood and for magic."

"Tell me how she came to be here, how she became captive."

"What knowledge I have is yours. It's not much. She was expelled from the haffling. Whether or not he survived, I cannot say. Perhaps that's why she was thrown out. It's possible—likely—that she killed her vessel. She is a creature of near pure magic. I grabbed her fast as she wriggled from the See back to the Unsee. My sister is brutal. I will not think what horrors would have ensued should she have passed through. Even here, I cannot stop all of her destruction."

"She wants more. She always wants more," Liam said, unable to take his eyes from the thing the once beautiful queen had become.

"Yes, power. It is her special, as mine is peace and Katye's is love. I cannot hold her here, Liam. I must learn how she was defeated. I need this information, and we do not have much time. You are traveling between worlds. The answers are in the See. That is where she did battle and was bested. I need you to do this, to be my hero. Tell me that you will, and in return I will give you—"

"No!"

Lizbeta turned, her expression incredulous. "You tell me no."

"I will take nothing. That is what I'm telling you. Let me continue on my way, and I will seek your answer. There will be no cost. Lizbeta, you hold back horror and destruction. It is I who owe you. Tell me what you will have of me."

"May, she is my sister. I will not harm her. I will not kill her…
but she must be contained. Even now she breaks my magic. It won't
be long."

Liam balked at the enormity of what was being asked. He eyed the
white monster as it paced on squat, heavy limbs. The ground around it
was littered with bones of magical creatures, the smell of fairy fire thick
in the air. *Given the chance, she will destroy us. Best to kill her. To be
done with this.* "Lizbeta, I will do what I can. I will do this. Tell me. You
say her bonds weaken, that your magic will not hold her. Tell me how
much time I have."

Lizbeta eyed her tethered sister. The luminescent queen's
expression was serene, but her words lit terror. "Not long. I cannot stop
her hunger. I cannot read her thoughts. The collar around her neck will
snap soon. I wish it were better news, and it's not. Now go. Hurry!
Though I fear no matter how quick you are, how true your course, we
are already too late."

MAY LISTENED and watched from her comfy circle of bones and
bits. With each passing day, her thoughts returned and her magic grew.
She knew who and what she was. *I am May, Queen of the Fey.* She
remembered the horrible black-haired boy and what he did to her. A
flame hissed through her lips. *I was tricked. Fool me once, shame on
you. Fool me twice… I'll eat you with rice.*

At first she'd not recognized her pretty whore. *Changed… but
the outside is still comely.* Recent events in the Mist coalesced. The
bright red truck, and—*This one was inside with a dark-haired human.
He has traveled between worlds. I have traveled. He is changed. I am
changed.*

Tricked, I was. But now I will trick. She curled on the ground, an
eye on Liam and her sister clothed in a swarm of tasty little fairies. She
hummed, and her mind traveled up and out through the Mist. She sang
as she again entered sweet Alice's thoughts. *There were three haffling
babes. Marked at birth they were. With a hey nonny-nonny and a twinkle
and a twirl. With hair of black and blonde and red. They traveled between
the worlds. With a hey nonny-nonny and a twinkle and a twirl.*

She looked out through Alice's eyes and marveled at the teen's
strength and speed as she battled with an Asian man, whose hands

moved like lightning and whose feet floated across the floor. *What are we up to, Alice?*

Her gaze widened as Alice practiced what she'd been taught by her kung-fu *sifu. I see, we train to be a warrior. Wonderful!* May watched and gently pressed at the edges of Alice's mind. She heard the girl's thoughts and mingled them with her own. The younger boy with the auburn hair was here, dressed in dull gray. May noted how his eyes seldom left Alice. *We have an admirer.* In Alice's thoughts, May tasted a delightful thread of the teen's uncertainty about the boy…. *His name is Clay. We like him. He's our best friend. He's too young. We still like him…. Do we like him in that way? I don't know. Then why do I think about him when I go to sleep? Why do I wonder what it would be like to kiss him? Too young. I'm fourteen. He's twelve. That's gross….*

Unlike the brutal takeover she'd performed on the girl's brother Alex, this time would be different. *Isn't this nice, Alice? See how well we fit. There's some of you and some of me… and bit by bit, there's more of me and less of you. Until one day it's all of me and none of you.*

Fifteen

AFTER FINN showed up at Slotnik's office with a warrant, a couple of guys, and a truck to box up the records and computers in the rental office, Charlie called his older brother Michael, an NYPD detective.

"What's up, Charlie?"

"I need to track someone down."

"You plan to get me in trouble?"

"Not my intent. I just need a number."

"Fine. Why?"

Charlie hesitated. He thought about lying, but the truth was too convoluted. "I'm trying to track down the guy I got out of that building."

"Right, Naked Chihuahua Guy. Are we talking boyfriend material, here?"

"Maybe… I don't know. I just need to know if he's okay."

"Name?"

"Liam Summer, but I've got a feeling he won't have a phone."

"Everyone has a phone, Charlie."

"If he does, great… but the one I think might know where he is, is kind of famous. Guy's name is Alex Nevus."

"Right… I know that name, because?"

"He was on a reality show a few years back."

"And this Alex Nevus knows Naked Chihuahua Guy?"

"Maybe."

"Okay, then, brother, give me five minutes, and I'll see what I can do for you. And in exchange—"

"Here it comes…."

"Hey, you want a favor, it's going to cost."

"How much?"

"You pick up Gran and take her back tonight."

"Done."

"Awesome!"

True to his word, Michael got back to Charlie with Alex Nevus's cell number. "And you're right about that Liam Summer... lots of Summers, fewer without the *S*, but not a Liam to be had. I don't know if I'd trust someone who doesn't have a phone. Those off-the-grid guys are usually a few apples short of a bushel."

Charlie smiled. Between Gran's weird rambles over brunch and the bizarre paintings inside the wardrobe in the burned-out apartment, there was a possibility that not only was Liam off the grid, he was.... "Thanks, Michael." And he hung up.

Without pause he tapped in Alex Nevus's number. He waited, wondering if the guy screened his calls, and if he left a message, what was he supposed to say. *Hi, you don't know me, but I'm a firefighter who was in your old apartment, and I saw the freaky painted closet, and I was wondering....*

"Hello?"

"Hi. You don't know me. My name is Charlie Fitzgerald. I'm a firefighter with the FDNY."

"Look, I'm a student. I've got no...."

"I'm not looking for money, and please don't hang up. I was in your old apartment on East Third."

"Right... I saw it on the news. You the one with the naked guy holding the dog?"

"Yeah... guess it went viral."

"It did."

Charlie heard a shift in Alex's tone. "So it's kind of why I'm calling, and it's going to get strange."

"I'm used to strange. Is this something we do over the phone, or did you want to meet?"

"I'm on East Sixth," Charlie said.

"You want to meet in Washington Square? I'm at the NYU library. I could use a break, and it sounds like you've got questions."

"I do."

And Alex said something that let Charlie know this was not a goose chase.

"You know that questions cost?"

His hand shook. "I'd heard that." And they hung up.

Fifteen minutes later, winded and anxious, Charlie stood in front of the white arch that opened onto the start of Fifth Avenue. He scanned the Sunday scene for the dark-haired boy who'd nearly won *IT* a few years back and whose videos from that talent show had exploded on the Internet. *I should have told him what I was wearing.*

His attention caught on two men, both in jeans, both wearing shades, one with curly blue-black hair, the other's sparking with red and gold in the afternoon sun.

Charlie raised a hand, and they headed toward him.

"Alex?"

"Charlie, this is my boyfriend, Jerod."

They shook hands, and Charlie was struck by the closeness between Alex and Jerod. It had nothing to do with public displays but the sense of them communicating without words.

The three walked toward an unoccupied stretch of benches across from the fenced-off dog run.

"I saw it on the news," Alex said, referring to the fire. "That place was a dump, but it was our dump."

Charlie wondered how to broach the topic of the weird paintings inside the closet. "The guy with the dog was in your place."

"Okay... I don't see what—"

"I don't think he was living there. No one was. The place was being torn up... rehabbed."

"Of course, makes sense," Alex said.

"How's that? You moved out over two years ago."

"There's all of these rules around rent-stabilized and rent-controlled apartments. I know them all, and if you want me to bore you, I can recite chapter and verse."

"He can, and he will," Jerod warned. "Alex is an idiot savant around rules and regulations."

"Watch it, buddy. I may be a savant, but I ain't no idiot." He looked at Charlie. "Here's the deal. The landlord leaves the place empty for a couple years, documents a certain dollars'-worth of renovation, and presto chango, no more rent stabilization."

"But you were getting housing assistance."

"True, but based on a low rent. I found that place when I was eleven. It's a long and not terribly interesting story, but as shitty as that place was, it saved my sister and me. No bad feelings, and I'm sorry it burned. But that's not why you're here. You've got questions. And someone around here is baking cookies, and I *really* want one."

"Yeah," Jerod said. "What is that smell?" He took off his shades and looked at Charlie. "It's coming from you."

Charlie nodded. "You both smell it?"

"Of course," Alex said. "You have cookies in your pockets?"

"No... the fire, the one at your old place, that's what you're smelling. And not everyone does."

Alex pocketed his shades. He looked at Jerod. "And this is where things get weird. So tell us, Charlie Fitzgerald, why do you smell like cookies, and what did you see in that fire that has you burning up with questions?"

"What was that?" Charlie startled, his focus pulled by a blur between the two men, like something hovered back and forth around their shoulders. He had the strangest sense that Alex and Jerod weren't the only ones in on the conversation. He thought of Gran and her tales of the good people. The blur gained substance. He squinted and caught movement, fast, a flash of a vivid orange-and-black wing, like a butterfly. "What is that?"

"Tell me what you see," Alex said.

He's talking like Gran was around Liam. He spoke the line from his dream. "Ask no questions here."

"Tell me what you see," Alex repeated. "You tracked me down, and it's not for my autograph. Tell me what you see, Charlie Fitzgerald."

"It's nothing." *Has to be the light.*

"Then it's nothing," Jerod said.

Charlie thought of his dream, Liam cowering in the bathtub of an apartment that wasn't his. *Was he squatting? Why was he there?* "There was a closet in your old apartment. The inside was painted. It was beautiful, and.... Who painted it?"

"My mother did. She is... was an artist."

"She's dead?"

"No, not exactly, but she doesn't paint anymore."

"The people… the things in the painting." Again the blur on Alex's right shoulder. He narrowed his gaze. *There's something there. Alive, so fast.* A flash of butterfly wing, but what it was attached to…. *Not possible. Maybe this is a dream. Maybe it's all a dream.*

Alex smiled. "Fitzgerald is one of the old Irish families. So is Nevus. They say odd things run in our blood."

"That's something my Gran would say. I think it's just a product of all that marrying cousins." *Just say it, Charlie*, because the more he let the weirdness of the last day and a half wash over him, the clearer the impossible thing making faces at him from Alex's shoulder became.

Jerod spoke. "You know, the first time I saw her, I was convinced I'd lost my mind."

"Tell me what you see, Charlie," Alex repeated. "If we're to have this conversation, you need to take a leap. For a man who makes his living walking into buildings on fire, it shouldn't be hard."

Charlie blurted, "There's a bare-chested pitch-black fairy with swirly gold tattoos and butterfly wings on your shoulder."

The moment he said that, two things happened. All haziness around the six-inch-high creature vanished, and she darted across the space that separated him from Alex and kissed him on the tip of his nose.

"She likes you," Alex said. "Her name is Nimby. She's been with me from birth, and thinking you're going mad around her is par for the course. Now you've seen my fairy, and you saw the performances on *IT*."

"That was real?" Charlie asked. His attention pulled between the things they were telling him and the antics of the pirouetting fairy on Jerod's shoulder.

"It depends what you mean by 'real.'"

"Oh, stop already," Jerod interjected. "You're talking like one of them. And you." He turned to Nimby. "Taken up ballet, have we?"

She stopped in midturn and stuck her tongue out at him.

"I'm haffling. Hear me talk in vague riddles," Alex said.

"What's a haffling?"

"Half human, half something that comes from somewhere else."

Charlie stared at Nimby, who'd resumed her interpretive dance, and then at the two handsome young men, so connected, so comfortable with the impossible. And just like storming into a house on fire, he told them everything. At the mention of Liam's name, a worried look passed between Alex and Jerod.

"You know him. You know Liam Summer, blond, purple eyes… handsome… no, beautiful."

"Yes, we've met," Alex said without humor as Jerod pulled out his cell and brought up the viral image of Charlie carrying out the naked man, who in turn held a small dog tucked in his arms.

Jerod passed the phone to Alex, who enlarged the picture with his fingers. He nodded as Nimby fluttered over his shoulder. "It could be him. Different, though…. Great ass."

"Give that back!" Jerod snatched his phone away. He stared at the picture. "It is, isn't it? Damn!"

"And?" Charlie asked as hope and anticipation bubbled. *Not a dream. Weird as fucking hell, but not a dream.* Something in the two men's expressions gave him pause. *They're worried.*

"This can't be good," Alex said. "You pulled him out of my old apartment… and you looked inside Marilyn's painted closet. I should have destroyed it. I just couldn't, and it was too big to take. I should have smashed it."

"No. It's beautiful. The outside not so much anymore. But there were creatures inside… sort of like Liam, and others like your Nimby. She's gorgeous, by the way."

Which bought him a second kiss. The fairy alit on his shoulder, and using his ear as a ballet barre, practiced turns and kicks.

"And easily flattered," Alex said. "Look, Charlie, you're not going to like what I have to say. But you should stay far away from Liam Summer."

"Why?" *He sounds like Gran.*

Alex was about to speak and then stopped himself.

Jerod was less polite. "Because he can't be trusted. Because he does what's in his interest and his interest only."

The words stung, and Jerod wasn't done.

"Here's the deal, Charlie. Liam Summer was told to seduce my boyfriend, and he did his damn best to do that. From what I've learned about the fey, present company excluded, they have their own logic and their own ways. We stupid humans have to avoid the worst mistake we can make."

"And what's that?"

"Good question," Jerod said. He stared at Charlie. "Don't make the mistake of thinking Liam feels what you do. Liam Summer is a very handsome prostitute. It wasn't just that he was to seduce Alex but to glamour him to the extent—and here's where we go from just plain weird to lock-me-in-the-nut-hatch—Liam was the tool of someone so evil and mad for power, kind of like the fairy version of Hitler or the guys who go around chopping off everyone's heads."

"Queen May," Charlie said. "She's in the Mist."

"You've seen her?"

"In a dream… your second-to-last performance on *IT*." He looked from Alex to Jerod to the fairy on his shoulder.

Alex nodded. "That's right. Jerod pulled a giant white fire-spitting salamander out of me on national TV."

Jerod added. "Liam was to trap Alex so that May could just waltz in and steal his body. It didn't happen, and in hindsight, his failure cost her everything."

"That was her." Charlie wondered at what point the men in white coats would haul them away. *Mad queens, fire-spitting salamanders.* "But that's what I saw in my dream. That's what smells of cookies."

Not fully listening to their conversation, Nimby stopped in midarabesque. With a leg extended behind her, she leaned in and whispered in Charlie's ear, "Fairy fire. You smell of fairy fire, Charlie Fitzgerald. And after fairy fire comes fairy dust."

Charlie shook his head, which threw Nimby off-balance. She fluttered back to Alex's shoulder and shook an angry finger.

"Sorry about that. But what the hell are fairy fire and fairy dust?"

"Weapons," Alex said. "Just as Liam Summer is a weapon."

Charlie looked across as dogs frolicked in the fenced-off section of the park. He didn't want to look at the fairy on Alex's shoulder or think about the awful things they'd said about Liam, *which Gran kind of warned you about… and he told you himself. Shit.* "Let me get this straight… mad salamander queen sent a ball of cookie-dough fire to your old building, which is where I found Liam. So maybe that explains how he got there… like he rode on fairy fire. Would somebody please give me a shot of something?"

Alex spoke. "I think you're close. I was in her head, or more accurately, she'd taken over mine. I got images and bits of her thoughts. The fairy fire is power. It's made from magic. I think it's magic she steals. Fairy dust, not so sure what it's for, but I think it's like a drug to them."

Nimby clapped her hands. "It's delicious! Mmmm. But bad. Bad, bad, bad. Makes you go mad, mad, mad."

Charlie felt sick. "So maybe she sent Liam. But he seemed so afraid of her. And in the dream, it's like she wanted to kill him... to eat him."

Jerod interjected, "It's clear Liam's gotten to you. I'm sorry for that. But this fey-in-distress thing is an act. He can't be trusted. They say that the fey don't lie. I'm not sure of that. But I do know this—they sure as hell don't tell the truth. And, Charlie, you need to multiply that by a thousand when talking about May's whore, Liam Summer."

Sixteen

LIAM WALKED through the tunnel of mist Lizbeta formed. He turned back once but could no longer see her shimmering light or May's beastly form. He paused and swallowed. He tasted his fear, an emotion that had ruled his life. Like well-worn shoes, he'd lived with terror so long, he barely noticed. Fear of May, fear of tripping her temper, of saying or doing the thing that would leave him dead and gutted, his organs ripped out for dinner. *What would it be like to be unafraid?* He stared down the tunnel to its dark opening in the See. *What would it be like? To be like Charlie.... To be with Charlie.*

An idea rooted as he faced the threshold that separated worlds. *Your fear serves a purpose. It's kept you alive.* "'Tis true," he spoke aloud. "Fear keeps me alive and keeps me in the shadows and under her thumb. I am alive... but at what cost?" The sound of his voice was muffled by the mist. The tone rose into a question: *Can she hear that?* He listened for the beast's growl. There was nothing, just a hum in his ears and crickets and leaves in the wind through the black opening in the tunnel.

Fear keeps me alive. He came to the tunnel's end and stepped into darkness. Unlike his first trip to the See, there was no fire. He stilled as his eyes adapted. A branch brushed his face. He reached out a hand as forms took shape. He was in the dense bower of a great tree. His fingers traced the outline of heart-shaped leaves as his eyes separated shadow from shape.

He worked an opening through the dense entwined branches. Old twigs snapped and fell. Daylight pierced through, and he looked out on a park. A stone castle sat high on a hill and a great river below. On the distant bank, he glimpsed a city with steel-and-concrete buildings and hard, dark streets. He stepped out into the See, with grass and moss underfoot, birdsong and crickets, the rasp of frogs. He gazed back at the massive tree, whose branches landed like a waterfall on all sides, creating the cave-like space into which he'd landed. *Remember this place.*

He searched for Charlie's great red dragon with the spinning lights but did not see it. He ran his fingers across the tips of his ears and then along his teeth. *Flat... human. But the travel comes with cost. What is changed? What have I lost this time?* His hands ran over his face and up and down his body. *It feels solid.* He checked his fingers, toes, made certain he'd not had a sex change or other major life-altering event. *But I could be mad.*

His gut churned as he thought about the enormity of his tasks. To get word of Marilyn's children back to her and to learn of May's weakness. To find answers as to the how and the why her foray into the See had failed. *It is too much... and I will try.*

A breeze swept across his face. *At least I'm not naked this time.* Something about the gray sweatpants and red T-shirt that Charlie's gran had given him comforted him. Even the funny shoes with their laces and bouncy bottoms. *I look human.* He sniffed for signs of the Unsee, for the echo of fairy fire, but there was nothing, just the soft wind, the chatter of wildlife, and the dance of sun and shadow through the trees.

He heard footsteps, twigs and leaves crunching. A man in a dull green uniform appeared on a dirt path. "Are you looking for the Cloisters?"

The man's question startled him. He reminded himself that this was the human way, indiscriminate asking of information with no sense of cost. "No." Fear gripped his throat, and he wished it gone. *What would Charlie do?* But with no building on fire, the answer wasn't clear. *I will not give in to fear.... So do the thing that frightens you.* He asked a question. "How do I get to Staten Island?" He braced for pain, for the punishment and cost of the question.

"You're not from around here, are you?"

"No, and I need to go to Staten Island."

"Okay, then." The man in green pulled a folded map from the patch pocket in his pants and spread it on a flat boulder. "This is what you have to do."

Liam listened and nodded as the man traced the route in red ink from where they were, at the tip of the island of Manhattan, all the way down through the city, to a body of water.

"And that's where I take the boat," he stated, wanting to be certain, but there it was, in large letters. Staten Island, where Charlie lived.

"You think you got it?" Mr. Green Hat asked.

"I think so."

"A bit of a haul. You have family out there?"

"A friend," Liam said and hoped it was true.

"Okay, then." And the park ranger refolded the map and handed it to Liam.

Liam held the precious paper with the path to Charlie's homeland clearly marked. "Tell me the cost."

"Excuse me?"

Liam's free hand searched in the pockets of his sweats. He had nothing to offer in return.

Green Hat smiled and stepped back. "It's yours. No cost. Maps are free."

Stunned by his response, Liam clutched the city map—a gift from a stranger—and watched as Mr. Green walked down the dirt path where he'd first appeared. Before the ranger vanished, he turned and pointed toward an opening in the clearing.

"If you go through there, it takes you to the bike path. Then just keep going downhill."

"Thank you."

"Not a problem." And Mr. Green left.

The exchange troubled him—a gift in response to a question. *It could be a trick....* He held the map and looked at the path in red. He unfolded and refolded it. He felt the fear in his belly and how it wanted him to retreat into the sheltering bower of the tree with its heart-shaped leaves. *No... it's not what Charlie would do.*

With Mr. Green's instructions clear in his head, he followed the dirt path to a narrow black one, its surface smooth and hard as rock. With each step the noise of the city grew. If not for his brief time in the See, the sights would have left him cowering.

"Left!" a voice shouted from behind.

Liam turned as a helmeted man hurtled toward him on a thin-wheeled device. He pushed back into the hedge and braced for the attack.

"Thanks, guy." And he was gone.

His knees weakened as the two-wheeled creature flew down the path to a busy street. He stopped and tried to make sense of the noise and the metal dragons, none of them big and red like Charlie's.

You can do this. You have a map.

Putting one bouncy-shoed foot in front of the other, he left the safety of the park.

Always one with a strong sense of direction, he quickly figured the compass points. The park with the castle was at the north end of the island, and he needed to get all the way to the south, where he would board a boat, which would take him to Charlie's Staten Island.

He noted how men and women glanced at him and then averted their gazes, some with a smile and some with a second look. He caught his reflection in a store window filled with strange food and brightly colored packages whose contents he couldn't even guess. He stopped and stared. While his clothes were drabber than he'd like, he looked human. He wondered if there'd been further changes with this second trip…. *No.* The silver of his hair was still the color of ripened wheat, the tips of his ears and his teeth no longer pointy. Just his eyes remained unchanged from the Unsee, purple rimmed in lashes of dark gold.

A girl with fishnet stockings and skin covered in tattoos stopped beside him. She looked from his reflection and asked, "Purple, awesome! Where do I get contacts like those?"

He stared at her and at the colorful scenes painted on her skin. "I don't understand."

"Your eyes. The color is wild. Those are contacts, aren't they?"

"I don't think so."

She got right up into his face. "Holy shit! They're real. I'd kill for eyes like that."

Liam backed away. "Please don't."

"Just kidding."

"I need to find the A train."

"Easy." And for the second time, assistance was offered with nothing taken in return. It was bizarre, although Liam hurried away from the picture-covered woman who'd threatened to steal his eyes.

He stalled at the entrance to the subway. He watched as people descended and then climbed up from beneath the ground. This felt familiar. The fey were no strangers to dark places. Knowing how and where to hide were useful tools. What worried him was how the ground shook and then grew calm.

I will face my fear. I will be like Charlie… and maybe I will see Charlie. And maybe he will not be broken.

Swallowing dread and stomach acid, he followed a group of young women down the stairs and into the station. He watched as they slid plastic cards through metal slots and then walked through toothlike turnstiles.

One of them stopped and spoke to him. "You don't have a MetroCard, do you?"

"I don't."

She smiled, and as her friends waited, she pulled a plastic card from her shoulder bag. "I always carry an extra for out-of-towners." She reached back over the turnstile and slid the card. "You're good to go."

Liam copied what the others did and pressed on the bar. It wouldn't move.

"You've got to really push," she instructed.

And then he was through. "Thank you."

"No problem." With a wink and a smile, she returned to her girlfriends.

An older woman helped him find the A train, and another stranger made sure he got off at the right stop.

A Chinese man in a business suit and tie asked his name and walked him from the station to the ferryboat. As he turned to leave, the man asked, "You need money?"

Before Liam could respond, several pieces of green paper with intricate pictures on both sides were pressed into his hand.

"Thank you."

Without a word the man gave a shy smile, waved his hand as though giving money to strangers was an everyday thing, and walked away.

Aboard the bright orange-and-blue boat, Liam climbed to the top deck and turned around and around, wanting to take it all in as the ship pulled away from the dock. His fear was replaced by wonder. *Steel-and-glass towers, blue sky streaked with clouds, people who smiled without guile and helped and asked and answered questions without wanting anything in return.* He held tight to the rail and braced his feet wide, loving the feel of the dark gray waves as they lapped against the steel hull.

On a distant island, a giant green statue of a woman came to view, her brow encircled with a crown and one hand aloft with a flaming torch. He thought of Queen May and understood her passion for this world. Who wouldn't want to be here?

A little girl in a red-and-white-checked dress pointed at the green lady. "That's the Statue of Liberty."

The girl's mother, obviously pregnant, her eyes hidden behind dark glasses, looked from her daughter to Liam. "Daria, leave the man alone."

"She does not bother me," Liam said. "I am new here. I've not seen these things. I do not know their names."

"She's a symbol," the woman said.

"Of what?" he asked, each question through his lips a bit easier.

"Freedom. Your accent… I can't quite place it. Irish?"

He nodded, not wanting to lie but knowing the truth was not for humans. "Freedom matters here."

"Of course. It's what Americans treasure most. Give us liberty or give us death. A lot of us forget just how precious it is and how easily it can be lost."

He nodded, not certain what freedom meant. *Freedom from whom? From what? From a queen who dines on her subjects and steals their magic. From a world where wrong words can have deadly consequences.* "Freedom sounds like something worth fighting for."

"Yes." She lowered her shades. "That's both the terrible and wonderful thing about it. We call it a right. Something that comes with citizenship, but there's a price. As noble as it sounds and as that statue would have us believe, it's not free. It comes at a tremendous cost, and even today, not everyone has it. The thing I don't like to imagine is what would happen if we lost it. Some say we've already given up much of it, with new technologies and selling off our privacy. I just hope we don't wake up one day and realize we've sold our freedom and our liberty for an endless stream of cute pet videos."

He nodded, understanding but a fraction of what she'd said. His thoughts were troubled by other matters as the enormity of Charlie's Staten Island came to view. He pulled out the map from the man in green and looked from it to the shore, which stretched for miles in either direction.

The woman saw his distress. She stared at the line in red, which ended at the ferry. "Do you know where you're going?"

"No. I did not realize the size of his island."

"His?"

"A friend… I think. Someone who saved me from a building on fire."

The woman's gaze narrowed. "Your friend have a name?"

"Charlie…. Charlie Fitzgerald."

The woman stared at him. "I thought you looked familiar."

Liam froze. *She knows of me. She knows what I am.* He braced for the denunciation, for all to know that Queen May's whore was on the boat.

"You're Naked Chihuahua Guy. It's your eyes. In the pictures they looked purple… and they really are. Oh God…."

The little girl, who'd been focused on the approaching shore, spoke. "I knew that. You saved the doggy. And my uncle Charlie saved you. It was on the news."

Liam met the pregnant woman's gaze. The same blue eyes, her face a narrow version… and no dark stubble. He couldn't breathe, poised on the edge of hope and despair.

"So you're looking for my brother. You got a name?"

"Yes. It's Liam Summer."

"Too strange. This has to be fate… which is just the kind of shit my Gran says."

He nodded. "I've met your gran… and the cats. They don't like me."

The little girl perked, and her eyes brightened as she ticked off names, raising a finger for each. "Aldo, Andre, Lily, Lulu, and Crazy Daisy. Why can't we have cats, Mommy?"

The woman shook her head. "Okay, Liam Summer, I'm Annie DiCarlo, and my daughter Daria is obsessed with anything small and furry. So, how is it you met Gran?"

He felt the weight of her scrutiny. "The night of the fire, Charlie brought me to her."

"Does he know you're looking for him?"

"No."

"Will he be glad to see you?"

"I do not know…. I hope so."

"Wow! What are the chances?" The boat lurched as it pulled into the dock. The sun beat down on the deck as the passengers flocked toward the stairs. "You do realize that Staten Island houses the mother lode of cops and firefighters and about half a million people. And Fitzgeralds,

Murphys, Reillys, Hulains, the place is crawling with them. And… you just happen to catch the attention of Charlie's niece and sister."

"You are troubled by this. I mean him no harm." *And yet that's all I've done. And now here's his pregnant sister and young niece. I should stay on the boat. I should leave this place. I should…. And this cannot be coincidence?*

"I *am* troubled. I love my brother." It was hard for her not to stare. "He brought you to Gran's…."

"He did."

"Crap! Tell me you're not going to break his heart, Liam Summer. Forgive my bluntness, but without doubt, you're the best-looking man I've ever met. And guys—gay or straight—become idiots around a pretty face."

Daria interjected, "Mommy, Gran says boys are handsome and girls are pretty."

"Yes, sweetheart, and there are exceptions to every rule." She did not break eye contact.

Liam felt her love and concern… and something else. Protectiveness. "I will not hurt Charlie. If you think I should get back on the boat and…."

"Hell no." Her worry blossomed into a smile. "You know, he's never brought a guy home to meet the family. This should be interesting. Really, really interesting."

Seventeen

CHARLIE RODE across the Verrazano Bridge after a bizarre afternoon in the park with Alex Nevus, Jerod Haynes, and the wannabe ballerina fairy, Nimby. At first he'd chalked up his obsession with Liam as the damsel-in-distress thing firefighters were prone to, albeit with a gender change. Yet the more he'd listened and asked questions of Alex and Jerod—and even Nimby, or maybe especially her—the more he'd believed there was another world, similar to New York only built on different rules and populated with creatures like those inside the wardrobe. All those long-ago stories Gran would read, they'd all start with a statement of veracity—*This is a tale that is ancient and true*—and then throw you into a world of warring nations, some human, some fey.

His head swam. Mostly he worried about Liam. *Is he okay? Will I see him again?* It ate at him. The dream and Liam's disappearance from Gran's. *He's gone. Like to another world.* There was more too. Things Alex and Jerod had said about Liam, not just that they didn't like him, didn't trust him, but... *they said what he said—a whore.*

It was ten after five as he drove the last blocks. He glimpsed the water in the distance, turned onto his block, and stopped. In the drive were his brother Michael's pickup and Annie's red Prius. "Shit." He contemplated sneaking up to his over-the-garage apartment to digest the day. "Not an option." He'd promised Michael he'd get Gran back, and maybe the noise and bubble of his family would clear his head and get him to think of something other than Liam. Resigned to Sunday dinner at the Fitzgeralds', he got out.

His mother appeared behind the front screen door.

"Charlie, I wondered where you were. Flora said you left hours ago." She stepped out onto the stoop. "Annie met up with a friend of yours on the ferry and brought him over. I didn't think you'd mind, so I invited him to dinner."

"Who?" he asked, thinking it was someone from high school, or the fire station, or one of his sister's feeble attempts to find him a boyfriend.

Katie Fitzgerald glanced back through the screen. She scurried down the steps.

Charlie kissed his mom on the cheek. "What is it? You're like the cat with the canary."

"Is he your boyfriend, Charlie? Is there something you haven't told us?"

"I don't have a boyfriend, Mom. I'd tell you if I did."

Her smile vanished. "Oh... well, he's very handsome. Is he a model or an actor? He's got a bit of an accent."

"Mom, who's inside?" *Not possible.* Wondering... hoping.

"Annie said it's the man you got out of that horrible building on Third Street. That she and Daria met him on the ferry... that he was looking for you and didn't have your address. That seems odd... to come to Staten Island and not know where you're going. He probably wanted to thank you."

"Liam? Liam's inside?"

His mother's gaze narrowed. "Interesting. So this is him? Annie says there's pictures of you carrying him out of that building... that he was naked and carrying a Chihuahua."

Charlie looked up the stairs. *He's here.*

"Charlie? Charlie? World to Charlie."

He turned to his mom. She had on makeup, not just her usual swipe of lipstick and pinch of the cheeks. Instead of her usual Sunday dinner apron and ponytail, she wore her favorite green dress. She'd braided her salt-and-pepper hair and pinned it up in a bun. "What?"

She smiled. "Nothing. We should go in."

He nodded, his throat dry, his breath hot through parched lips. Sunday dinner with the family had just turned from a dutiful chore into a minefield. He walked up the steps and held the screen for Mom. He looked in. *Yes, a minefield... but bring it on.*

CHARLIE LOOKED around the dining table, draped in a cream-colored cloth and laden with familiar covered dishes—Mom, Dad, his brother

Michael, his wife, Dawn, who was also a cop, their five-year-old twins, Corey and Rory, his pregnant sister, Annie, her husband, Sal, little Daria, Gran, and of course, Liam. It felt claustrophobic, which had nothing to do with the remodeled dining room. Expectancy hung in the air, and the usual need to shout over one another to be heard was sadly missing. *They're all on their best behavior…. It won't last.*

As his mom delivered the last of the steaming red-enamel dishes, this one filled with string beans and almond bits, onto its trivet, he couldn't take his eyes off Liam, seated directly across, with Daria to his right and sister Annie on the left. He seemed less skittish, his long hair tied back, his violet eyes alive and expressive. Someone had dressed him a bit more formal in one of Charlie's blue flannel shirts and a pair of jeans, probably a leftover from his brother Michael. *How can he look so comfortable? How does someone do that in a room full of my family?*

Annie said grace, and as the round of "Amens" filled the room, he thought of Alex and Jerod's warnings about Liam, how he seduced strangers at the bidding of an evil queen. He sipped ice water, his mouth way too dry. The glass sweated, cool and wet in his hand. Was that what this was? *Have I been seduced by an evil queen?* The thought sent the water down the wrong pipe. He choked. Water snorted up his nostrils. He grabbed for a cloth napkin.

"Charlie," Gran said. "Tell me what's wrong, dear."

Oh no you don't. He understood her deliberate words and how they were intended for him and Liam. *I will not be the toy.* "Nothing." He hoped that would be the end of it. But in a room with three cops, his sister the nurse, Mom, who had thirty years with the city as a court social worker, and Gran, the games had just started.

His mom kicked it off. "So, Liam, what do you do?"

Liam paused. "At this moment I'm working to find information."

"From us?" she asked.

"I don't think so, although I hope Charlie can help."

"And how did you two meet?" Michael's wife, Dawn, who'd been the last to arrive with the twins, asked.

"He rescued me from a building on fire."

"It was on the news," Mike Fitzgerald said.

"And there's pictures all over the Internet," brother Michael added. "You know, they're calling you Naked Chihuahua Guy."

"Michael! Not at the table." Katie cast her son a warning glance.

"I'm just saying…. Where were your clothes, dude?"

"Michael, stop it!"

Liam wasn't thrown. "It's a good question. I don't have an answer." He took a bite of sweet potato casserole with candied pecans baked on top and sprinkled throughout. "This is delicious."

"Thank you," Katie said. "It's Gran's recipe."

Gran nodded. "Some traditions get kept. Others… not so much. It's interesting, though." From her vantage point of sitting next to Charlie and across from Liam, she took her shot, weighing just how much information she would share with the whole family and what she would keep to herself. "Tell me how it is, Liam, that you don't remember how you came to be naked in a burning building."

Liam nodded. He looked around the table and ended with Charlie.

It was freakishly quiet, every member of the Fitzgerald clan unsettled by the beautiful man's violet gaze. "There's much that I do not remember of that night. I do remember your kindness in letting me stay in your home."

"But you left without saying anything," Gran replied.

"I did…. I had to."

"Where did you go?" she persisted.

Liam glanced across at Charlie. "Someone took me home."

Gran looked from Liam to Charlie. "Who?"

Charlie nodded. "I think I did."

"What? Huh? What's with all the secrets?" Annie asked, aware that there was far more unsaid than spoken. "Where do you live?"

Liam looked at the various foods on his plate and at the still steaming sweet potato casserole. "I don't mean to be rude, but I think Charlie and his Gran would rather I not say."

"That's cryptic," Charlie's dad replied. He looked to his mother. "Why wouldn't you want the boy to tell us where he lives? You've got a bit of an accent. I'd guess Ireland, but unless you and Charlie have been doing the red-eye from LaGuardia, it's not possible."

"Dad, everyone, can we please just eat?" Charlie pleaded, the room way too close. His cheeks burned. *This is not going to end well.*

"Of course," his mom said. "It must have been so frightening, the fire. And that you were able to save that little boy's dog."

"His name was Max," Liam said.

"The boy?"

"No, the dog. And yes, very frightening. I would be dead if it weren't for Charlie. I'd like more of those."

"Of course. Michael, pass Liam the sweet potatoes."

Unaware of the eleven sets of eyes fixed on him, Liam spooned the delicious mash onto his plate, pushing aside the mostly uneaten brisket, green beans, and buttered roll. With a forkful in his mouth, he looked up. He swallowed the warm sweetness and crunched down on a candied pecan. "So good. So yes, the fire. You have a very brave son, brother, uncle, and grandson."

"You gave the dog back to the little boy," Daria said.

"Yes, though in truth, I found comfort in the little thing. I was sorry to lose him. But he wasn't mine to keep."

"It must have been terrifying," Annie said. "Do you think that maybe you're still in shock, and that's why you can't remember things?"

"It's possible," Liam said. "Much is confused."

Brother Michael lobbed the next bomb. "Three people died in that fire."

Liam stiffened. "I did not know that. Though I am not surprised. That is very sad." Tears welled, and he looked at Charlie. He put down his fork. "I did not know that."

"It was too late for them," Charlie said, not wanting to give the details of a mother and two children who'd not made it out, not with so many young ears at the table.

Looks bounced among the adults. This felt familiar. Death and tragedy were no strangers at the Fitzgerald table, which beneath its starched cloth bore the high-tide mark of Hurricane Sandy.

Mike Fitzgerald, who'd had the hardest time accepting his youngest boy was gay, had put the pieces together. "It's just the way it is," he said. "You can't save everyone. But he saved you, and you got a little boy his dog back. I always thought Charlie should have been a cop."

In unison, Charlie and his brother said, "Here it comes."

"No, seriously," their dad said, having worn this chestnut smooth over the years. "But"—with fork raised, he added—"you have to let your children find their own way."

"It's true," Liam said. "Forcing people to your will leads to unhappiness and assassinations."

Charlie choked on his brisket.

Gran, who'd stayed uncharacteristically quiet, spoke. "Michael, if Charlie is up to it, why don't he and Liam take me back tonight."

Brothers Michael and Charlie exchanged glances, having already cut that deal. "Sure, Gran," Charlie said, aware that the conversation that had begun when he'd brought Liam to her apartment and had continued through their boozy brunch was not finished.

His family's protectiveness, curiosity, and dogged pursuit of answers was palpable. Liam's every word, his grace, the foreign lilt in his voice, were like chum in a sea full of sharks. Yes, so far Liam had dodged the nutso stuff, but how long could that last? Charlie's best strategy was to throw them off the scent. "I saw Finn Hulain today. He's doing the arson investigation. The building has a shady history."

"Finn... we've not seen him lately," his father said.

"You should have invited him," his mother said as she looked across at her husband. The mention of their oldest boy's best friend was like dust falling on a grave.

"I didn't think of it," Charlie admitted.

"So what's the deal? If it's arson, it's also murder," Dad stated.

Charlie steered the conversation to the frauds perpetrated by the building's owner.

It worked for a bit. But five-year-old Daria was bored by the cop talk. She tapped Liam's arm and asked the question on everyone's too polite minds. "Is Uncle Charlie your boyfriend?"

Dead silence. Forks hung in midair, mouths in midchew.

Liam looked at Daria. "I am unworthy of your uncle's love. I hope we might be friends."

Charlie was taken aback. The answer hurt. He looked around at the awkward expressions of his adult family members, none of them willing to look him in the eye, as though they'd all become fascinated by their food. Liam's response had done the impossible: shut them up.

Gran smiled and took a deep draw on her second, possibly third, glass of lager.

Corey, the twin on Charlie's left, asked the obvious follow-up. "Why? Why aren't you worthy?"

"Shh!" his mother hushed him.

Gran looked at Liam, her right brow cocked.

Liam nodded. "Because your uncle Charlie races into buildings to save strangers. I'm more likely to do the opposite."

"Enough," Mike Fitzgerald said from the head of the table. "Liam is our guest and has been through an awful experience. So, Michael, your turn. Anything interesting at the precinct?"

As KATIE, Annie, and Dawn got up to clear the dishes and get dessert, Charlie seized the moment. He looked at Liam "You want to go for a walk?" He felt the weight of his dad's and brother's gaze and didn't care. *Please say yes.*

"I'd like that."

"And you'll be back in time to take me home," Gran said.

"Yes."

Without further discussion, Charlie headed out with Liam. "I'm sorry about that," Charlie said.

"No need. You have a beautiful family. They all love you."

Charlie looked down the quiet street and, with Liam at his side, crossed to the shore. "I still can't get over that you're here," he said.

Liam gazed out at frothy waves. "It reminds me of home."

"Which would be where, exactly?"

"Charlie, enough with the questions, especially when I think you know many of the answers."

"Right. So here's one I don't understand. How did you come to be in Alex Nevus's old apartment?"

Liam startled. "Not possible. That building... not possible."

"Truth."

"I do not know." He looked at Charlie and ached. *I'm so sorry.* Charlie was in love... with him. He knew the signs well, the way his dark blue eyes sought out his, the deference in his words and gestures, his hunger, barely restrained. *I am sorry, and I could swim in those eyes forever.* "I should not have come here, Charlie. I did because I need help, and you're the only one I know."

"Not feeling special here."

"Charlie, I am unworthy of you, and that is truth. I don't know how to make you understand, and yet I must. What you feel for me is glamour. It's not truth. The travel between worlds took my magic, but that remains. I am a whore, Charlie. It's been my truth since I was a child. It's what I was raised to be and to do."

Charlie's jaw twitched. "I see. So what you're saying is my feelings aren't real, and that you're just here to use me."

"Yes. Correct."

Charlie stood side by side with Liam as he looked out at the water. "Fine… whatever, but I still want to know how you came to Alex Nevus's apartment. Do you know him?" Charlie couldn't figure why he felt so furious, why he was deliberately trying to trick Liam, to catch him in lies.

"We have met. Not here."

"In the Unsee."

"You know things today you did not know at the fire."

"Yes, I tracked down Alex and his boyfriend."

Liam perked. "They are well? They are alive!"

"Yes."

"I must see him."

"He said you tried to seduce him."

"'Tis truth."

"And that you tried to have him abandon his dying boyfriend."

"Enough, Charlie, I told you what I am and what I have done."

"You did."

"Do you still intend to seduce him?" Charlie asked, remembering Jerod's cryptic warning—*The fey don't lie, but they certainly don't tell the truth.*

"No. He was immune to me. I need to see him, Charlie. I bring a message from his mother. I have information he will be glad of, and I need to know things of him."

"So your coming here tonight…. I suppose it was to see me, but not for—"

"Charlie. No. I have tasks to perform, and there is little time. I have hurt you… I hurt you now. I'm sorry."

Charlie's cell rang. He pulled it out and saw *F. Fitzgerald* on the screen. "Gran?"

"It's getting late. You ready to drive me home?"

"Sure. Be right in." He hung up and looked at Liam. "Alex and Jerod said some wild things. I saw a real fairy… a little bug named Nimby. Daria and my nephews would go bonkers if they knew she existed. What kind of tasks are we talking about? According to Alex, where you come from is a dangerous place."

"We shouldn't keep your gran waiting, Charlie."

"You don't want to tell me. I suppose that's your right."

"I promised to do you no harm, Charlie, and I've done the opposite. Please, let me think a bit. Bring your gran home, and then…."

"And then what?"

"I don't know, Charlie." And without giving a response, Liam turned and walked back toward the Fitzgeralds'.

Eighteen

GRAN SAID her good-byes to the family, with hugs and kisses and the extraction of a promise that everyone would go to Mass.

All appeared normal, and Charlie knew it wasn't. Gran had held her tongue for hours. It would not last. With trepidation, he took her arm and helped her up into the front of his truck.

Liam hung back, not intending to join them.

"Oh no." Gran pointed a finger at him. "I want two handsome men driving me home." And in a voice meant for just Charlie, "We have things to discuss."

As they backed out of the drive, with Liam hidden in the shadows of the backseat, she started. "Liam, tell me where you've been since leaving my home so abruptly and so rudely. I believe you are one of the good people, the Tuatha Dé Danaan. You are fey, and you will tell me the truth." She flipped down the sun visor and flicked the mirror open, her gaze on Liam.

Her bluntness struck Charlie dumb, again with the odd phrasing, a question embedded inside a command.

"I apologize for my rudeness." Liam sensed her intellect, her curiosity, and her fear—of him. "I returned to my home."

"I see. Tell me of your travels."

Charlie's eyes fixed on the road, his attention riveted to Liam's response.

"I rode home on a dream... Charlie's dream."

"So it's true?" Charlie asked. "That dream was true."

"Charlie," Gran cut in. "There are rules with the good people that are different from ours. They don't like questions, or rather, they view them as a sort of currency. Every answer exacts a price."

"It's truth," Liam said. "But here, I find, questions have no value. People give answers and expect nothing in return. The dream was true… all of it."

"I kissed you in the dream."

"Yes, and as I said then, you should not have."

"And the thing is done," Gran stated. "It's obvious Charlie is infatuated with you, Liam Summer. You will cause him great pain. You will break his heart. I could kill you for that."

"Gran! Stop. I'm an adult."

"He's not human!"

Liam nodded. "She is right, Charlie. You wanted to know of my travels…." He told them of the trip through the Mist and back to the Unsee. Of mad Queen May trapped as a white salamander, yoked by her sister Lizbeta. "It is why I must find Alex Nevus. Lizbeta's yoke will soon snap. May is a raging beast. She will not calm. She will escape."

Gran listened, intent on his every word. "Queen May. Tell me her other names."

"Mab, Maeve."

Gran gasped.

Charlie looked at her. "You know about this?"

"Of course…. The thing about our people, Charlie, is that history and folklore twine together. Where one starts and the other ends is difficult to say. Queen Maeve was a warrior… and more than a thousand years since her stories began, she survives."

"She is not human," Liam said.

"I have many books about Maeve and her lover and enemy Cuchulain. They were constantly stealing one another's cattle, battling to get them back, and then making love, only to war again in the morning."

"Hulain? Like Finn Hulain?" Charlie asked.

"Possibly. Hulain was a man who killed a beast, which turned out to be a king's hunting hound. To repay his sin, Hulain became the king's hound. Eventually the king embraced him as his son, and when the king passed, he ruled." As though this information was normal, Gran barreled on. "Maeve had sisters. This Lizbeta is one. There is another."

"Yes… Katye. They each embody a major magic. It's called their special. May is power, Lizbeta is peace, and Katye is love."

"Lizbeta, the peaceful one, has trapped her sister," Gran stated. "But she sends you here to find how she can contain her. Interesting. Just like in the books, where fey starts and human begins is not clear."

"Not at all," Liam agreed. "Alex Nevus, half human and half fey, embodies our connection. There are three of them as well."

"Three of what?" Charlie asked.

"Hafflings. Alex has both a sister and a brother. The little boy, Adam, is with his mother, Marilyn, and his father, my uncle Cedric, back in the Unsee. His sister, Alice—if she lives—she is here."

"She lives," Charlie said. "She called Alex while we were in the park."

"That is good news." From the back, Liam could not read Charlie's expression. A situation that Flora Fitzgerald made difficult, as each time his eyes tried to catch Charlie's in the rearview mirror, she pulled him back to the conversation. *What does he make of this? Of me? I have told him the truth, not the best of it and not the very worst. Does he hate me?*

For Flora, the conversation was a revelation. It brought whiffs of her childhood. While different from the little fey she'd played with as a child outside of Limerick, Liam was proof of what she'd experienced. That in fact she'd not made it up. It had not been the imaginings of a little girl. But with validation came danger. *If this is real….* "It's May's motive that is not clear. You see, the minute we believe your story, Liam, is the minute we believe her threat."

"You do not believe."

"I do," she said. "So what I know of Queen May—Maeve, Mab, whatever name you use—she was a warrior. And she led the Tuatha Dé Danaan in a protracted war against the humans. The tales say it lasted a thousand years."

"What did they fight over?" Charlie asked.

"The world," Flora said. "And if you take all the stories and attempt to pull them into one, this is how it settled out. It came down to the forces of Queen May and those of Cuchulain. Lovers and enemies. After more than a thousand years of bloodshed and battles, they called a truce. They came together to determine the conditions of a peace."

"A thousand years? It's absurd," Charlie said.

"Charlie, if you want logical things, this is not that story. If what Liam tells us is true, then logic must stand side by side with leaps of faith and belief in the unbelievable."

"I saw a fairy today," he stated.

"Tell me."

"Small, no bigger than my hand. Her skin was black as coal and covered with swirling gold designs. She was mostly naked, and her wings looked like they came from a swallowtail butterfly. She was with Alex and Jerod. But you were getting to the part where May and her boyfriend made up." Charlie glanced in the rearview mirror and caught Liam's eye.

Gran continued. "Yes, they made peace, and a treaty was signed whereby the humans would take half of the world and the fey would keep the other. But Cuchulain—the Hound—was crafty, and the document, once done, created a wall between two worlds."

"After a thousand-year war, sounds like a good thing," Charlie stated.

"Yes, but it was not a fair truce. The humans took the top of the world—the See—and the fey were forced into the ground and under the ground—the Unsee. If I were May, I would be furious. It wouldn't have been the first time she was tricked by Hulain."

"Hell hath no fury," Charlie said.

Liam spoke. "It is so. We too have those stories. And Flora Fitzgerald, you may have gotten to the soul of May's ambition. She would rule both worlds. She would take back that which she feels was stolen."

"It's a theory… a scary one," Flora added as Charlie headed up Fifth Avenue and took the right onto Twenty-Third. He parked on the street across from her building. "Perhaps there's more to it."

With the engine off, Charlie unbuckled and turned to Gran. "What are you thinking?"

"That you're right, Charlie. Think of what it feels like to be cheated."

He paused. "It doesn't really happen to me…." He stopped. "I take that back. Oh God." He thought of his brother Rory and his uncle Charlie, both killed in the line of duty on 9/11.

"Yes," she said. "Think of what it feels like to have something—someone—you love stolen from you. The fury, the sadness, the pain, and this horrible feeling like you should be able to do something, and you can't. You have no power." Gran's voice cracked. "This May might be mad, but she has her reasons."

Charlie got out as Liam fumbled for the door handle.

"It's there," Gran said in the darkened cab. "You put your fingers inside and pull it toward you."

Before he could figure it, Charlie walked around and opened the doors. He gazed at Liam, bathed in light from one of the nineteenth-century gaslights that had been converted to electric. He knew he should look away, that all this ogling Liam was no good. He couldn't stop. He wondered if once Liam had the information he'd come back for, he'd vanish. He studied the planes of his face, his strong jaw, the curve of his cheeks, and the way his lashes curled beneath those beautiful eyes. *Dude is so far out of my league.*

Liam spoke. "I'm sorry for your dead, Charlie... Flora. I know this pain."

"Yeah." *Do you? Who have you lost? Or is this part of the lies... the glamour?* Charlie broke his gaze as Liam got out, and he helped Gran down.

The trio crossed the street in silence, each deep in thought.

Gran greeted her doorman and fished her keys from her pocketbook. "Walk me up, Charlie."

"Of course."

"I can wait," Liam said.

"No, you too," Gran said.

He nodded and followed.

In the elevator up, Liam braced for the attack of her cats and thought of what Flora and Charlie had said about May. The Hound of Hulain was an oft-told story, apparently both in the See and the Unsee. Yet if true, it explained much. To have the one you love betray you, trick you.... *And isn't that what you do? Have done.* He felt the weight of Charlie's gaze and caught him staring in one of the fish-eye mirrors mounted up in the corners. *This has to stop. I have to get away from him. It's hurting him.* Other thoughts intruded as he looked into Charlie's true blue eyes. *He's not broken. He crossed between worlds. He got out of his red metal dragon in the Unsee. How is this possible?*

They followed Flora to her apartment and waited as she undid the double locks.

Liam strained for the sounds of the cats. There was nothing.

She opened the door, and standing like sentries in the middle of the bookcase-lined hall were the two tabbies, and behind them the older black-and-white sisters, with the little Siamese winding her way around them. Her long tail, like an arabesque, whipped one way and then the other. They neither hissed nor moved.

Gran looked at her feline army. "There's something you don't see every day." She turned to Liam. "At least they no longer want to rip your eyes out."

"Don't be the toy," Charlie said.

Gran smiled. "And don't be the perp. Come in, boys."

"Gran, we should get back."

"I know." She brushed past her cats, who didn't budge from their posts. "You sure you can't stay for a cuppa?"

"Not this time, Gran."

She turned to the two men, her Charlie with a good four inches on Liam in his borrowed clothes and tied-back hair. He looked like some eighteenth-century prince caught out of time. *He will break Charlie's heart... and I can't stop it.* She looked back at her cats, with five pairs of eyes on Liam, neither attacking nor backing away. *It's different tonight. Something has changed.*

"This is just creepy," Charlie said as he pushed through the cats to get to Gran. He wrapped her in his arms, smelled the lilac in her hair. "I love you, Gran."

"And I you."

As they embraced, the smaller and bolder of the tabbies broke formation and walked to Liam. He butted his fuzzy head against Liam's ankle.

Liam froze as Gran and Charlie separated.

"He wants you to pet him," she said.

"I don't want to be the toy."

"I don't think Aldo will hurt you. Just rub the top of his head," she instructed. "Let's see what happens."

Liam crouched as the bushy-tailed cat brushed back and forth against his ankle. He put his hand gently on the fluffy fur and rubbed. The cat purred. "He's so soft," Liam said.

"Yes, they still have a bit of kitten in them."

The bigger tabby followed the action closely. He apparently decided Liam was safe, so he followed his brother's lead and demanded attention.

"This means something, doesn't it?" Charlie asked.

"It does," Gran agreed, her eyes on Liam, who shifted from crouching to sitting cross-legged on the floor with two purring cats. One by one, the remaining three approached.

Charlie watched Liam play with the animals. He thought back to the fire and the little dog, who would have certainly died had it not been for him. "So tell me, how come one night they sound like they could rip him to shreds, and now…."

"I'm not certain… unless…."

Liam turned, aware of their attention but enjoying the fuzzy antics and different feels of each of Flora's animals. "Please tell me what you're thinking."

"I think you're more human now. They still sense the fey, but it's faded…." She looked from him to her grandson. "Liam Summer, I see that you are trying to mend your ways. My offer of hospitality still holds. And now that my cats don't want you for their supper, you are welcome to stay with me."

Charlie shook his head. "No, Gran. It's late, and Liam, I want you to stay with me."

Liam, from his nest of cats, looked up at Charlie. *She wants me away from him. She's trying to protect him, and she's right.* "Charlie, I can stay here. You needn't—"

"Just stop, okay? The both of you." And aware of Gran's attention, he didn't care. "I get it. You don't want me macking on you. I'll keep my distance. I've got a pull-out sofa."

"I have no idea what that is," Liam said.

"You'll see. It's comfortable, and you can stay as long as you like."

Liam grew quiet. He looked from Gran to Charlie. "You don't see me for what I am, Charlie. She does… and your family will talk."

Gran spoke. *Some things you cannot fight.* "Of course they will… they already are. Charlie, it's about time you gave them something to talk about. But before you go, let me give you some reading. It could help." She grabbed a couple of books from a near shelf and handed them to Charlie. "I'll be right back." She vanished for less than a minute and returned with another half-dozen volumes. A couple looked like children's books, and the others were antiques with titles like *Among the Sidhe*, Yeats's *The Celtic Twilight*, Lady Gregory's *Gods and Fighting Men: The story of the Tuatha De Danaan*, and one slender leather-bound on *Cuchulain*.

She loaded them into Charlie's arms and gave him a last kiss. "Call me when you can, and go to Mass."

He kissed her cheek and promised he would.

Liam extricated himself from the furry pileup and stood by the door.

"Come here, you," she said.

He approached, with a tabby on either side.

Gran drew him into a hug and whispered in his ear, "If you break my Charlie's heart, I will cut out yours."

Nineteen

THE RIDE back from the city, across the Brooklyn Bridge and then over the Verrazano Narrows, was the first real chance Charlie and Liam had to talk alone. It was awkward at first.

"So what was it like growing up in… fairyland?"

"Don't be a snarkling. It's called the Unsee or Fey. And now that I'm not there, I see my life in a different light."

"Tell me," Charlie said, his eyes on the road but wanting to look at Liam, afraid that at any minute, he'd again vanish.

"My life was spent in her court. As a child, it was clear that I was to be raised with a purpose. My parents knew this. It's what led to their death… to their murder. They attempted to get me away from May. I can barely remember them."

Charlie thought of his own parents, of how fiercely they loved their children. Of how more than ten years after the horror that killed Rory, they still grieved. "What happened?"

"They trusted a relative to hide me. Instead he took their money, and the night I was to vanish into the backlands, the soldiers came. They brought me and my mother and father before May." Liam grew silent.

"I'm sorry, Liam."

"No, Charlie. It's just I don't think about these things. I go through life with doors in my mind that I do not open. If you don't look, maybe it never happened…."

"Then don't."

Liam braced against the leather seat. "She made me watch as she ripped them open. Father first… then…. She did not do it quickly."

Charlie's eyes misted. He could not find words. "I'm sorry."

"You did not kill them, Charlie. You have nothing to be forgiven for. I, on the other hand…."

"Stop! You didn't kill them either. You were a child. That was not your fault!"

"But it was. If not for me, if not for them loving me, they would be alive. So yes, it is my fault. I caused their death."

"Hell no! Parents love their children. They tried to protect you, and some evil fuck killed them. It is *not* your fault."

"As you will. The facts stand. To save me, they died… were murdered, and I was not saved. You asked me of the Unsee. It is beautiful, there is no doubt, but filled with fear and terror. That was my life. She killed my parents, and she would have killed me… at least, that's what she said." He stared out the window as they crossed a second great bridge. Like time had never passed, he was there, May lovely in a silver gown, her hair swept up with jewels, resplendent over the bodies of his mother and father, their bellies ripped open, blood and steam rising from their guts, the smell of fairy fire thick in the air. "She told me, 'Liam Summer, you may follow your parents in death, or you will swear fealty to me, for now and forever.'"

Charlie waited.

"I was weak… and young. I did not want to die. I wanted to kill her, but I did not have the strength, and I knew it. I was a coward, Charlie. I gave her my pledge."

"No." He struggled to drive through the tears. "No, Liam, that's not cowardice. That's survival."

"It is both. In time I realized she had always intended to kill them. They were not obedient, and they were strong. I was raised by my uncle Cedric and his woman, Marilyn Nevus."

"Alex's mother."

"Yes. Cedric and I are much alike."

"Is he the one who turned in your parents?"

"No, a cousin, and he too found himself at the pointy end of May's sword, though that came later. I don't think of these things, Charlie, and yet… I suppose I have to. The fear that rules the Unsee—she will bring it here. And beyond the horror of what happened lies bits of my life with my parents. I can't seem to get to one without going through the other. My mother, Ileana, I think she always knew. I can remember sitting on her lap and playing with her hair as she'd tell me stories and teach me about magic. My father, Cullen, of him I remember little, other than he looked a lot like Cedric but in my mind's eye is taller and stronger."

"They sound like heroes, Liam. And bad stuff happens here too."

"I see that. Buildings catch on fire."

"Or are lit. We go off to war in countries that have little to do with us. We say it's for principals and freedom, but it's often not. More about oil and politics, money… drugs. We have our own crazy queens and kings who slaughter thousands and even millions. God, this is depressing."

"Then let's talk of other things," Liam offered.

"Like how beautiful your eyes are."

"A woman today told me she'd kill for them. I don't think she was serious, and she did help me find the right subway."

"About that," Charlie said. "How the hell did you find your way to Staten Island? And that's one hell of a coincidence, you meeting Annie and Daria on the ferry."

"People are kind here."

"Are you kidding? This is New York City."

"No, everyone today was kind. The woman who wanted my eyes, she walked me to the subway. From there another girl slid a piece of plastic through a metal lock and took me to the right train." He reached into his pocket and pulled out a wad of bills. "I assume this is money."

"How did you get that?"

"A man who showed me where the ferry was gave it to me."

As Charlie pulled onto his street, he glanced at Liam and the money in his hand. "There's got to be over two hundred bucks there. People don't just give strangers that kind of money, unless…."

"I did nothing for this money," Liam protested, aware of the direction Charlie's thoughts had taken.

"I'm sorry, I didn't mean to—"

"No. I have told you what I am and what I've done. You were right to think that."

More than anything, Charlie wished he could take back his unspoken accusation. He pulled into the drive. It was ten past midnight. The light was on in his parents' bedroom. Mom, possibly Dad as well, were still up and reading their shared guilty pleasure of romance novels. An entire upstairs bedroom was filled with shelves of bodice rippers and period stories of the plucky shopgirl and the jaded duke/earl/count/baron/CEO in need of her redemptive love.

He parked the truck, acutely aware of the man at his side. Between them lay the stack of books from Gran. "Liam."

"Yes, Charlie."

"I told you that I wouldn't bother you... you know, in that way."

Liam nodded, the air in the truck heavy. He read the hunger in Charlie's eyes. *But you feel something too. Do him no harm.* "Yes."

"Gran said the damage is done. You said the same thing and a lot more about how horrible you are, and... just so you know, you're not. And if you are... I don't care. But here's the thing." Charlie heard the ramble in his head. *Just go for it.... No, ask for it.* "One kiss, Liam. Right here, and once we go in, I promise to keep my hands to myself. Just one."

Liam felt the space between them and Charlie's smell, human and musky. "Yes." And he felt, rather than saw, Charlie come to him, his hands tentative on the sides of his face. Charlie's fingers at the back of his neck, his heat, his strength, and a heretofore unknown thought—*I love him.* And then the kiss, unlike any before. Always the one in control, Liam tumbled and fell into Charlie's embrace, all bad thoughts and memories replaced by Charlie's lips on his. *I don't want this to end. I don't want this to ever end.*

Twenty

LIAM'S BODY hummed as he sat in the Greenwich Village Greek diner and waited. Charlie had given him a MetroCard, and he had plenty of money from the man who'd brought him to the ferry. More importantly, there'd been another kiss. Not like the one in the dream or the one last night... in his truck, the sound of the waves in his ears, the realization that *Yes, I, Liam Summer, can love, do love. I love Charlie.* The morning kiss as he'd handed Liam the MetroCard and drawn a different route on the map he'd gotten from the man in green, was the best kiss of all. Yes, there'd been passion, hunger, and a bit of tongue, but there was no doubt. A kiss of connection, of *I am yours and you are mine. Charlie, what have we done?* He thought back through last night, Charlie's hand in his as they'd walked along the shore before going upstairs. Charlie had stayed true to his word—*damn him*—of just one kiss. But that walk, gentle waves and sand beneath their feet, hands connected, and the moon's silver light across the water. He replayed each moment, and when they'd finally gone up to his little house, and he'd turned the sofa into a bed. What sweet agony, lying there, knowing Charlie was just feet away in his own bed. *Just one kiss.*

A waitress in a red-checked uniform materialized with a berry-filled pastry and a foam-topped coffee. "It's from the woman over there."

Liam nodded and smiled in the direction of his patroness. In that instant, his buzz vanished. *It's glamour.* He looked at the sticky treat and the pretty woman in her dove-gray business suit, who'd sent it his way. He heard May in his head. *"You are my toy, Liam Summer, as is your uncle. Pretty toys to play on the affection, to snare and entrap. Your magic is the cruelest of all. You trick in love."*

That's what I've done with Charlie. He spooned sugar into the white-capped mug of coffee. *He said he doesn't care.* It was no use. They all said that. Once glamoured, the victim's reason was gone. Glamoured love was blind, deaf, and more than a little dumb. His mood darkened. He didn't want to think about what had become of those he'd snared for her, most of them ending up gutted on her kitchen floor, their usefulness to her gone. Their magic ripped from their bodies.

His appetite ruined, he pushed away the pastry and the sweet milky coffee laced with chocolate. While he'd lost his magic in the travel between worlds, the glamour remained, and while it made strangers help him on the subway, give him money, and buy him treats in diners, he wanted rid of it. *I don't want to be me—not that me. I am done with this.* But May was deep in his mind. *"The leopard does not change its spots, boy. You are mine, Liam Summer. Liam the whore."*

A flitting motion from outside the diner window drew his attention. A black Nevus fairy with vivid orange-and-black wings and beneath it, Alex Nevus and Jerod Haynes.

Liam inhaled as he spotted the men. He stood as they approached. He'd wondered if they would show. They'd both matured, no longer boys but tall and handsome men, Alex with hair the color of a crow's wing and Jerod's chestnut kissed with red and gold. "You both look well."

"You look different. The trip across changed you," Alex stated, clearly not eager to join him at his table.

"Thank you for coming. I bear messages from your mother, Marilyn, and your father, Cedric."

"Tell me of my brother, Adam."

"He is well. He is younger than you remember. Some of the years May stole were returned to him. Please, sit with me. I will buy you something to eat."

The waitress reappeared. "No you won't," she said. "Before that woman left, she gave me a hundred bucks for whatever you wanted. I get to keep what's left for a tip."

Liam shrugged, and Alex and Jerod took their seats.

"It happens to Alice too," Alex said. "People always give her stuff. It's kind of freaky."

"It's glamour. I do not do it deliberately… at least, not lately." He realized that Alex knew the truth. He'd been on the receiving end of Liam's glamour, though his love for Jerod had protected him.

Alex nodded. "Good. It sounds like you're doing the twelve-step thing. You said you had word from my parents. Let's have it."

Liam felt the weight of Alex's distrust, and the facial expression on the little fairy that perched on his shoulder spoke volumes. *They hate me… and with reason.* As for Jerod, if looks could kill, Liam knew he'd be cold on the floor. "Yes, they are both well and strong. The Mist that devoured the Unsee has stopped its growth. In spots, it has retreated." He paused. "Marilyn would know that you and your sister are safe and happy."

"We are," Alex said. "So you're going back."

"I suspect so, yes." Liam sensed the powerful bond between the two men. "You do look well and in love. It makes me feel… strange."

"Jealous?" Jerod asked.

"Perhaps, but not in the way you think…. Hopeful."

"Charlie Fitzgerald," Jerod said.

"No, he is too good for me." Heat rose in his cheeks. He grabbed his coffee and could not look at them. "As you're aware, Alex Nevus and Jerod Haynes, I have done much that is shameful. I was set to harm you, Alex."

"Yeah, about that," Alex said. "In the end, it didn't matter. You failed, and May still got what she wanted."

"It did matter. It is important, as it's a piece of why she failed. That is the other thing I must do…. Queen May is not dead."

Nimby fluttered at the mention of the mad queen.

"She turned into a giant white lizard and then vanished," Jerod said.

"An amphibian, but yes, a salamander, and she is not gone but trapped by her sister Lizbeta in the Mist. She grows strong, and she is hungry. Lizbeta's collar will not hold. I must know how you defeated her. For once she breaks free, she will seek vengeance, blood, and thrones, both there and here."

Alex looked at him dead-on, "Tell me, Liam Summer, servant to the queen, how are we supposed to trust you? How do we know it's not May who sent you, who's looking for a way to succeed where before she failed?"

"You are right not to trust. I no longer belong to May, and there's no reason for you to believe that. I cannot say it plainer, other than when and if she returns, she will kill me." He ran his hands through his hair, struggling to find the words that would make these two believe him and even trust him, if just a little. "You know me for what I am." He looked from one to the other and did not flinch from the disgust in their eyes.

Alex snorted. "I think somebody needs self-esteem therapy." He turned to Nimby. "Can I trust him?"

"He is not lying," she replied. "But do not trust him."

Alex shook his head. "Great…. Maybe we can help each other. Have you seen the video?"

"No. I do not know what that is."

"Then come with us. There's someone you need to meet… the other sister."

Twenty-One

KYLE SCHMIDT shot a stream of water into Charlie's face.

The cold and wet shocked him. "Hey! What was that for?"

"Earth to Fitzgerald. You've been standing with that sponge, staring at the same spot for, like, five minutes. The truck ain't going to clean itself. What's with you?"

Charlie looked from the side of the engine to the warm soapy water dribbling down his hand onto the cement floor. "It's nothing."

"Yeah, right. What's his name?"

Before Charlie could answer, his cell rang.

Schmidt chuckled. "I'll get it out of you... and it's about time, Fitzgerald."

With his free hand, he dug out his phone.

"Charlie?" Finn's voice spoke on the other end.

"What's up?"

"We need to talk."

"About?"

"Your Liam."

Charlie was about to argue that Liam wasn't his, but even thinking *not mine* made his stomach hurt. That plus the tone of Finn's voice braced him for bad. "What about him?"

"Can you get away? I'd rather do this in person."

"Now you're scaring me." He looked at Kyle, who was doing his best to eavesdrop while pretending to hose the truck. "You know, Schmidt, people say women gossip, but really? Give a guy some privacy." He hurled the sponge at Kyle's head, and before Kyle could retaliate, he ducked out the open bay of the station house into a warm spring day. He put the phone back to his ear. "Where are you?"

"Pulling up."

Charlie turned as Finn angled the red-and-white Bureau of Fire Investigation SUV into one of the reserved spots. On its back window was the agency's gold seal with the Latin *Veritas ex Cineribus*—Truth from the ashes.

Finn rolled down the window. "Get in."

Charlie pocketed his phone. The expression on Finn's face ratcheted up his anxiety. "We going somewhere?"

"I don't want to be overheard."

"Got it. So what is it you're going to tell me that I don't want to know?" His head filled with worst-case scenarios, like maybe Liam started the fire, which considering it was arson, would mean three counts of homicide.

"Did you find him?"

"Liam?"

"Yeah, Charlie. And by the way, thank you for softening up that scumbag Slotnik."

"My pleasure, and yeah... I found him." *And I kissed him, and we walked in the moonlight, and I wanted to do a whole lot more, and it took everything I had to not jump his bones last night, and please don't tell me he's a suspect.*

"Where is he?"

Charlie looked Finn dead-on. "Why?"

Finn nodded and didn't speak. "Here's the deal, Charlie. Nothing about that fire adds up... including naked Liam. I need to talk to him. You know that. He was the closest person to whatever took out that building."

"You think he set it."

"I don't know, and you're putting me in a bad spot. Tell me where he is. This isn't a negotiation. And I already called your Gran, and she said he wasn't there anymore, and then she clammed up."

Charlie smiled. Gran might not like or trust Liam, but she was no snitch. "He's with me...."

"At your place.... What's that mean, Charlie?"

"He needed a place to stay. He's on the couch."

"Is he there now?"

"I don't think so. He was going to meet someone."

"Enough with the half answers, Charlie. Don't be the perp."

Charlie looked at Finn, who'd been there his entire life. Growing up, he and Rory playing ball, making a raft out of logs they'd tied together and fishing off it in Saint George Bay. They'd always been so much older, the decade plus that separated them had seemed like a lifetime to Charlie. Always on the outside of his boisterous big brother and redheaded best friend, who probably spent more nights at the Fitzgeralds' dinner table than his own two blocks away. Charlie had been five when they'd both joined the FDNY after high school, and eight when Rory died. Finn Hulain was family to Charlie, though the years since 9/11 had seen him pull away. "Finn, Liam didn't set that fire."

"I hope you're right, but you know I have to talk to him. You found him naked in a vacant apartment. So maybe he didn't start it. But if it hadn't been for you, he'd be dead. So what I think is that maybe he didn't set it, but he could have been the target. One way or the other, he's got information."

"What if you don't believe the stuff he has to tell you?"

"What aren't you telling me?"

"A bunch. And it's beyond weird. Remember that closet?"

"Yeah, I'm having it taken apart and brought in. While it may not be evidence, it's beautiful. I'm pretty sure it was made by Alex Nevus's mom. In going through the files, it seems she was an artist, and mentally ill. Which might explain how fucking strange it is."

Charlie wondered how much Finn could take. He blew out a stream of air and went for it. "What if the stuff inside is real?"

Finn shook his head. "You high? I mean, seriously."

"I don't even know where to start, Finn. So let me give you the parts you'll believe and can check out. From there, if you want more, you're coming with me down the rabbit hole."

"Okay, Alice."

"No, I'm not Alice... but I've a feeling we're going to meet her before this is over. Her name is Alice Nevus, by the way. She and her brother Alex... Alex Nevus, lived in that apartment and moved out about two years ago."

"I know... the kid on that singing show."

"Yes, and I had no clue you liked talent shows."

"Charlie, there's a lot of stuff you don't know about me." His expression clouded. "Stuff that died with Rory, and now is not the time."

Charlie read the pain on Finn's face at the mention of his brother. A thought skittered to mind, and before he could censor it, he blurted, "Were you in love with Rory?"

Finn flushed. It happened in the beat of his heart, from his neck all the way up his ears and his cheeks—beet red in the way only the superpale can do. He turned away and looked out his window at the station.

"I'm sorry," Charlie said. "Not my business."

"Yeah, it kind of is," Finn said, unable to make eye contact. "Yes… I loved Rory. And growing up, when I didn't start to like girls and realized I wanted to be more than best friends… yeah, I loved… and was in love with Rory."

"Were you guys…?"

Finn turned to Charlie. "No. Rory wasn't gay. He knew I was. I never told him how I felt. There was no point. I didn't want to risk our friendship."

"That sucks."

"It does, it did, but not as much as losing him. So there," Finn said. "The thing I don't share with another soul is yours, Charlie. Now return the favor. Call Liam."

"He doesn't have a phone."

"Of course not, because you're going to tell me he walked out of that closet and…." Finn stopped. "Shit, no, Charlie. You're not going to tell me that closet is a portal to… whatever crazy mind painted that closet."

"I hadn't thought about that, but now that you mention it…."

"Don't," Finn warned.

"Look, you want to do this, you got to get ready. But you'll see. Liam went to meet with Alex Nevus—some stuff he needed to tell him." He retrieved his cell, flipped through the history for Alex's number, and called. As he waited he looked at Finn, his cheeks still red, his hair the color of fire, the revelations of the last few moments like flipping the lid on something he and the rest of his family tried to keep shut. *Finn loved Rory. Of course he did…. How did I miss that?* He bit his lower lip and tried not to think of just how much that would have to suck. To be in love, to not have it returned, and…. Alex picked up.

Twenty-Two

LIAM WALKED between Alex and Jerod through the bustling city of Manhattan. Nimby rode on Alex's shoulder, occasionally flitting into the air to catch a fly, mosquito, or other tasty winged treat.

It was all new to him, the trees in iron cages, their leaves the bright green of spring, the air scented with flowers and car exhausts, and the sun high and not too hot. He listened as Alex told him the story of May's sister Katye.

"She's the real deal," Alex said. "And somehow she kept a bunch of her magic on this side of things."

"Tell me more," Liam said, not knowing where to let his eyes rest, every block different from the last. Buildings festooned with carved heads or with walls of steel and glass, no two alike. "I know some of Katye. She and her sisters are legend. Though May is the only one who remained in the Unsee. Katye vanished long before my birth. They say she traveled for love through a mirror."

"Sounds right," Alex said. "It's her and Lance, as in Lancelot of the round table."

"I don't know that story," Liam said.

"Well, I think it got a bit twisted with the frog prince."

Jerod snorted. "Poor Lance, he definitely got the short end of the stick."

"I'm not certain about that. When he's not a frog, he's a stone-cold fox."

"You did not just say that," Jerod said.

"Whatever. When he's not green and hoppy, he's the poster child for Italian *Vogue*," Alex stated. He looked across Liam at Jerod, whose shoulder doubled as Nimby's perch. "And you can't overlook the fact that he's probably more than a thousand years old. So spending a few years here and there as a frog may be not the worse deal."

"I am confused. Katye, one of the three great sister queens, is in love with a frog?"

"Yup. It's freaky. They're connected. One of them stays young while the other grows old, and then at some point they run out of juice, and he turns into a frog. That happened three years ago."

"Yes, he croaked," Jerod deadpanned.

Alex rolled his eyes. "And he's still a frog. Katye says he remains like that for the span of the frog's life, and then, one day, he'll be good as new. And then wash, rinse, and repeat, about once every hundred years. She says they get a few years where they're both young together… and then it's about love and loss, which, I don't know, it's both beautiful and sad."

Jerod broke ranks and hugged Alex from behind. He whispered, "He doesn't have a thing on you. Though you and he were cut from the same bolt, and not just your looks. He's a hero, as are you… and you're mine."

They kissed.

Liam watched, unable to quell the war of emotions—whiffs of jealousy for what Alex and Jerod had together, a pang in his chest, and the tingle of Charlie's full lips on his own.

The little black fairy hovered and then lit on Liam's shoulder. She chattered in his ear. "They do this all the time…. It's love."

"Yes." Liam twisted his head to face her, the tiny thing no more than three inches from his nose. "And you. It's just you. Tell me of your swarm."

Her jewel-red eyes clouded. Her smile fell. "Just me. Just Nimby."

Liam studied the tiny creature, with her swirling gold tattoos festooned across coal-black skin. She was similar to creatures of the Unsee but not exactly. "Tell me what you are."

Jerod and Alex, still locked in an embrace, turned.

"I am his… now theirs," Nimby stated.

"She's been with me since birth," Alex clarified.

"She was sent," Liam stated.

Alex broke from Jerod's arms and walked up to Liam, his attention on Nimby. "By whom?"

The fairy shook her head. "No, no, no. I do not know, know, know."

"Do you?" Alex asked Liam.

"No, but as you're aware, the fey are best judged not by words but by action." He held his left forefinger like a perch. Nimby hopped on. She gazed into Liam's eyes, unable to look away. "It's her markings that are different. She's a warrior. But unlike any I've seen."

"The woman, or whatever she is, we're going to see—Katye—she called Nimby a Nevus fairy. I'm not sure what that meant. And other than being a bit of a pest at times, she's always had my back. Alice's too."

"She's of your family… and she's but one. Fairies like this come in swarms, flocks, and gaggles. One alone…."

Tears of blood streaked down Nimby's cheeks.

"Tell me your sorrow, little one," Liam whispered.

"I am one," she replied. "I am one, and I am alone. There is but one Nevus fairy, and she is I. When I go, there will be no."

Liam nodded. She took to the air and returned to Alex's shoulder. "I am his," she said, and in words barely audible above the traffic of Fifth Avenue, "and I am alone."

"What does that mean?" Alex asked. "She won't tell me anything about where she's from. She says she doesn't know."

Nimby stamped her foot on his shoulder. "I do not lie. I do not know."

"If I had to guess—but it's just a guess," Liam said as they resumed their progress up Fifth, "I'd put my money on your father, Cedric."

Alex muttered, "More riddles. So, here's something I'm trying to figure out. You and Katye and my dad all have the same last name." He stopped. "I hadn't even thought about that. We're somehow related. Or is Summer like Smith over there?"

"We are related," Liam stated. "Your father is my uncle. That makes us cousins. As to the bloodlines with the three queens, it's ancient history. But yes, the sidhe of Summer are family."

As the three walked abreast, Jerod observed the effect Liam had on strangers. "You, Katye, and Alex's sister all have that glamour thing. You notice how many people turn their head to look at you."

"It seems to be the only magic of mine that's left."

"About that," Alex said. "You know that Charlie is totally caught up in that… in you."

"It was not my intention."

"Maybe so, but the thing is done. He's on the hook. When you get set to haul ass back to the Unsee or whatever it is that comes next, what happens to him?"

"I do not know for certain. I hope it will fade. I hope he will find someone who will love him, someone good." But Liam did know, and he prayed that things worked differently here. Because in the Unsee, once glamoured, the victim was trapped in love for life. They would pine for the object of their affection. They would waste away, starved for love and not caring for food.

"You have feelings for him," Jerod said as they reached the apartment of Katye Summer.

Alex's cell buzzed. "Speak of the unlucky devil." He pulled out his iPhone as they headed through the motion-sensitive revolving door. "Charlie, what's up?"

"Liam still with you guys?"

"Yeah."

"Good. I'm with the fire marshal. He's a friend, and he needs to talk to him about the fire. Where are you?"

Alex gave him the address. "It's a friend's place, someone who I hope can give us some information. We'll be here awhile." He heard Charlie over the line talking to someone.

"We'll meet you there. Give us ten minutes."

Alex snorted. "Really? You think you're going to make it through midday midtown in ten?"

"It's called lights and sirens. See you in ten."

Liam perked, and his pulse quickened at the sound of Charlie's voice. *What is happening to me?* His fingers tingled from the remembered touch of last night's walk along the shore. *He will be here in ten minutes.* He stared at his reflection, his hair tied back, dressed in borrowed clothes, his eyes bright. But like a brick to the head, he remembered the truth…. Charlie was glamoured. And while using his power had once given him value and kept him alive, now it made him sad.

Inside, Frank, the doorman, dressed in dark blue with gold epaulets and brass buttons, greeted them with bad news. "Ms. Summer had to go out of town for a while. She left this and a set of keys. And you want to know the weirdest thing? And you know I love that woman."

"What's that?" Alex asked, taking the envelope and keys.

"She had a cat carrier with her, so I snuck a peek."

"And?" Jerod asked.

"No cat…. Frog—huge. Just freaky. But a woman who looks like that…. She could have a cobra for a pet and no one would think twice."

"That's Lance," Alex said to Liam as they headed to the elevator. "Quite the good-looking man, and as frogs go, not hard on the eyes."

On the ride up, Alex slit open the envelope and read her note aloud.

> *My dear Alex and Jerod:*
>
> *May is not done. She means to bring war. It is an ancient struggle, and I must take Lance and myself to safety. Were he in his human form, he would fight me on this. But frogs are easily tucked into pocketbooks and cat carriers, though he does fuss.*
>
> *That you've come seeking help underscores the truth of my words and the growing threat. Feel free to use my apartment and the texts you will find within. Alex, I have made arrangements for the expenses on your sister's and mother's—who is not really your mother, although she sort of is—apartment, so do not worry.*
>
> *I can give one answer, and because it is central to who may rule the fey, I believe it explains my sister's choice to go into a salamander. They regenerate lost limbs. To rule the fey, one must be whole. And as we know, the travel between worlds takes pieces from us. For me, it was much of my magic, which is why I am no match for my sister, though I hope my travels with Lance might remedy that.*
>
> *Again, I apologize for needing to run, but sometimes that is the only course to take if one hopes to live and to fight another day.*
>
> *With love, always,*
> *Katye*

"That sucks," Jerod said as he keyed into Katye Summer's light-filled apartment.

Liam stopped in the doorway and stared. "It's like the inside of a seashell. So much pink." Hundreds, if not thousands, of shades of that color, filled the space, from the inlaid rose marble in the foyer to the lavish but fading bouquet of peonies that dropped their petals on the carved table.

"It suits her," Alex said. "She's crazy beautiful. People stop to get a second or third look at you, Liam, but she stops traffic… literally. Even when she's old and withered, she's mesmerizing."

They passed through the foyer into her living room with its soaring windows, which overlooked Central Park ten stories below. A spacious balcony with potted trees and a frog pond wrapped around the building's corner. "I can't believe she took off," Alex said as his cell rang.

"Alex, we're downstairs. Can you let us up?"

"Let me talk to the doorman."

He hung up and looked at Liam. "He's bringing someone who wants to talk to you about the fire."

Liam smiled.

"You really do like him," Alex said.

He nodded. "Yes. I would have died in that fire. He saved my life."

"That's not what I'm saying…. Tell me, Liam Summer, are you capable of love?"

Alex's question burned. He thought of Uncle Cedric, who grew to love his Marilyn. He thought of his parents, who loved their son enough to die for him. "I do not know. I hope so."

Alex shook his head. "This is not going to end well." And he headed back through the foyer and opened the door.

CHARLIE AND Finn, who'd both been inside hundreds of Manhattan apartments and townhouses, were dumbstruck by the lavish pinkness of Katye Summer's airy home.

Charlie caught Liam's eye. He grinned. "Liam, this is my friend Finn Hulain. He's the marshal investigating the fire. He needs to talk to you."

Liam, increasingly used to the greeting customs of the See, walked up to the man with the flame-red hair. "I am Liam Summer."

"Good to meet you," Finn said and shook his hand. The marshal struggled to find words between the drop-dead blond guy, whose bare ass had been all over the Internet, to the millions upon millions of dollars this apartment represented. Nothing here was in his comfort zone, including the two handsome young men, one who'd had his fifteen minutes of fame on a TV talent show, who stood holding hands as though it were the most natural thing.

Charlie made the introductions as he tried to get a grip on their surroundings. "So what the hell does this friend of yours do?" he asked. He caught Alex's eye and stopped himself from adding *Or is this something you make out of magic?*

"I'll show you," Jerod said, letting go of Alex's hand. "This way." He led them into a two-story library with a coffered ceiling inset with murals of winged creatures, lovers in the woods, and sea monsters—half dolphin and half horse—pulling gods and goddesses in chariots.

This room was not as pink as the others, with tufted red leather chairs arranged in groupings and the walls lined with books. "Here." He crossed to two bookcases filled with hardcovers and paperbacks, all with the name Katye Summer on the spine. "She writes romance novels, like two or three a year, all bestsellers. A bunch have been made into chick-flick movies. She's not hurting for cash."

"Are you related to her?" Finn asked Liam, torn between getting his answers about the fire and trying to make sense of what they were doing in this lavish apartment. *Okay, so maybe this Katye Summer is his aunt or something. God, she's written a lot of books.* His eyes tracked up the shelves, as the titles and styles of the books shifted from the kind you get at the airport to ones bound in fabric and others with her name embossed in leather on the spine, which had to be more than a hundred years old.

"Distantly, yes. But I've never met her."

This makes no sense. What is going on? He looked back at Alex and Jerod. "And you two?" he asked, trying to piece together the connections between the three young men and Charlie.

Charlie sensed Finn's confusion and had a pit-in-the gut foreboding. Worse even than the feel at Sunday dinner with Liam in the lion's den of his family. He worried that Finn would think Liam had set the fire or that Liam would say something that would…. *Crap. Not good.*

Liam stood by his side. "It's okay, Charlie. I'll answer your friend's questions. Though we both know he'll leave with more than he came."

"Why's that?" Finn asked, noting the attraction between them and the odd impression that they were holding hands, but they weren't.

Liam smiled and met the redhead's gaze. "Let's find out."

Caught in Liam's eyes, Finn couldn't focus. "What's happening?"

Alex interjected, "Liam, stop it!"

"Sorry. I will try." He searched deep inside for the source of his glamour, like a wellspring in his chest.

"What are you talking about?" Finn asked, feeling a fog in his head when he looked at Liam. *He has such beautiful eyes.*

"I can have an effect on people," Liam said. "I'm trying to not have it happen. Maybe it's better you don't look at me."

Finn was about to remark on Liam's high opinion of himself. *But he's right. The guy is so beautiful.*

Charlie looked at Finn. "You sure you want to do this? I wasn't kidding about the rabbit hole."

Finn froze. He looked from Charlie, to Liam, to Jerod, to Alex, to… a little black fairy with butterfly wings and gold tattoos on her mostly naked body, smiling at him from Alex's shoulder. "What the hell is that?" His finger shook as he pointed. "What is that?"

Alex followed the direction of his gaze. "She's not a *what*, but a *who*. You're going to want to sit down for this."

FORTY-FIVE MINUTES later, Charlie's cell startled them. It was Kyle Schmidt at the fire station, wondering what had happened to him.

"I'm still with the marshal. Will be for another couple hours at least."

"Uh-huh…. Investigating Naked Chihuahua Guy?"

"Schmidt, you're a pig."

"Oink-oink, and you owe me, Fitzgerald."

He hung up and caught Finn slack-jawed and staring at Liam. His friend's expression bordered on comical. His mouth opened like a landed fish, about to ask a question. Then he'd glimpse Nimby, and the question died before it made it to his lips.

For his part, Liam was candid. He laid out all that he knew, which made things worse for Finn.

"A salamander," Finn finally muttered. "You're saying that the fire on East Third was caused by something spit out of a fire-breathing salamander."

"Yes." Liam smiled. He looked to Charlie. "You saw her too."

"I did, Finn."

The marshal tore his gaze from Liam. He looked to Charlie. "You got to help me out here."

Alex interrupted. "Finn, you saw my second-to-last performance on *IT*?"

"Yeah, the one where… holy fuck me! The one where you did all that pyrotechnic stuff and…."

"Just say it, Finn."

"Something came out of you. But that was special effects. That was…."

Jerod walked over to Katye's writing desk and booted up her computer, with its large curved-screen monitor. He clicked on her browser and flicked over to YouTube and the video of the performance. With nearly a billion hits, it was an Internet favorite with thousands of comments, which ranged from speculation on how it was done, to the power of love, to angry rants on how Alex had been robbed of the *IT* title because of some technical crap.

They watched in silence.

For Alex, who had lived the nightmare of being possessed for months by the fairy queen, it was the first time he'd seen the video. He'd never wanted to, and now he heard her singing in a lilting tenor through his mouth, her—his—fingers graceful and sure on the piano. Then it all went awry, at least from her perspective. Lance the frog hopped onto the keyboard, disrupting her performance as Jerod moved through the audience, declaring his love and demanding that she leave a body and a soul that belonged to another, to him.

Liam stared with rapt attention, his breath hot between his lips. "This is what she wanted. To be worshiped in this world." He watched her magic unravel as Jerod boomed out, *"Alex is mine, and I am Alex's."* The audience took up his chant and amplified the power of his love and his prior claim to Alex. "Love… you defeated her with love. They say it's the only true magic left in the human realm."

Finn stared at the screen. He'd seen the performance, both when it had first aired and more than once on the Internet, when a friend or family member would share it on Facebook. "Shit, Charlie, you weren't kidding about the rabbit hole." He braced for the video's climax, where a massive, writhing fire-breathing white salamander spewed from out of Alex's mouth. It was fascinating and grotesque. *This can't be real*, Finn thought. Like everyone else, he'd speculated at how the trick had been done.

On the final show, the producers had disqualified Alex for using unapproved pyrotechnics and special effects. It had sounded plausible.... It had all been lies.

The video ended.

"See," Liam said. "She's a salamander, and Katye's letter tells us why. She means to rule, and to do so, she must be whole. It's brilliant. She may be mad, but she's a genius."

Charlie looked at Liam and then to Finn. "You were right."

Finn shook his head. "About what?" He sank into one of the red leather chairs and stared at the now dark monitor.

"Liam didn't start that fire, but his being there, it being in Alex's old apartment, it's no coincidence. She sent that fireball with a purpose. Liam, don't you remember anything about how you got there? Please, try."

"Charlie, I have tried. It's a blank."

"Great," Finn said.

"No, it's not." Liam shook his head. "It's not great.... It's dust! I was dusted."

"Say again."

"That's why I don't remember. The fire—tell me what you smelled."

"Cookies," Finn replied. "Fresh-baked cookies."

"I smelled it too," Charlie said.

Nimby flitted across the space and sniffed at Liam. Her wings fluttered as she darted from his shirtfront to the hem of his jeans.

"What's with her?" Alex asked, used to his fairy's antics, but this was new.

"I said the *D* word." Liam smiled.

"And today we learn something new," said Jerod. "Explain, Liam."

"Dust," Liam said. "Why I didn't make the connection before... I guess with coming to the See and all, I didn't think about it. But yes, May sent fairy fire. Whether I was the intended target or got snagged by mistake, I don't know. It's too much to be a coincidence. So let's argue that I was the target or part of the target." His eyes widened. "I remember something. I was at the Mist's edge, and I heard screams from within. It had been happening more frequently. Like ogres being tortured... or eaten. And then, yes, I saw and felt it at the same time. A tunnel ripped into the Mist, and something pulled me through. She might have known I was there. She might have sent it for me. And then I woke to the building on fire and to Charlie and his ax. And maybe this is important, but in the

Unsee, fairy fire is highly prized, not for itself but for what comes after. When the fire burns out, dust remains."

"This is where I've got to draw the line," Finn said. "After fairy fire comes fairy dust?"

Liam nodded. He held out his forefinger for Nimby. She perched on it. He looked into her eager red eyes. "Sorry, little one. I have no dust for you."

Her shoulders sagged, and she took to flight. She circled him, sniffed his ears and under his ponytail. Disappointed, she flitted back to Alex.

Liam looked at her. "You do not want her getting her hands on any, either."

Nimby shook her head emphatically. Her tinny voice insisted, "I don't have a problem with dust. I can stop any time. I just want a teensy taste."

Liam nodded. "Of course you can. And best not take that risk. Fairy dust is the most addictive substance known to the sidhe. It causes dreams and forgetfulness in some. Others it makes silly, and some get dangerous. Under its power you can go to sleep for weeks, months, and even years."

Charlie asked, "Is it just the sidhe it affects, or humans too?"

"I do not know," Liam said. "There are tales of humans enchanted by fey who are sprinkled with dust and waken decades later, to families who don't recognize them."

"Rip Van Winkle," Charlie offered.

"I don't know who that is," Liam said. He crossed to a wall of glass-fronted cabinets filled with leather- and vellum-bound volumes. He opened one of the doors, reached in, and pulled out an ancient tome. "Her note said that we might find answers." He looked back at the others.

Charlie followed him and looked at the book. "It's in Gaelic. Do you know how to read this?"

Liam looked at the floor.

"What?" Charlie sensed hurt in his expression… and something else. Shame.

"Just a little, Charlie. My education stopped after she killed my parents. She viewed it as unnecessary for her purposes." He opened the page and stared at the bold black letters and intricate gold-leaf calligraphy that ornamented the corners. He placed the book flat on a table and turned to an illustration of a battle. Some of the soldiers were human, and the opposing army was made up of a broad array of the sidhe. "Your gran, Charlie."

He nodded. "She would love to see these."

Liam heard a catch in his voice. "You are frightened for her. You don't want to bring her into something that is dangerous."

One by one, the others came over and selected books from the cabinet, even Finn.

"Great," he commented. "Latin. I had to take that in high school. Don't remember any of it, other than the teacher was a sadist who wore polyester leisure suits."

Liam repeated, "We need your gran, Charlie."

"I know… it's just…."

"It's dangerous. But here's the thing." He looked at each of the men and then Nimby. "The danger comes, whether Flora Fitzgerald helps or not. That is certain. Give her the choice, Charlie. I've lived in a world ruled by May. I would not wish it on my worst enemy. She means to be queen again, over all. We must know why. I thought I knew, that it was all about power. I'm less certain now. There's something more. We need to learn how she can be stopped. Alex and Jerod did it once. We need something stronger. Something to not just defeat her but to hold her, to keep her from ever doing harm again."

"Why not just kill the witch?" Finn asked.

Liam looked at Charlie's redheaded friend. "Yes. That was my thought, but her sister will not have it. It's not certain that she can be killed. But there's something else, something about the three sisters, that all are needed to maintain balance. If one were to die, the balance would be destroyed. I think it no accident that each resides in a different realm."

Charlie nodded. "I'll call Gran. If she says no, then it's a no, Liam."

He dialed. Flora picked up on the second ring.

"Illustrated manuscripts… in both Gaelic and Latin." Her excitement was palpable.

"Gran, there's more to it. It could be dangerous. You don't have to—"

"I'm getting my purse now. I'll wait downstairs. I am so excited about this!"

Charlie turned to Finn. "Feel like giving me a ride?"

"Sure thing. Feel like helping me write this report?"

"Good luck with that, but maybe just focus on all the fire code violations so that Slotnik and company are on the hook for both the criminal and civil. The place was a firetrap."

"True, but now we know they didn't set it. They're scum, just not the murdering type… at least this time."

"No." Charlie grinned at Finn. "Just put down that it was started by a fire-breathing fairy queen."

"Shut up," Finn said.

"Liam, I have to get back to the station. I'll be home in the morning. Please be there. Can you find your way back?" There was doubt in his voice and an ache around his heart that Liam would once again vanish.

"Charlie." Liam took his hand. He looked up into trusting blue eyes as his fingers squeezed. "I will find my way back to your Island." And this time it was Liam who pulled the tall firefighter in for a kiss. And so only Charlie could hear, "And into your bed."

Twenty-Three

THE GREAT white worm writhed in the mist. She spat out two fireballs that pierced holes, one to her left and the other to her right. Her sister's enchanted collar dug into her slick skin. Rivulets of acid-green blood trickled from its steely bite. She growled and worked the wretched restraint deeper into her flesh. Violently she threw her head first one way, then the other. She used Lizbeta's magic like a knife to cut her hide. As she did, pricks of flame appeared between her tearing flesh. She thrashed. The pain was beyond words as her skin caught fire. *Faster. It's coming. Faster.*

Her eyes now red, now amber, ever more awake, tracked her fiery projectiles as they tunneled through worlds. *Little Alice, little Alice, come to play. Are you ready? Are you waiting? Have you greased the way? Are you pretty? Are you polite? When I knock, let me in tonight.... Here it comes.*

She clawed the dirt and smashed a severed leg from yesterday's troll. It was to be a snack for later. *But no.* Power surged inside her. *I am strong. I will wear pretty dresses. Little Alice, let me in, let me in. A little more, a little more.*

She opened her mouth and felt it start. Her jaw unhinged, the corners cracked open. A seam of silver flame appeared down her side, and like a snake shedding its skin, the great white salamander split open. It screamed and howled as it slipped Lizbeta's collar, and in the shell of its former self, covered in green blood and bathed in fire, were not one, but two perfect identical copies of herself.

The Mist, sensing her escape, swirled down and tried to capture the slick white creatures. In unison they reared back on squat, powerful haunches, and as if a starter's gun had been fired, one shot down the fairy fire tunnel to the right, and the other vanished down the tunnel to the left.

We are free*!* With minds joined as one, they shot like rockets through the Mist. *I am free! I am powerful.* She felt the tunnels she'd created attempt to close around her. *No!* She ran with all her might. Flames licked at her new flesh, hardening her skin to a rubbery smooth perfection. *I will be free. I will wear pretty dresses. I will take back all that was mine.* That thought, like gas exploding on fire, sped her legs and hurtled her to freedom.

A WORLD away, Alice Nevus looked up from her tablet to Mr. Kayden, her biology teacher. He was laying out the material to be covered on Friday's exam. Five more minutes till the bell, her thoughts fixed on her locker and her backpack. As she'd done since first tasting that incredible powder, she'd wondered how much longer its effects would last. *Is there more? I should go back and look. Maybe there was some on the ground I didn't see. Maybe there's more. There has to be.* The last few minutes to the bell were pure agony. *I should have brought some with me. But then it's going to be gone. I should go back. There's got to be more. I'll go after school.* The thought quieted the hunger as the second hand on the clock crawled from the one to the five. *Is this class ever going to end?*

She looked at the page on her tablet, the stages of cell division. Meiosis, mitosis, the lining up of the DNA, the splitting apart, one cell into two, two into four, four into eight. She knew this stuff cold, interphase, prophase, metaphase, anaphase, telophase, then back to interphase, *and start all over again.* Amused by the singing voice that seemed more and more frequent since… *that delicious powder.* The hand crept past the eleven. *Only four more minutes.* She looked down. There was a tiny speck of white under the nail of her right forefinger. Without thought, she stuck it in her mouth and licked it free.

Her eyes widened as the treat connected with saliva. *What is this stuff?* Her nostrils filled with the scent of cookies as she sang through the material for the test in her head. *Zygote, morula, blastula, gastrula. Make me a frog, make me a snake, make me a person, or make me a salamander that breathes fire….* That was just strange. She flipped from her textbook to the Internet and typed in *fire-breathing salamander.*

Thousands of references and images appeared. A fire-breathing serpent, kind of like a dragon without the wings, a crown above its head and flames shooting from its mouth. References to Frances I of France, who had it as his symbol, and then earlier Gaelic references and something about St. George and running the snakes out of Ireland. That caught her attention. It took up the remaining three minutes of class as she read through a blog post that claimed it wasn't really snakes that St. George ran out, but the Druids and the ancient religions of Ireland, which had snakes and other fantastic creatures worked into their stories and legends. Stories, she knew firsthand, were based in fact.

The bell rang. She bolted for the door.

"Alice!"

She turned at her name to see blond and handsome Leif Swann trying to head her off.

"What's up, Leif?" Her tone was abrupt.

He stopped and bit his lower lip. "I was wondering if you're going to Friday's dance."

The little singing voice was amused. *This is the third one to ask. Will we go with blond, or red, or brown? Will we wear a pretty dress or pretty gown?* "I'm not sure yet. I've got to run."

Before he could muster his courage to ask her out, she was gone. Not quite running but on the cusp of, she bypassed the elevator and flew down four flights to her locker.

The voice in her head sang as her fingers whipped the combination wheel on her locker.

Fairy dust, fairy dust,
Tasty, yes, to some,
Fairy, fairy, fairy dust,
Eat it up, yum.

Twenty-Four

FLORA'S PULSE raced as they flew crosstown with lights and siren. *I can see why they like this.* Her eyes were bright as she rode with Charlie and Finn from Gramercy to Katye Summer's West Side apartment.

As they pulled up, she looked through the back window at Alex, Jerod, and Liam, who were waiting for them. She clapped and pointed. "It's one of them!"

Charlie followed her gaze. "You see her?"

"Yes... and so can you." Tears welled. "I've not seen one since I was a child. I thought...."

"Her name's Nimby."

Finn turned off the lights and parked the SUV in front of the building. Charlie got out and opened the back door for Flora. He gave her his hand and waited as she got her legs steady on the ground.

"This is my gran." He introduced her to Alex and Jerod, though the one who held her interest was Nimby.

"She is the most beautiful one I've ever seen."

"You did not say that." Alex groaned, knowing he'd have a big-headed fairy for weeks to come.

"No." Flora held out her hand. "She is lovely. Black and gold and swirly. She is special."

Nimby did not need a second invitation. She lit on Flora's hand and put a finger to her lips.

"What is it?" Flora asked as she lifted Nimby to her ear.

The fairy whispered, "I will help you."

Gran nodded. "Yes, I would like that."

Nimby continued, "If we do not stop her, she will eat us all."

Gran startled and looked at her grandson, who was climbing back into Finn's truck.

"I can't stay," he said.

"Of course. It's a workday. Call me." She looked from him to Finn, to Alex, to Jerod, and finally to Liam. Deep in thought and with a fairy on her shoulder, she muttered the thing stuck in her head. "When I was small, I played with the fey. Not as pretty as you, Nimby... but then I came here, or maybe because I was older, they were gone. I did look. I called for them, and nothing. But now... you on my shoulder. Liam." Her gaze then landed on Alex. "Something about you...."

"Haffling," he said in a low voice. "I'm half-and-half."

She nodded. "Yes, something big is happening. Something is in motion."

Finn's truck pulled away.

"Do we call you Gran?" Alex asked.

"Gran, Flora, both are good. Nevus is an old name. You do know what it means."

"Yes, it means birthmark."

"Marked at birth," Liam added.

"So, show me these books," Gran said. She sniffed deep. Her mouth watered. "Do you smell that?"

"Cookies," Jerod said. "It's been everywhere the past few days."

"Not cookies," Liam corrected as they went through the revolving door. "It's fairy fire, and we don't have much time."

BACK IN Katye's apartment, Gran gaped at the incomparable library. It cast her own collection into a dim light. "Never have I seen... so many." Her hand touched one of the manuscripts opened on a marble table. Her focus went from the exquisite gilt-and-ink Celtic knots in the corners, to the carefully penned dark letters, the hand of the scribe sure and strong. "Amazing." She looked back and spotted the little fairy back on Alex's shoulder. She motioned to Nimby, who flitted across the room and alit on the table. "When I was little," she told her, "my mother insisted the sidhe did not exist. But she left a saucer of milk on the windowsill and tossed the heel of every loaf from the oven into the yard. Of course, you and I both know that the fey prefer sweet things. But the milk would be gone, and the birds took the bread." She fumbled in her purse and found a wrapped butterscotch.

Nimby smiled. "Yes, please." She took the hard candy, and with a decisive crunch, her needle-sharp teeth made quick work of the sweet that was half the size of her head.

"She needs to see the YouTube thing," Liam said. "It'll let her know what we're up against. At least a taste of it." He looked at Nimby, whose wings trembled with the first rush of sugar. He smelled the butterscotch, and his mouth watered.

Flora followed his gaze. "I have another. Would you like it?" She fished a second candy from her pocketbook.

"Oh yes." He popped the glass-hard treat into his mouth. The flavors were rich, buttery, sweet.

"I always brought them sweets." Her voice sounded wistful as Liam led her to the desk with the computer. He pulled up a chair with arms for her to sit.

"Thank you."

And as he'd seen Charlie do, he held the chair steady as she gripped the tufted leather arms and eased down.

They replayed the Alex-vomiting-out-a-salamander video from *IT*, as well as the performances that led to it, where each week one or two contestants had been eliminated.

"She was obsessed with this stuff in the Unsee," Liam said.

"Explain," Gran prompted.

"The years before her possession of Alex, she was furious to discover...." He thought back through the studios May had created, uncreated, and recreated in her palace.

"What?" Gran urged.

"This." He pointed to the screen, now paused on a still of Alex at the piano, with Lance the frog about to mix up the performance. "This is what she wanted. To gain followers.... This little box does that. You said there have been nearly a billion views. You gain power from others. Like Jerod and Alex harnessing first their love and then amplifying it with the people in that room. The chanting, whether or not you realized it, was magic, an incantation that gained strength with numbers."

"I remember," Alex said. He shuddered and shook his head. "When I was there... in the Unsee. She was doing some kind of cooking show. There was a cupcake with cherries, and she didn't like it. She threw it on the floor and stabbed the fairy who'd had the idea for the cupcake. She killed it."

Jerod was out of the chair and at his side. "For a cupcake? Seriously?"

Alex nodded. "She ranted about needing something new, something people hadn't seen. The cupcake didn't cut it. But it looked delicious, even though I thought I was losing my mind. I can still see that poor thing, with a pencil jabbed in its forehead, dying on the ground."

Liam spoke. "Here's more you need to know. The fey she killed— and I was there that day—was then taken to a kitchen not made for cupcakes. But one with a stone floor and hoses to wash away blood. The fey she murdered, like all the others, was both an object lesson for the living and a snack for later. A powerful strain of magic comes from our blood and our organs. She has gorged on her subjects. Her power is immense."

"Liam, that is important." Gran glanced at the monitor as they replayed the televised extraction of the salamander. "Hold it there."

Jerod hit Pause. Flora stared at the moment when the massive creature lost physical contact with its haffling host. "That's where her magic broke."

Liam nodded. "She needs the physical contact with a haffling. It's what tethered her to the See."

Gran looked from Nimby to Alex. "Your little fairy—you seemed surprised that I could see her."

"Yes, no one does, although…."

"Although what?"

"Lately that's less true. Growing up, it was just me. I tried to tell people I had a bare-breasted black fairy with squiggly gold tattoos on my shoulder. It did not go well. Once I realized that I was the only one who could see her, I shut up. I even learned how to block her out."

Nimby, now recovered from her butterscotch buzz, flew at Alex's head. "You were bad, bad, bad."

Gran smiled. "I understand. I grew up seeing fairy circles in the woods outside my home in Limerick. Others did not see them…. I learned to not speak of them."

Alex whispered to Nimby, "I'm sorry, little bug…. When I was little, I'd talk about her. When you're real small, it's not such a big deal, but with a mother who hears voices, people looked at me funny. They'd wonder if my imaginary friend was the apple of Mom's schizophrenia not falling far from her crazy tree."

"But others see her now," Gran prompted, her eyes on Nimby.

"Yes. Jerod, my sister, Alice, Charlie, Liam… even Charlie's friend the marshal could see her. That doesn't happen."

"Finn saw her?"

"He did."

"Finn…. Hulain. How could I not have seen this? This is no coincidence. All of this matters." Gran grasped the chair arms and stood. Her rubber soles squeaked as she turned in place. Her mind skittered over the bizarre: the monitor frozen on the giant white beast, the walls filled with magnificent books, a little black fairy, a man who claimed to be—was—a haffling, and of course, Liam. She looked at the purple-eyed one, with his perfect face and easy glamour. She shuddered. *He was the queen's weapon. Is he still? Can he be trusted?*

Liam came to her side. "Flora, I think I know the wander of your thoughts. It is important, all of May's plans, her cooking shows and flea-market contests, and then that… singing through Alex's body."

"She needed us to believe in her," Gran said.

"Yes, and they did believe, just not in her. Jerod, please take it back again."

"Sure." He moved the status bar back to the start and hit the Play arrow.

"Make it louder," Liam instructed, and standing next to Gran, he watched and listened as first Jerod claimed his love for Alex, and then the audience picked up the refrain and chanted louder and louder. "It's them—Alex and Jerod—that the audience believe in. They believed in love."

Alex snorted. "I'm sorry, that just came out a little too after-school special."

"I thought it was sweet," Jerod said. "And you know he's right. You sidhe—hafflings included—think you have the market on magic, but we have some. It's love, and Liam is dead right. All of the other pyrotechnic-frog-morphing-fairy-queen bullshit doesn't come easy. May tried to force too big a pill down everyone's throat. That's where she screwed up."

Gran spoke up. "Not entirely, as evidenced by more and more people seeing darling little Nimby. This is an important piece to tuck away…. For May to conquer the human world, the blinders must come off. You can't be conquered by someone you can't see."

"Right," Alex said. "It's like *Peter Pan*, that if you don't believe in Tinker Bell, she doesn't exist."

Gran wandered to the book-filled cabinets. Reverentially, she opened the one that housed the oldest volumes. She breathed the perfume of parchment, vellum, ink, and leather. Her fingers traced the spines and settled on one with intricate Celtic embellishments in tarnished black silver. "All these stories, even the most unbelievable, are rooted in both worlds. That's the path we have to take. Like you, Alex, the way between the worlds is neither fey nor human but both. May knows this… and you are not safe. Though how she can again attempt to possess you, I do not know. For the thing that ousted her before, your love for Jerod, is strong."

"Shit!"

She cocked an eyebrow. "Language, young man."

"Sorry. It's just, I'm not the only one. I have a sister and a brother."

"That's not good. I mean…."

"I know what you mean."

He pulled out his cell. There were no texts from Alice, something they usually did a couple dozen times a day. He checked the history. Her last texts were from yesterday morning. Nothing from last night, and no morning check-in. *Not like her.* He knew she'd be in school and sent one anyway. *What you up to?* He stared at the screen. "She's probably in class."

"I'm sure she's fine. Wait till school's out," Jerod said, his tone less certain than his words.

Alex nodded and wondered if he should hop a subway down to Stuyvesant and check on her. He hit the GPS locater app on his cell and entered her number. He waited as the red target appeared.

"See," Jerod said, a hand on his shoulder. "Right where she's supposed to be."

"She's been acting weird the last couple days." He turned to Liam. "Since you showed up."

"Tell you what." Jerod grabbed his cell. "I'll text Clay. He gets out half an hour earlier than she does. You know anything Alice related, and he's up for it."

"I don't want her leading him on."

Jerod chuckled. "Yeah, well, that ship sailed the moment he met her."

Gran looked from Alex and Jerod to Liam. *Can he be trusted? He looks so human... and he's not. And do I have a choice but to trust him?* She laid the manuscript beneath a goose-necked lamp. "This is the epic tale of Cuchulain, a kind of Irish Hercules. It's where the name Hulain comes from." She opened the hinged cover and gazed on pencil markings that documented the book's prior owners and prior sales, the last from a major auction house. "This is the real thing, maybe twelfth century, maybe earlier. The first written manuscript of Hulain's battles is eighth century. Which, considering all these stories began as oral traditions, eighth century just hints at its true age. The tale started well before Christianity."

As she turned the stiff vellum pages, with images of mythical beasts and warriors caught in the swirl of Celtic knots, she translated. Even Nimby was entranced by Hulain's adventures, starting as a small boy going on to defeat a god-king's army. "The stories don't have a continuous narrative," Gran remarked. "There are tales of how Cuchulain fell in love with a fairy queen—Maeve, Mab, May. Though in some stories she is human and he is sidhe. They're more like chapters, with bits of his life missing in between. Each tale is both whole unto itself and part of a larger body. There's one where he kills a king's hunting dog by accident and in return offers to be his hound. There are hundreds of those stories in which he is simply referred to as the Hound. And while his relationship with May was filled with passion, they both delighted in tricking one another. Lots of cattle stealing and plaguing one another with curses. And everything on a scale too big to be believed. Thousands of cattle stolen in a night. Hulain single-handedly defeating an army." Flora came to the center page and unfolded the oversized sheet. She gasped. "This should be in a museum." It showed a great battle between a human army and creatures that ran the spectrum from men and women to beings comprised of animal, insect, and human portions, along with red-faced ogres and bright blue and green trolls.

"It's like the pictures Mom used to paint," Alex said.

Gran looked back at him. "So your mother is with a…."

"Fairy. My dad is a fairy."

Liam nodded. "'Tis true. Uncle Cedric."

"And your mother, where is she?" Gran asked.

"With him and my little brother, Adam, who I've barely met. They're in the Unsee, and she pretty much can't return. She's crazy on this side and perfectly normal on the other."

"Right…. That's another piece," Flora remarked. She pointed at the battle scene before them. In the center of the sidhe contingent was a beautiful blonde queen astride something that had the lower two-thirds of a praying mantis and the head and shoulders of a man. In the creature's mouth was a severed human hand, to which the artist had added drops of blood, which pooled on the ground. "There…. In the war between the humans and the sidhe, Hulain lost a hand. He was no longer whole and so could not rule. Much blood was shed in the war, which they say lasted a thousand years and was a draw in the end. A truce was struck and a treaty drawn in which the world would be divided. Hulain tricked the fey, and the land was divided between above ground—the See—and all beneath the earth's surface—the Unsee. But deals are deals, and the fey hold true to contracts."

She flipped to the book's end and shut it. She stared through the light-filled windows at the treetops of Central Park. "Her magic is growing, and she is persistent. I believe she intends to reunite the worlds, with her as the ruler over all. She tried it by taking your body and working magic on TV in front of millions. It's why more people can see Nimby. It has something to do with your being here." The latter was directed to Liam. "None of this is coincidence, and she is many steps ahead of us."

Liam spoke. "She's poking holes in the Mist. She burned one with fairy fire, and it sucked me in."

Gran scanned the open cabinet and grabbed a second smaller volume, this one bound in white kidskin with a tight golden knot on the cover. It was filled with miniature illustrations, almost like the cells in a comic book, albeit with medieval clothes and the now familiar mix of beast and man. "This one's even older. It shows the signing of contracts between May and Hulain." She paused, struck by a thought. "Could such documents truly exist? If the treaties are real, who possesses them?"

"They both signed." Alex stared at the page. "If they both signed, it's a binding contract. One thing I learned about the fey—they stick to their rules. Without breaking the contract, she can't rule here."

"You are correct," Liam said. "Somewhere, someone possesses the treaties. If the image is to be believed, there were two. Hulain would get one and she the other. Unless—"

"Tell me," Gran said.

"A contract need not be written. Like Alex and Jerod's love, it need only be sworn to bind."

"Yes, let us tuck that away." Gran turned the page to a split image of the human world above and the sidhe cast into shadows, woods, and caves. Above, in the light of the sun, Hulain, his hand replaced by one made of silver, sat in a castle with a redheaded wife and seven redheaded children. Below, surrounded by fire, was blonde May, her eyes rimmed with blood.

Liam looked at Alex and then at Gran. "The two of you are both of ancient families. If the Hound still exists, he does so in the blood of his children. She will look for them. They will not be safe. My head, it swims." Memories, horrible scenes from his life in May's court, passed through his mind. Things he'd learned to block out. The screams, the pleas from those caught in the crosshairs of her fury and her hunger…. *She will bring that here. It cannot be.*

"It's a lot," Gran said. "And we haven't even pieced together the bits of the three sisters." Her eyes glittered as she looked around the library. "Yet we know more now than an hour ago. I don't think this Katye would mind my staying here. These books hold answers. And one thing I've learned in my long life, if you want to solve a problem, you must first understand it. My place is here." One by one she looked at the men and the little fairy. "None of this is coincidence… the ancient families coming together. And Finn, Finn Hulain. I have no doubt but he has the blood of the Hound."

Liam nodded. "She means to start a war."

Flora risked looking into his wondrous eyes. "Yes, Liam. And we must all find our courage, prepare for battle, and fight for those we love."

Twenty-Five

FREE, FREE, free. The two white salamanders, their skin not yet fully hardened, ran free from Lizbeta's yoke.

We are whole!
We are free!
We are two,
It's all me.

Their long necks arched back as they glanced at each other one final time. Then in unison they dug deep into their guts and spat forth one ball of fairy fire after the next.

They reared up and stared down the tunnels burned into the Mist. One shook her head, sniffed at the entrance, and like a puppy trotting to its master, scampered in. She stopped at the opening between worlds. She stared into the bright blue sky of the See. She shook her hind legs and wiggled her plump belly. *Just enough, Alice....* Her thoughts flew through the air. *It's time.* The teen came into view, the girl's thoughts calm and receptive. Her body crackled with fairy dust. *Perhaps you need a wee bit more.*

FAR GONE into the addiction of dust, Alice reached across her bed for her backpack, her mind buzzed and numb. *Just a little more. A wee bit more.* She pulled out the Ziploc baggy of the incredible white powder. The sadness of her dwindling supply was gone. *I wonder why? What will I do when it's gone?* She dipped her fingers in, let the sticky powder coat them, and stuck them in her mouth. *So good.* The rush of dust, the feeling... no, the certainty that everything was okay, that the world was a beautiful place, and that nothing or no one could ever harm her. *So good. So perfect. Nothing bad can touch me.*

MAY KNEW. *It's time. She is perfect. Not like the other.* Her emotion darkened at the thought of the brother. *But we will get him, and he will be delicious. I will grind him into a paste and....* She snorted flame through her nostrils, amused by how much troll and ogre she'd dined on. *Though truth be told, the bone grinding... not so bad. But soon it would be time for party dresses and payback. Alice, knock, knock, knock, let me in, let me in.*

LOST IN euphoria, Alice heard the singing and sang back. *Not by the hair of my chinny chin chin.*

May laughed and coughed up a final fireball. As it flew up her neck and out her mouth, she clamped down tight with her jaw and hung on for the ride. The night air, the sky filled with smoke, felt so good against her hardening skin as she hurtled toward the roof of Alice's building. She landed hard. She dropped the fireball from between her teeth and watched it burn through tar and wood and beam. *Then I'll huff and I'll puff and I'll blow your house in.*

Flames burst orange, white, and hot as the fireball fell to the floor below. Like riding an elevator, she climbed on top of her fiery treat and dropped floor by floor, sizzling through steel and concrete like a knife through butter. She hopped off on nineteen, in the bedroom of the haffling, Alice Nevus.

Alice stared first at the fire burning through the ceiling in her bedroom and then at the impossible lizardy thing that landed on the floor. *I should be afraid.... I'm not. It's kind of cute. It's talking to me.... I'm hallucinating. It's the powder. I need to stop doing the powder. But it feels so good.*

"Of course it does," the white salamander said. "It's fairy dust. And now it's time, Alice."

Alice struggled to find words. *Something is wrong. I know that voice. I know what she wants. She wants....* But the drug was too strong. She could neither move nor resist, only watch as the salamander's jaw unhinged and her mouth opened wide, wider, wider still.

She's going to swallow me.
And she did.

MAY BURROWED into Alice, keeping the teen's pretty outside while taking control of the haffling's insides.

Free. May's molecules raced up and down the girl's spine and grabbed control of her brain, tapping her thoughts and her memories. *Free to wear dresses and take back what's mine.* She paused over the image of an auburn-haired boy. *That's the one you like but think is too young. Interesting, and age is just a number. Still, not the one for us.*

She recoiled at scenes of Alice with her brother Alex. She hissed.... *That one... that one we will kill. And his boyfriend too.*

Twenty-Six

IT WAS barely 8:00 p.m., and Charlie had passed exhausted at their third fire, two fires ago. Now it was all nerves and shots of caffeine. The morning's weirdness, from taking Finn to Katye Summer's apartment to those wonderful moments with Liam, had been replaced by the smell of cookies, fire, and tragedy.

His company, like every engine and hook and ladder in the five boroughs, was under siege.

They barely managed to snuff one blaze when the call came for the next. And he knew, by the smell and the holes burned from tar and tin roof through to the basement, that these were all set by the same hand. Not the kind of thing he could, or would, voice to his station mates. *Yeah, fairy queen wants to conquer Manhattan.*

He heard the frightened rumors among the crowds, and even the usually unflappable Kyle was on edge.

"This is terrorist shit!"

Charlie didn't argue, just stayed the course, not wanting to look up at the night sky for fear he'd see another fireball. He wished he'd had time to get Liam a cell phone and worried about his brother Michael, 'cause it wasn't just the FDNY but every first responder—cop, firefighter, medic, ER doc, and nurse—who were under fire.

He focused on the tasks before him, hoping Alex, Jerod, and Liam would keep Gran, and one another, safe. Wherever he looked, the sky was filled with smoke plumes rising from Manhattan and far into the boroughs.

The air was thick. More and more people caught the smell. Before, it was just a few who thought a bakery was burning. Now, even Kyle sensed it. "What the fuck is with the Betty Crocker smell?"

As night dragged on and the fires kept coming, Charlie noticed something else. Perhaps it was fatigue or his experiences since meeting Liam, but from the corner of his eye, he'd catch a flash of wing, a woman's ears and teeth that seemed too pointy, like the creatures in that fantastic wardrobe. A gnawing sense grew that something below the surface, something dark, was on the rise.

At 10:00 p.m. his company was called to a high-rise on Lexington and Thirty-Sixth. At the wheel, he spotted the by-now-familiar column of smoke, like a chimney burned through the thirty-story structure.

It was bad. Families on the street, wide-eyed children, and shocked residents. Oxygen-rich flames shot high through the roof, far too high for any cherry picker or even a crane, if they could get one.

Charlie knew this was a night no one would forget. Residents frightened out of their homes, not knowing when the next building would be attacked. Like London during the Blitz, only there'd been no air-raid siren, and there were no well-drilled home guards directing people into shelters. Even Charlie, who'd been through dozens of disaster drills, was at a loss as to what to tell the desperate mother who'd grabbed his sleeve a couple of fires back and asked, "Where is it safe? Where are we supposed to go?"

"Get out of the city, if you can."

"What if they take out the bridges and the tunnel?"

"Ma'am, if you can take you and your kids and get out, I would."

People crowded streets and parted like waves before the screaming assortment of ambulances, fire trucks, and cops. Smartphones were affixed to everyone's hands, thousands of videos uploaded through Instagram and Facebook, headers typed with trembling fingers and thumbs. *Buildings on fire, fireballs from the sky.... Apocalypse!*

Charlie, at the wheel of Engine 25, Kyle next to him and six guys crammed in the back with full gear, were the first on the Murray Hill scene. He prayed others would follow but knew that even with companies pulled in from the entire eastern seaboard and en route from as far away as Chicago, it might just be them and the lone squad car parked fifty feet from the blaze.

Jumping down, he spotted Alex and Jerod running toward him. "What are you doing here? Where's Gran? Who's keeping an eye on Gran?"

"She's okay," Alex said. "My sister is inside."

"Okay, we're on it. Try to get them on your cell. What's the apartment number?"

Alex couldn't focus. He stared past Charlie as people, some he knew from the building, poured out the doors. He looked up and saw others trapped in their apartments. They screamed for help through open windows. The inrush of oxygen fueled the fire.

Bouncing on the tips of his sneaks, Alex, with Nimby on his shoulder, felt like he was losing his mind. He'd tried to reach Alice dozens of times. Not even Clay had been able to locate her, and now….

Before Charlie could stop him, Alex tore off into the building.

Jerod shouted after him, "Alex, *no!*"

"You, stay here," Charlie yelled to Jerod. "What's the number?"

"They're on the nineteenth floor, first door on the right as you face the elevators."

Charlie gauged Alex's lead. The night was chaos, and the worst thing he could do was break ranks, abandon his post, and go after Alex, who'd stupidly run in… *to save his sister and mother.* He shouted back to Kyle that he was going in. Not waiting for a response, which would be, *What the fuck do you think you're doing, Fitzgerald?* he raced in.

Residents in the building's hundred seventy apartments ran down the stairs as Alex, and three floors behind him, Charlie, headed up. Like salmon against the stream, they stumbled over and around abandoned suitcases, children's toys, all the things people thought important enough to grab but not important enough to lose their lives over.

Alex's thoughts were fixed on Alice as he ran, on why she hadn't returned his texts or voice messages. *Is she okay?* Nimby, on his shoulder, tried to speak, her chatter not making it over the noise and the sirens. In his gut he knew the fire in this building was no accident. Just as the one in their old place in the East Village had been deliberate.

May needed a haffling. *How could I not see this? How could I have left her alone? Stupid!*

His feet pounded up the stairs. The fleeing tenants grew fewer the higher he climbed. His eyes tracked the signs for the floors. *Eight, nine*…. Legs burning, *ten, eleven, stop looking at the signs. Thirteen, fourteen, fifteen. Charlie's behind me. Crap…. What if I get all of us killed? Sixteen, seventeen.* The smell of cookies and smoke dense in the stairwell from a fire door propped open on fifteen. His lungs burned. Charlie's heavy footfalls got closer. *Eighteen, nineteen, thank God!* He threw open the fire door and stood in the hall. The smoke was not so bad, many of the apartment doors wide open.

He jammed his hand into his pocket and grabbed the keys. He undid the dead bolt and opened the door. An unexpected wall of dense black smoke and heat burned his face, like getting too close to an oven. "Alice!" he shouted and doubled over as the smoke invaded his lungs.

Behind him Charlie cleared the fire door. "Alex! Get out! It's too hot."

He coughed and ignored his warnings. "Charlie, she's in here. She's frightened. I know where she'll be." Alex gulped air, barreled into the smoke-filled hallway, and stumbled blind toward Alice's room.

Charlie, who'd gone in without helmet or respirator, ducked low and followed. He wrapped a kerchief around his nose and mouth. "Stay low!"

The heat was intense. The fireball had passed through this unit. As with Finn's pointed questions to Liam, he knew the target here was Alice Nevus. And if a fireball burned through her room or had landed on her bed, there was probably a real bad reason why she'd not returned Alex's calls or texts.

His theory proved correct when Alex threw open the door to his sister's bedroom. Flames shot out, and Alex, unprepared, was almost immediately overcome by smoke inhalation. He crumpled unconscious to the floor. Nimby raced around his body in frantic circles. She looked at Charlie and screamed, but between the sirens, the roar and crackle of the flames, and the pulse pounding in Charlie's ears, her tinny voice was lost.

Charlie knelt by Alex. This was obviously his sister's bedroom. The fireball had done its work, the hole, not in the bed but in the middle of the floor, ringed with fire. *If she'd been in here, no way she's alive.*

He scooped up Alex as Nimby grabbed his ear and shouted, "She's in the closet, and she's not she, she's sidhe!"

He hoisted Alex over his back. The door of the closet cracked open. He startled. *Thank God.* "Alice, I'm here to get you out of here."

"Run!" Nimby screamed.

Charlie shook his head, prepared to coax a shell-shocked fourteen-year-old out into a room on fire. "Come on, Alice. You can do this. I've got Alex. We have to get out of here."

The closet opened wide, and Charlie caught his first look at Alice Nevus. A pretty teen with straight blonde hair and clear blue eyes, dressed in what looked like a ballet outfit, with a wide pink tutu covered with sparkles. *That's just weird.* "Come on, Alice. Stay low. Stay away from the hot spot."

She did the exact opposite. With her highly flammable tutu and fluffy top, she straddled the flaming hole in the middle of her bedroom floor.

"Get out of here!" Nimby screamed. "She is not Alice! *Run!*"

The teen spoke. "So brave. I think we've met, and look at what you've brought me. Thought I'd have to hunt that one." She waved a dainty hand in his direction.

Charlie, with Alex across his back, could not move. He fought back panic. *What's going on?* He tried to lift his foot. "What the fuck?"

The teen's eyes were on him as she sauntered across flames, which should have sent her up like a candle.

It's not touching her—not possible.

Pointing to Alex, she clapped her hands and spoke. "Let that one burn. Stay with him…. You may both burn."

Charlie panicked. "I can't move!"

She brushed past him. "That's because you're paralyzed, stupid." She stopped and looked at Alex, draped over his back. "Too perfect, too wonderfully, marvelously perfect. Yes, you can both burn." She paused in the door. "But never let them say that Queen May was cruel, though I am, of course. But here, my brave soldier of fire, let me cloud your thoughts and give you peace. There, so much better."

And, humming the tune to *Disco Inferno*, she was gone.

Nimby, who'd hidden in the collar of Charlie's coat, tried to break the spell. It was no use. May had frozen the firefighter and blanketed his mind in forgetfulness and fog. "Move, Charlie Fitzgerald. *Run, run, run!* Take Alex and *run, run, run!*"

Orange flames licked up through the hole in the floor, and somewhere deep in the building's guts a gas line, which they'd not yet turned off, exploded.

The fairy dived at his head. "*Try, try, try,* Charlie Fitzgerald, or you will die, die, *die!*"

It was no use. Charlie willed his body to move, but nothing happened. It was like he'd been filled with plaster, which had hardened on the spot. *Why am I here?* He heard Alex's shallow breath from his back. *Who am I carrying?* "Liam, is that you? I can't move." He thought of how they'd met. *We're in a fire again.* "Liam, I can't move. I have to get you out of here." The fog in his head receded a bit. *I can't move. I'm never going to kiss you again or tell you what I feel. I should have told you. Tell him now, you chickenshit moron.* He remembered that it wasn't Liam over his shoulder but Alex. The thing he had to tell Liam rang like a bell in his mind. *I love him. I love Liam.* His right foot broke free. *I love Liam.* His left inched back.

"Move. Move. *Move,* Charlie Fitzgerald!" Nimby screamed.

"Liam," Charlie spoke aloud, the soft syllable like an incantation. "Liam." He remembered the feel of his hand in his, his lips. *Why the fuck didn't I do more? Because you love him, moron. Because you asked for one kiss, and you got two. I want more.* The more he focused on Liam and what he felt, the easier he moved. He had no time to ponder, was it Liam, *or this feeling? Great, so I'm going to die just when I fall in love. I do love him. And it has nothing to do with his fucking glamour. Well, then, get the hell out!*

With Alex on his back and Nimby dive-bombing around his head, he backed out of the bedroom and kicked the door shut behind him. Unable to see through the smoke and knowing he'd been stupid to leave without a helmet and breathing apparatus, he fixated on Liam. His eyes, the way he chewed his bottom lip when he was nervous. He remembered how he'd freaked out Gran's cats, and then the next time he hadn't. It helped. He repositioned Alex on his right shoulder as Nimby rode shotgun on his left. *I am going to see him again. I will tell him I love him. And when he comes back with all those bullshit reasons why I shouldn't, I'm going to kiss him. I'm not going to stop!*

He made it to the stairwell, his head still clouded with May's magic. He halted and tried to remember what had just happened. It was useless, and knowing there wasn't time, he recited one of Dad's mantras. "Get the job done." So with Alex Nevus passed out on one shoulder and Nimby on the other—*Get the job done*—he hauled ass down eighteen flights and got them out alive.

Twenty-Seven

ALICE STEPPED daintily out of her closet dressed in a rhinestone-studded tutu, white cashmere sweater, and ballet slippers to a world of smoke and fire. *She is inside of me.* Though that seemed not quite right. A tipping point had passed. *She is in control.*

Of course I am, May thought as she spotted the tall firefighter with an unconscious Alex Nevus over his back. Her spirits soared. *Goody for me! Here but moments and already brought tribute. Too wonderful!*

Alice tried to stop May from casting the spell over the firefighter who'd come to save her and who had hoisted Alex like he was a sack of potatoes. *She's in control. I can't.* She'd watched and listened to the horrible words leaving her mouth. "Let that one burn. Stay with him.... You may both burn."

Alice knew. *This is what happened to Alex, and now she's done it to me.* Only unlike her brother, she had no true love to break the spell or to harness the powers of thousands in the audience and millions of live viewers who'd cast May out of his body.

Not this time. May's thoughts hissed like steam on burning coals. *We shall be great friends, you and I.*

From her brother, who had been possessed for months, Alice knew he'd been unconscious for most of it. *I'm still here. I'm still awake.*

Of course you are. And it's wonderful. You feel better than you've ever felt. More powerful, more alive.

As horrible as leaving her brother and that brave firefighter had been, Alice agreed. She felt light, unafraid... ecstatic.

Fairy dust, my love. You shall never want for it.

Alice remembered her backpack, forgotten upstairs in the fire. *We have to go back for it... and maybe we can save Alex.*

May hissed. *He burns, and smell the night, child.*

A firefighter ran toward them. "Are you okay?"

"Of course I am." May smiled bright and shone Alice's clear blue eyes into his.

The man stumbled. "You're sure?"

"Of course, and thank you for asking." *I am so hungry.* May breathed deep. The scent of fairy fire was everywhere. *And after the fire comes the dust. You will never go hungry, Alice. I will show you. So yes, we will be together, besties forever. You will tell me all I need to know of the See, and I will feed you mountains of fairy dust. Sorry about your brother... though he had it coming.*

Yes, of course, Alice thought, her mind clouded with the wonderful smoke and the promise of fresh dust. *He did.*

Too excellent! How I love this city. May threw out her arms, and with her head back she twirled, loving the feel of the stiff pink skirt, which sparkled with streetlight and the flashing reds, yellows, and blues from the police cars, ambulances, and fire trucks. *This is all my doing.* A stage fit for her, filled with smoke and lights. Just minutes into this new body—pure joy. *This time is perfect!*

She skipped down the street, trying to take it in, her gaze pulled to dozens of near and far plumes of smoke. Her mouth, or rather Alice's mouth, watered. *So hungry. I could eat them all... and maybe we will.*

She spoke aloud, loving the sound of her words through Alice's voice. "This reminds me of home.... This once was my home. This all belonged to us." With her slipper-clad feet firm on the pavement, she sensed the Unsee beneath them. *Like layers of a sandwich.*

Alice listened in to May's thoughts. *Can we see the Unsee from here?*

"What a marvelous question. And because you are part of me, it comes without cost. Let me see if I can see the Unsee." May shuddered, and gooseflesh popped along her arms. "I see the Mist. It doesn't touch the See but comes right up to it. Yes, like a sandwich, where the Mist is the filling and the See and Unsee are the bread. I am starving...." She didn't want to look at the Mist, at the place where she'd been tethered inside the body of the beast. *How dare she! My own sister. This is much better... and she will pay. They will all pay.*

I know some good restaurants, Alice offered. *And then you'll get me dust?*

May laughed aloud. "You will have dust, and I will feed."

Alice mused at how weird it was to hear her own voice, but it wasn't her thoughts steering the ship. Rather than frightened, she felt relief. *So floaty in here… safe.*

"Sweet Alice, I doubt they serve the food I seek in restaurants. Though that would be nice. Perhaps in the future. Then again, I'd be the only patron."

May scanned the street. She spotted a lone Asian man taking pictures of the fire on his phone. She approached.

Just as with the fireman who'd tried to save Alex, Alice watched May glamour the man. *Watch and learn, sweet Alice. This is how it's done.* "Give me your hand, and walk with me," she told him.

He pocketed his phone and took the teen's hand, the connection of his flesh to hers like a vacuum hooked to his life force. They headed south down Lexington. With each step he aged a year. By the end of the block, he clutched his chest and fell to the ground.

While not nearly as succulent as dust, Alice felt the swirling eddies of the man's vitality flow through her body.

Inside her head, May chuckled. Crocodile tears flowed, and she cried out, "Oh, help! Help me. My grandpa is having a heart attack!"

A crowd gathered.

Phones came out of pockets, and 911 calls were placed. "What's taking the ambulance so long?" a woman remarked.

"No telling," a man replied, and under his breath, "I don't think it's going to do any good."

Dressed in rhinestones, tulle, and cashmere, May slipped away. *That was tasty, but the problem with Chinese takeout—five minutes later and you're hungry again.* "Come." She glanced at a plume of smoke a block east on Park. "Time for something more filling and all the dust we can carry."

Goody for me! Alice thought.

May knew she had succeeded where with the now-crispy Alex Nevus she had failed. She cloaked her thoughts from the dusted teen. *Yes, goody for you. Dusted you are, and dusted you will stay. Goody for you, and goody for me.*

Twenty-Eight

BACK IN Staten Island, Liam heard it before he saw it. The high-pitched sound drew him from bed, though he'd not been asleep. *No. Please, no!* Dressed in fleece-lined sweats and a tee that smelled of Charlie, he got off the changey sofa bed where he'd slept the night before and stepped onto the deck that overlooked the drive and the whitecapped waves across the street.

He stared at the red streak in the sky. *Fairy fire!* It raced over the water, screaming as it went. *She's found me.* He froze. *Nothing can outrun fairy fire.* But run he did. This was Charlie's home. *She can kill me, but she will not take his home or hurt those he loves.*

Barefoot, he raced down the stairs, and aware of Katie and Mike Fitzgerald in their beds, he shouted, "*Fire! Fire!*" Before he could yell it a third time, the missile hit not Charlie's garage, but the Fitzgeralds' home.

"*No!*" He ran up the front steps as the glowing fireball melted and burned through the shingles, the plywood, and the joists below. "*Fire! Fire!*"

The home was lit from inside, as this was a night where no one slept, all glued to their televisions and computer screens, aware that the city was under attack. All assuming it was the religious fundamentalists who had attacked before.

"*Mike, Katie! Fire! Fire!*"

Her eyes wide, Charlie's mom came to the door. "Liam? What's—?"

"Your house." He grabbed her hand and pulled her down to where she could see. The flames rose high in the sky as they gobbled wood and tar.

Mike Fitzgerald followed, his expression unreadable as flames spread across the roof of the house he and his family had rebuilt.

"Grab what we can." And Mike vanished inside.

Katie looked at Liam. She shook her head and followed her husband. Liam did the same. The house reeked of baked goods as Liam pulled framed photos from the wall. Some he recognized from Sunday dinner—Annie and Sal, Charlie. Two teenage boys on a raft with fishing rods and a white-plastic bucket, a younger redheaded Finn, and someone who had to be Charlie's older brother, their expressions carefree. Finn holding a fish, the other with his legs dangling in the water. Liam grabbed them all, careful to not break the glass. He clutched them to his chest and ran as neighbors spilled from their homes, stood, pointed, and tried to help.

"Has anyone called 911?"

"I did."

"I did too. They said there are no trucks."

"Then get some fucking buckets! And hoses. Everyone get your garden hoses!"

From either side of the Fitzgerald home, neighbors dispersed, and like honeybees fixed on a central purpose, hoses were collected and connected. Every portable fire extinguisher that could be found was raced across lawns and passed over fences.

"Why does it smell like cookies?" a frightened child asked.

"What are you talking about?" his mother replied.

"It does," another onlooker said. "Cookies. What the hell?"

Liam caught snippets as he, now joined by the neighbors, did what they could to save anything of value as the fire devoured and spread.

The fiery missile bored through the roof, undeterred by the puny streams of water from too small hoses.

He followed Katie Fitzgerald into her bedroom. "What should I take?"

She pointed at a box in her closet with clear plastic sides—her wedding dress.

"Got it." Beside it was a suitcase that looked old and out of place. He snatched that as well and piled on suits, a plastic-wrapped uniform, and whatever else he could manage.

His thoughts were tortured as his lungs choked on smoke. *This is my fault. She came for me.* He ran out and deposited his load at the bottom of the drive next to the growing wall of Fitzgerald belongings. A man grabbed him by the shoulders. "You can't go back!"

He turned as the portion of the roof over the living room collapsed. On either side of the house, ladders had been erected, and garden hoses poured their sad streams onto the raging ball of fairy fire.

"Where are the fire trucks?" a woman cried. "Where are they?"

Liam searched for the Fitzgeralds. He panicked. "Mike! Katie!"

They found him. "We're okay," Mike gasped, barely able to catch his breath.

"I'm so sorry," Liam said.

Katie nodded, too choked with emotion to speak.

"It's just stuff," Mike Fitzgerald said, his jaw tight, his arm around his wife as they watched their home burn. "It's just stuff, Katie. We put it back together once. We'll do it again."

Finally, a siren, and then a second.

Liam wanted to scream *This is my fault!*

Katie, her face streaked with tears, looked back at the pile of her belongings, which stretched across the yard and much of the driveway. She pointed to the cardboard child's suitcase next to her wedding dress. "You got my doll," she said to Liam. "Thank you." She stared at the flashing lights as they neared. A small engine, with a lone firefighter, finally appeared at the end of the street.

Liam had no words. He watched the crowd part as the engine drove up. Several of the men and a few of the women pitched in and uncoiled the thick hose and hooked it up to a hydrant. Like a giant python, it swelled with pressurized water.

He watched them battle the ball of fairy fire. He knew it was useless. It would burn until it had devoured itself. Nothing or no one could extinguish it. At best, they might contain the peripheral damage. He thought of Sunday dinner and how proud Charlie and his dad had been of their hardwood floors, crown moldings, and the new powder room, which as far as he could tell held no powder. *My fault. This was meant for me.*

Then, as if Charlie were inside his head: *This is not your fault. You did not set fire to Katie and Mike's home. You did not do this.* A fire of a different sort kindled in his brain. Things he'd never considered lit up. *You did not kill your parents and force a small boy to watch. This is her. It has always been her.*

Old habits die hard. His shame and guilt, like old pals, demanded to be heard. *You were her whore.*

He stared at the fire and at the neighbors, who clustered around Mike or Katie or helped steady the hose or balanced on ladders with garden hoses. *I have to make this right.* He looked at Charlie's little house over the garage. The fire hadn't touched it, so at least Katie and Mike would have a place to stay. *I have to make this right.* He wondered why she hadn't taken out the garage, if in fact this had been aimed at him. *Or was it?* Charlie had passed between the See and the Unsee and made it back again without being broken. *What does that mean? Even so... her aim was off. She is not invincible. Alex and Jerod defeated her. She can be bested. This was meant for me. And she missed, and she hurt Katie and Mike... and Charlie. What will he think? He'll know this is my fault.*

Without conscious thought, he moved farther and farther down the front yard. He walked behind the wall of furniture, clothes, and pictures they'd salvaged. *I have to make this right. I know her best. I know what she likes. I know what she eats... who she eats.* His mind played over all they'd learned in Katye's apartment. Something clicked. This fire and all the others, yes, they were meant to take out her enemies, but that was secondary. *How did I miss this?*

He turned from the Fitzgeralds' house on fire and traced a path back to the island of Manhattan, uncertain if the ferryboat ran this late at night or if it would run at all on a night filled with such horror and danger. It didn't matter. He knew what was needed. The path before him was now clear.

As neighbors and family did what they could, he ran into the night without money, without MetroCard, and without a plan, other than find Queen May, stop her from taking Alex's haffling sister, Alice, and—or—die trying.

Twenty-Nine

CHARLIE WAS still at the smoldering Murray Hill fire where he'd nearly died with Alex, who'd been grabbed by a pair of paramedics. As they'd done their quick assessment, Charlie knew there'd be bad burns, but at least nothing on his face or hands. *He should be okay. Please, let him be okay.* He startled at the sound of his cell.

He glanced at the screen. His head was still in a fog with whatever spell May had tossed at him. It took him till the third ring to connect the name on his phone to a real person... his dad. He picked up. "What's up?"

"Charlie, I wanted to get to you before anyone else."

Over the sirens, he heard the pain in Dad's voice. His pulse raced. "What's happened?"

"The house...."

"Are you and Mom okay? Is Liam okay?"

"Yeah. No one's hurt. It's just stuff."

Katie Fitzgerald came on the phone. "Charlie, we're okay. No one got hurt."

"What happened?" Charlie asked, though he knew.

"One of those fireballs landed on the roof. Liam must have seen it. He got us out. If it weren't for him, we wouldn't have been able to save anything.... And your apartment and the garage weren't touched, just smoke on the siding."

He felt sucker punched. The entire night had been a weirdfest marathon. *No one got hurt. They're okay. Liam's okay.*

"Let me talk to Liam." He needed to hear his voice, to tell him the thing he should have said last night. Then it would have been perfect. Now....

"Sure," Katie said.

Charlie waited as a text came from his brother Michael and another from his sister Annie. Bad news traveled fast. He looked across at the building on fire. He needed to get back to work and battled a sense of futility that nothing they did tonight could possibly be enough. Lives were being lost, but at least Mom and Dad were okay. Liam was okay.

His mom's voice returned. "Dear… I can't find him."

"What do you mean?" His gut clenched.

"I know he's okay," she said. "But he was in the yard just a few minutes ago, and… maybe he had to take a walk on the beach or something. He was very brave, Charlie. I like your Liam. He saved the case with my old doll. I know it's not that important, but…." She cried. "We're going to stay in your place tonight."

"Of course." He knew he needed to get back to work, but all he could think of was Liam. "Mom, when you see Liam, call me or text. Just let me know he's okay."

"He is, dear. And I will. I promise."

He hung up, then read the texts from his brother and sister.

Michael: "Everyone is safe. House is totaled. Guess we can finally get the tiling right in the bathroom. City is a zoo. Got to go. Stay safe."

Annie: "Horrible. Everyone safe. You be safe. I love you. Stay safe. I mean it, Charlie!!!!!"

Why didn't I get Liam a phone? He felt helpless and pulled between wanting to get the hell out of there, check in with his family, and find Liam. *Where would he go? He doesn't know anyone, just me and my family.* He replayed the day and pressed Gran's number.

With the cell to his ear, he waited. Fear nipped at his thoughts. *Pick up. Please pick up.* Seconds passed, dread grew. *Pick up.*

"Charlie?"

"Gran, you're okay."

"I am. This is her work. This is all May."

"Do you know why? Did those books tell you that? Did they tell you how to stop her?"

"She wants back into this world," Gran said. "And not as a salamander. Liam and Nimby told me about fairy fire, and there was more in those books. Fairy fire, after it burns out, leaves a drug residue… fairy dust. For some fey, and apparently humans as well, it's more addictive than heroin. So when all these fires burn out, there's going to be drugs.

I wonder if she plans to create an army of drug-addicted followers, with her as their only source."

Despite all, and the pressing need to get back to his station mates, Gran's hypothesizing made him smile. Next to old Irish tales, Gran loved her crime shows. "Seriously, CSI: fairyland?"

"Charlie, don't make fun. And true, it doesn't tick enough boxes. She wants her body back... or somebody's body."

"Oh God. That's it!"

And like poking a hole in a balloon, the last of the spell May had cast, which had nearly cost both his and Alex's lives, vanished. "She took the girl. She's inside Alice Nevus. And she did something to me."

"Tell me."

"Yeah." He looked at the building, now nearly out, and his station mates. They'd finally figured how best to fight these blazes and had spread the word. They'd start in the basement, where the projectile landed, and while nothing seemed to extinguish it, if they could contain the peripheral damage, then the building was left with a ceiling-to-basement hole but still upright and structurally viable. "She hit the building where Alex's mother and sister live."

"You know she's not really his mother but a changeling."

"I didn't, and I.... Too weird. So Alex raced in, and I went after him. We got up to their place, and his sister was in the closet, and then she came out, and she was in some kind of ballet outfit, and she walked right through the fire. Not just through it, but stood over it. Her dress should have gone up like a rocket. It didn't touch her. Alex was out cold, and she looked at me, and she said something and did something, and I couldn't move, and she was in my head to where everything was dull. I couldn't remember anything. She meant to kill us."

"Charlie!"

"Nimby kept buzzing my head and tried to get me to move. I couldn't. But I thought about Liam—and I know you don't like him, Gran, and you don't trust him, but I love him—and that's what helped. And the more I realized it was true, and that I had to tell him, the more whatever she did went away. I could walk again, and I got us out of there.... And now he's gone.... Do you know where he is?" Hope blossomed. "Is he with you?"

There was silence.

"Gran? You there? Hello!"

"I'm here, Charlie. You nearly died tonight. I will not lose you."

"I don't intend to get lost."

"Said the man who runs into burning buildings and nearly gets enchanted to death by a fairy queen. I have no illusions, Charlie, about you or any of our boys, and now even our girls. You do these things to help, and I love you for it. But why couldn't some of you become accountants? Or even a doctor would be nice."

"Do you know where he'd go? Please… tell me."

"I do, and Charlie, I know you love him. I think he has feelings for you as well. Though I'm uncertain if he even knows what they are. I do know this—he's changed here, and you're a part of that. He's the one who raised the alarm at your parents' house. I will always be grateful for that."

"They're okay," Charlie said, parroting his mother's words and those of thousands of disaster survivors. "It's just stuff. They're safe."

"I think I know what Liam intends… because he wants to be like you."

"What are you saying?"

"He's going to go after her."

Charlie thought of the blonde girl in her pink tutu who walked through the fire, said a few words, and nearly killed him and Alex. He gasped. "He's no match for her."

"I know. I'm sorry, Charlie. It's what he'll do. He's going to try to stop her, and he will fail."

His cell buzzed. He glanced at the screen—Jerod.

"Gran, I have to take this." He told her that he loved her, that he'd stay safe, and he hung up.

Jerod's words came fast and frantic. "Charlie, you got to talk some sense into him. He's trying to leave against medical advice."

Before he could respond, Jerod was replaced by Alex Nevus's almost unrecognizable smoke-damaged voice. "She has Alice."

"I know," Charlie said. "She tried to kill us. She nearly did."

"This is bad," Alex wheezed. "You don't know what she's capable of."

"Above and beyond setting a couple hundred fires in one night?"

"Just the start. She's got Alice…. She's going to go after everything she thinks was taken from her."

"Which would be?"

"The world. With a haffling body… she has all her magic." Alex's voice weakened.

"I think Liam is going to try to go after her. I think he has."

Alex rasped, "Then he's dead, Charlie. I'm sorry, but it's why he came back."

"What the hell are you talking about?"

"Liam. I've been too hard on him. People can change… if he's even a person. He came to try to make good for all the crap he's done."

Over the line, Charlie heard him sip something to try to ease the burn. He waited.

Alex cleared his throat. "I've learned a lot about the fey and the Unsee in the past three years. What matters most to them is balance. He wants to be good… clean, and the only way he believes that will happen is by completing what he came to do."

"Alex, just say it!"

"Okay. He has to bring word to my mom—real mom—that Alice and I are okay. That's not possible. The second is to get information to May's sister Lizbeta about how we defeated May—it's fuzzy at best. Which, if I were him, leaves one option. Take her out himself."

Charlie knew Alex was right. "He's no match."

"No one is, but we've got to try. Better together than alone."

"Alex, you have to stay in the hospital."

"Not an option."

"Shut up and put Jerod on. We've got to be smart about this. We're not going to get a lot of chances." He pictured Alice Nevus in her tutu and fluffy sweater. *She was on fire…. She didn't burn.*

Jerod's voice. "He's ripping out his IV."

"Where are you?"

"Bellevue, still in the ER."

"Keep him there. We've got to stay strong. It's the only way, and I get that he's got someone he loves on the line… so do I. But here's the thing. It's the first thing they teach in probie school—a dead hero is no hero. We're not going to help anyone if we're not smart. I'll get there as quick as I can, but there's something more about these fires—Alex's old apartment, the one here, my parents' house, where Liam just happens to be staying. These aren't coincidences, and they may give us an answer, or at least a direction. Can you hold him there?"

"I'll do my best, but hurry."

"You got it." And knowing he was putting a job he loved on the line, he turned his back on the under-control fire and, worse, on his station mates. *Abandoning a post is grounds for immediate dismissal. Shit.* He stared up the avenue, another blaze four blocks north, a dwindling plume to the east. *You have no choice. This is war, and you must fight.* He broke into a run and sprinted north toward Bellevue.

Thirty

HIS ENTIRE life, Liam had been aware of May's power and presence, her eyes on his every move. She was a prickle on the hairs of his neck, a twist in the gut, and the surety that if he were to run and hide, she would find him. He felt that now, though with a difference. He wasn't running or trying to blend into the background. He was frightened. *I will not run.*

As he rode the ferry, all eyes and ears on board fixated on the sirens and the flames, mostly in Manhattan, but as he listened and learned, Brooklyn, the Bronx, and Jersey City had also been hit.

There was a strong wind and chop in the water. Passengers pointed and speculated. "It's 9/11 all over again."

"Why can't they leave us alone?"

"I'm getting out of the city. I can't take this crap!"

"And who the fuck is baking cookies?"

They scanned the night sky. "They've stopped."

Liam looked up. Indeed, since the fireball that hit the Fitzgeralds' home, there'd been a lull in May's attacks.

As the ferry made it to the Manhattan docks, the hairs on his nape bristled. He knew what the cease-fire meant. May had broken free from the Mist. She was here, and what had started bad was about to get far worse.

He disembarked and headed to the closest subway. It was closed. Standing at the mouth of the station, he felt her presence. *Not near... but on this island.* He wished Charlie were here. *No, you don't. This won't end well. Better that he be far from here, far from me.*

A block north, he came to a park and climbed a bronze statue of a masked woman holding scales. He gazed out at the city filled with flashing lights, smoke, and sirens from engines like Charlie's and shorter ones like the navy clan had driven. He had no doubt. *She is here. How do I stop her? She can't be stopped. Not helpful. What do you know? There must be something.* He stared at the sky. Here and there a faint star was visible through the smoke and lights. *I know that fairy fire pierces the Mist. What else? She needs the haffling—Alex's sister... or the little boy, Adam.* He thought of Marilyn and Cedric but mostly May. Given a choice, she'd come after the teen and not the boy. *She'll want to dress up. But why so much fairy fire? It would have come at cost. And why Charlie's house...? Because I was there. And I was in Alex's old apartment, where the first one landed. But I'm not in these other places. So who is? Alex has his Nimby—are there others? Were these bombs sent to homes of sidhe? But why? You know why.* He did. *To frighten, to cow us into submission. To kill those who resist. To steal our power.*

From his vantage point atop the statue's base, he counted plumes of smoke and fire, some still burning red and gold, like the tips of candles. He stopped at a hundred. *Not possible, and yet it is so. So much power.... She will need more. She will be hungry. She has come to conquer worlds, and she will need to feed.* He looked around at the towering buildings and thought of the brave men and women inside. *They have armies that will fight her... and she has magic. They won't see it coming. They won't know how to battle her.*

He felt the folded map, like a talisman from the man in green, in the pocket of Charlie's sweats and pulled it out. He held it in front of him, fixed his current position and the vicinity of Katye's pink palace to the north. If he was right about the fairy fire having been directed, he suspected Katye's lovely home with its priceless books would be gone. *Would she attack her sister?* He climbed down, folded away the map, and started to jog and then to run. Lizbeta's directions to him seemed impossible. She wanted the means to stop her sister but had made clear her intent was not to kill her. *Would May feel the same? Not likely. Her power comes from death.*

His legs pumped, and his nostrils filled with the delicious reek. At the corner of Pearl and Fulton, he came to a smoldering four-story brick building. A lone engine pumped water into the basement. There was no flame, but waves of dark gray smoke flooded the street. Frightened tenants looked on. All so familiar as he searched the crowds, his eyes peeled, like doing one of the puzzles in the books his mother would get at the fair. *Find the troll, the ogre, the thing that doesn't fit... and there she is.* She looked human enough, a blonde in her late twenties, tall, thin, her luminous eyes wide as she watched her home burn.

Careful not to scare her, Liam worked his way toward her. She was taller than he by three or four inches. *Nearly as tall as Charlie.* Tears streaked her cheeks, and the only thing she'd managed to save was a frightened ball of red fuzz in a blue-plastic pet carrier. Its inhabitant was some sort of dog with a long body, fluffy auburn fur, and short legs.

He edged through the crowd until he stood at her side. Each glance confirmed his suspicions. With his voice low, he said, "Tell me, this was your home."

She turned, and he knew. Her teeth had been filed; they were pearl white and perfectly human. Her long hair was tied back and revealed human ears, but they'd been altered.

"It was." Her attention riveted to Liam as recognition blossomed. "Tell me your name."

"I am Liam Summer."

"You don't look like a Summer."

"You don't look like a sidhe... and you are."

"I had work done."

"Interesting."

Her hand clenched the handle of the little dog's case. Liam wondered if she would run. He eyed the strange creature in the carrier and wondered if it might be fey.

"He's a Maltese," she said. "His name is George."

Liam nodded, unconvinced that something so odd could be a native of the See and not the Unsee. "I mean you no harm, but we are in great danger."

"Yes. I smell it." She shuddered. "Few creatures are capable of fairy fire, and none of so much."

"There is one, and she is ravenous. You need to leave the city, take George, and get as far away as you can. Though if she achieves her aim, I don't know how far is far enough."

The women shook her head.

He noted how many in the crowd openly ogled her, as well as him. "Tell me your name."

"Lianna, and I will not run. This is my city. It's where I choose to live. My house is gone. I will find another. I will not run, Liam Summer.

So tell me the name of the creature that attacks my city and destroys my home." She leaned in to him.

He whispered, "Queen May."

Lianna shuddered. "Of course. Because of her I fled through the Mist." She stared back at the smoldering building. "These fires were sent for us."

"I believe so."

"And you, Liam Summer, you appear to run toward a danger rather than away."

"Yes, and I must continue. You should flee."

She shook her head. Tears glistened in her eyes. "Tell me what you intend."

For a moment he wondered if this lovely creature, with her fluffy dog, could be a spy. *But no, she is in exile, just as I. Just as all these others who May is trying to burn out.* "I will not say. But you are in danger. You need to get away."

Lianna arched her neck and looked over the crowd. "Wait here, Liam Summer." She ran toward a mother and her teenage daughter. She spoke and handed the girl the pet carrier. She opened the door and pulled out George. His bright pink tongue lapped at her face, his tail wagging as she kissed him and ran her cheek across his fur. "Keep him safe," she instructed and handed George to the girl.

She returned to Liam. "Whatever you intend, Liam Summer, I will help. This is my home. She ran me from one. It will not happen again."

"No. You mustn't. The thing I intend will not make me a hero. It will likely leave me dead."

"Tell me."

He edged back, turned, and ran north. *I will not drag her into this.*

Lianna was just as fast and kept apace. "Tell me, Liam Summer, for I intend to help."

Liam sprinted, but the long-legged sidhe with her surgically altered ears and filed-down teeth stuck to his side.

"She will kill us both," he argued.

"I am aware. Tell me the plan. At least that way, I'll know when we have failed."

"We'll know when she kills us and dines on our hearts and livers."

"I'm not leaving."

He couldn't shake her. *And perhaps two are indeed better… stronger than one*. He voiced the thing that would get them killed. "She has stolen a haffling child. She will be new in its body, weak, and not at her full power. This fairy fire has cost her magic, even for one as powerful as she. She will need to feed, and feed a lot."

"You know her." Lianna slowed her pace. "And I know you, Liam Summer."

He braced for the accusations. She'd not recognized him at first, and now she did.

"You are of her court."

"I was."

"You know her better than anyone in the See."

It was not the response he'd expected. "It's possible," he said without slowing.

With a burst of speed, she was back at his side, their strides in sync. "Tell me the plan."

"She will be weak inside the body she stole, though weak for May is stronger than a hundred of us. There will be a sliver of a chance. I intend to take it."

"Stop dancing around. Tell me your plan."

Liam recoiled from the thing he intended, where either success or failure would leave him hated and alone. Both paths would cost him any hope of seeing Charlie and of telling him what he'd figured out. He would stand with Alice Nevus's blood on his hands, and Charlie, the man he loved, would hate him for it.

"Tell me!" Lianna demanded.

"I mean to kill the haffling girl with May inside. She will break without the body, and before she has the chance to flee back into the Mist or the Unsee, I will end her."

Lianna didn't flinch or slow. "Yes. You are right, Liam Summer. It is the only way. I will fight with you, and if need be, I will die. But here's the thing." She pointed to a plume of smoke, three blocks north on Broadway. "Two are stronger than one, and three are stronger still. She means to kill us."

"She means to eat us and take our magic."

Lianna sprinted toward the building where flames shot through shattered windows and danced high upon the roof. "Then we save who we can, and we fight. I fled once. You did the same. I am of this world now and have nowhere left to flee."

They stopped at the edge of the orange plastic barriers and searched the crowd. Liam spotted him first, a tall man with dark close-cropped hair, dressed in drawstring pants and a *Blondie* T-shirt with the sleeves torn off to reveal muscular arms. Like Lianna his skin shone a bit too pale, even for New York, his lustrous blue eyes a bit too bright. Without pause he went to him. "I am Liam Summer."

The man looked from his house on fire to Liam. He swallowed and for a moment seemed about to run. He met Liam's gaze. "I am Frederick Flowers." He pointed at what was once his home. "This is not my imagination. This is fairy fire."

"Yes, we are under attack."

"She comes."

Liam nodded. "She does."

"Tell me, do you run from her or to her?"

Lianna came to Liam's side. "Hello, Frederick."

"Lianna, she has found us."

"Yes, and I will not run. Liam Summer means to kill her. I will fight at his side."

Frederick looked from Lianna to Liam. "You were her vicious thing. And now...."

Liam smiled. This Frederick, like Lianna, knew what he was and what he'd done. "I'm better now."

"Then I will follow you, Liam Summer, and I will fight."

And two became three, and a block north... four. They swelled to ten by Fourteenth Street, and with May's fires to point the way, their little troop grew, each aware of the danger, and each, like Liam, prepared to fight and willing to die.

Thirty-One

CHARLIE ARRIVED at the Bellevue ER, still in his full turnout gear, covered with soot, and smelling freshly baked. The doors whooshed open, and he entered chaos. Burn victims on stretchers were parked two deep on either side of the broad corridor. Doctors, nurses, and aides moved among them, their expressions blank, exhausted. One resident pulled a hand through his hair.

"They've got to stop coming. We have to go on diversion."

"We can't," a senior physician told him. "It's the same everywhere. Just focus on one at a time, Tim. It's all you can do."

Good advice, Charlie thought as he pushed past the reek of blood, feces, and pastry. With everyone too busy to notice a random firefighter, he strode through the ER and stopped in front of the electronic patient-tracker board. He saw *Nevus, A*, connected to *Trauma Room D*. Standing still in the middle of people crying for help, passed out from drugs, or possibly dead, he turned and checked the numbers over the doors and curtained-off cubicles. A sign with an arrow and the word *Trauma* seemed a good bet, and he headed down a patient-packed corridor.

"Water," one woman cried out, two-thirds of her face blistered and slick with a hastily applied antibiotic salve. He knew she'd need skin grafts and stiff doses of narcotics, and for the rest of her life children would point and stare. He knew too that many as badly burned as she would choose to never again leave their home... *if she even makes it home.* While there to find Alex and figure their next move, he stopped in an occupied cubicle, grabbed a paper cup, filled it, and handed it to the woman.

"How bad?" she rasped, her vocal cords hoarse from smoke inhalation.

"Just rest," he said, not wanting to lie.

"Thank you." And clutching the paper cup, she lay back.

He glanced at her IV bag and was relieved to see it contained a potent narcotic to mask the pain. As he passed, hands reached out for him.

"I need a nurse."

"Have you seen my doctor?"

"I'm sorry, no." He checked the letters above the doors and found Trauma D.

He heard them from the hall. Alex croaked, "Jerod, I have to find her."

Without pause Charlie pushed through the doors. There were six patients jammed in a room meant for two. Alex was closest to the door, Jerod with a hand tight around his wrist, trying to keep him in bed. He was dressed in a johnny coat, with an IV in his arm and thick white trauma pads taped to large areas of his back, shins, and thighs. Charlie didn't want to think about how close he'd come to dying, how close they'd both come.

He started at the memory of pretty Alice in her fluffy sweater and ballet outfit, commanding him to stay and burn. "Shit!"

Jerod turned to Charlie. "You got to help me. He thinks he can find her. He thinks he can stop her."

Alex stopped struggling. He couldn't mask either the pain or his desperation. "We have to! We have to get her out of Alice."

Charlie nodded as Nimby flew to him and, hovering inches in front of his nose, said, "She will kill us all."

"Not helpful," Charlie replied as he came to Alex's bedside. *This is bad.* If even a third of the area concealed by the trauma pads was burned, Alex was headed toward months and even years of grafts and rehab. At least his hands and face hadn't been affected. But if he were to leave... the wounds would become infected, and an awful situation would turn fatal. "Alex, a dead hero is no hero." He thought of Gran's stories. *We have our own banshee.* "Before this night is over, we'll all be counting our dead. We have to be smart."

"She's my sister."

"I know. But right now May has control of her, and we don't know how, though we're getting a better sense of why."

"I can't stay."

Charlie glanced at Alex's IV bag. Like the woman in the hall, he'd been dosed with narcotics to numb the pain from thousands of nerve endings burned raw. "You can't even stand, Alex. We'll find Alice." He glanced around to make certain there were no doctors or nurses in view and cranked up the rate on Alex's drip.

"But how?"

Jerod glanced back at him as Nimby returned to Alex's shoulder and kissed him on the cheek. "You rest… you sleep," she cooed. "You sleep, Alex Nevus. Sleep, sleep, sleep."

Charlie wept. He hated this sense of helplessness, of not knowing what to do. This wasn't a fire, where he'd been trained and knew the course of action. Like the overwhelmed intern, his thoughts ricocheted from Alice to Alex to Liam, out there trying to do God knows what. Even Nimby's panicked words crushed him. *There has to be a way.*

Jerod spoke. "He said she tried to kill you… both of you."

"She did."

Jerod nodded. "I saw her come out the front door. I knew it wasn't Alice."

"Did she see you?" Charlie asked.

"No, I wanted to go to her… but…."

"But what?"

"I've been to this rodeo, Charlie. I know what May can do and that life—human or fey—doesn't matter to her. She headed south. And then you came out with Alex. Thirty seconds earlier and she might have seen you…. Thank you, Charlie. I know he's hurt. Shit!" Jerod's jaw clenched, and tears spilled. "Thank you. He's alive, you both are, and that's what matters."

"It's not," Alex croaked, though the drugs made it hard for him to speak and to keep his eyes open. "It won't matter if we can't stop her. Alice. I should have known. I'm sorry, sorry… sorry." His lids fluttered. He sank into the mattress. The pain of his burned back caused him to wince and then relax.

"Thank God," Jerod said. He gazed on the man he loved, who had nearly died, and if not for the potent narcotic, Dilaudid, would be prowling the streets in search of his possessed sister.

Charlie pulled out his cell and called Finn. "I'm at Bellevue."

"Are you hurt?"

"No. I pulled Alex Nevus from a building on Murray Hill. Look, Finn, are you someplace you can talk?"

"Yeah, I'm in my truck. We've been instructed to take whichever scene is closest, and if there's already a marshal there, move to the next and call it in."

"It's... her. All of this."

"Yeah, I get that. And Charlie, if you're not hurt, what the hell are you doing at the hospital?"

"I think you know."

"You're worried about Liam, and I heard about your folks' house."

"It's bigger than that, Finn."

"Tell me."

"How many fires tonight?"

"Last count 132."

"Okay, so we know that the first one on Saturday, where I pulled Liam out, was probably meant for him."

"Got it. Not a coincidence."

"And then Alex's sister's place, and ready for the rabbit hole?"

"Already down here, but look, there's a trap door."

"His sister is possessed by Queen May. She tried to kill us both, and she nearly did."

"Crap! What saved you?"

Not expecting the question, Charlie paused. "Liam."

"Wait, you left out something. Liam was there?"

"No. I don't know where he is, and I'm freaking out that he's going to go after her himself and get himself killed."

"Whoa, Charlie. Chill. How could Liam save you if he wasn't there?"

"I love him, Finn. He doesn't know that, and as I thought about him... really thought about him, it did something... like, broke the spell." The words choked in his throat.

There was silence.

"Finn?"

"Thinking... that's what saved Alex the first time. Apparently love really is a kind of magic.... Not that I'd know. So that's two things, right? We know these fires are deliberate, your home, the Nevuses' apartments old and new, and likely all of these others."

"They could be diversions."

"True, but it's the only lead we've got. Look, I can be at Bellevue in twenty. We can check this out."

"So what does it mean that she sent missiles to 132 buildings in the five boroughs?"

"What we've always known, kid. New York City is filled with weird shit, and we're about to find out how much."

"Finn, she's dangerous. She just looked at me, said a few words, and I froze, as in could not move." Charlie heard Finn inhale and then the crisp snap of the marshal turning on the siren.

"We don't have a choice, do we, Charlie?"

"Not seeing one."

"Wait for me outside. I'm pulling up a schematic of the fires. Any way of narrowing things down? You know, like where she's more likely to be?"

Charlie glanced at Jerod, who stood sentinel over the now sleeping Alex. "Yeah, she was headed south from the Murray Hill fire."

"Good. I'm cutting across on Thirty-Fourth. I'll be there in five."

They hung up.

"I've got to go," Charlie said.

Jerod glanced up. "Be careful, Charlie. She's going to look like Alice, but…."

"Yeah, I know." Charlie looked at the fairy parked on Alex Nevus's shoulder. "Nimby, I don't know how this works… any chance you'd come with me? I could use someone who knows about magic."

The fairy's pointed ears twitched. Her bloodred eyes fixed on him. She looked from Jerod and then to Alex, the man she'd been attached to since his birth nineteen years ago. The times they'd been separated were so painful, like a piece of her had been ripped off. She nodded, kissed Alex's cheek, zoomed across and did the same to Jerod's, and with a blur of orange-and-black wings, lit on Charlie's shoulder. "We go to war. We go to fight. We likely die, but we do right."

Thirty-Two

MAY GAZED in the window of a dress shop filled with glittering gowns. She caught her reflection in the glass, wonderfully smooth skin, china-blue eyes, and hair the color of ripe wheat. "I am pretty again. Pretty, pretty... and hungry."

She fluffed the stiff tulle tutu she'd found in Alice's closet. *It's not right... not at all. It doesn't fit. I look like a little girl... but I'm not.* She examined her long toned legs and breasts that swelled beneath soft white cashmere. She felt her toes squished in the too small ballet slippers. *This is no look for a queen.*

Torn between her hunger and the need for a better outfit, she flicked her forefinger against the thick plate glass. A spider fracture blossomed. She blew on it. The window shattered into thousands of glittery shards.

The cool smell from the shop spilled out and beckoned. The burglar alarm wailed, adding its impotent scream to hundreds of others. Carefully she lifted one dainty foot and then the other and climbed into the mannequin-filled window. Her hands flew up the sides of something floor-length, shimmery, and green. *Lovely, but too mother of the bride.* She rested her cheek against a cherry-red strapless number. *Velvet, so soft.* She worked it free from the mannequin when her eye caught on a recessed lit display in the back of the shop. Her breath caught as she stepped down from the window and into the store. *Perfect. Midnight-blue satin, corset top, black lace overlay.* Even the satin pumps. *Yes.* Knowing it would fit, she stripped naked in the shop, and like a snake shedding its skin, she stepped into a tea-length gown of blue satin and black lace. She twirled in the mirror, letting her silken hair fall across creamy white shoulders. *I will let this body grow a bit longer but not too long.* The swell of her young breasts was perfect for the dress that nipped in tight at her waist and flared out at midcalf. *I am a beautiful dark flower.*

From a display of fringed shawls, she grabbed one of a matching blue worked through with gold thread. *Perfect.* And with her hunger near insatiable, she threw the shawl around her shoulders, stepped over broken glass, and emerged like the queen she was onto the street.

A handsome stranger approached. "Are you okay?" he asked.

She turned her blue-eyed gaze toward him. "How kind." A window exploded down the street.

"It's not safe out here," he said, his eyes fixed on hers.

"Walk with me."

"My pleasure."

Her hand found his. *So young, so vital.* And just as she had with the Asian man, each step robbed a year from him. *Sweet and tasty.*

Filled with the lovely blonde vision in a dress of deep blue, the man never noticed how his life flowed from him into her. He dropped to his knees, a man who'd started the day as a twenty-nine-year-old commodities broker and died that night as a nonagenarian.

Alice, trapped in her head and in addiction, stirred from a dusty dream. Clay was in it. He needed to tell her something. She looked at the old man dead at her feet. *Where did I get those shoes? They look like they hurt.* She knew the dead man should bother her. He didn't. The wonderful feeling she'd been wrapped in since first tasting that sticky powder, *more like a resin*, was losing steam.

I know, sweet. Never fear, Queen May is here. And you're right, these mortals make a tasty snack, but nothing more. Amuse-bouche on the way to fatter fare… and fairy dust.

May's thoughts settled Alice. *But for how long?*

The drugged teen fretted. *Why didn't we take my backpack? I need dust. I need it now!*

"You're out of your mind," May said aloud as she abandoned the dying man, and walked as fast as her satin pumps could manage. *Alice, dear child, I will get you dust, but I will not ruin this outfit with a backpack! And you are right, there's little point in empty calories. You need dust, and I need….*

She stopped, well away from the crowd who'd gathered around the shriveled corpse. She sniffed the air. The tall buildings obscured her view. She listened to the sirens, knowing enough of this world from two prior visits that they were like locator spells for tragedy. She paused and reflected. *This is all my doing. And I'm just getting started.* Like a starlet taking the stage at the Oscars, she was filled with pride. *This is all me, and this time no one is going to fuck things up!*

Dust, Alice whimpered. Her wonderful feeling, the euphoria of all being well, was unraveling. Sirens and images of Alex in the arms of a firefighter—*She killed them.*

No, May thought, feeling the teen's panic. *You will not infect me with fear. I told you you'd have dust, and so you shall. You will always have dust, buckets of it.*

Goody.

May spotted her target in a smoldering brownstone on West Twenty-Eighth. Dwarfed between two high-rise luxury condominiums, the fire had burned hot, leaving nothing but the brick shell of the nineteenth-century home. That and, of course, *fairy dust.*

Yes, please, Alice thought. *I need it.*

May surveyed the scene. Orange plastic barriers, warnings to stay back. A lone police car, none of the big red trucks. *Other fish to fry. Look at what I've done. And think of what I'm going to do. Just the start.*

Dust, please.

Yes. Careful of her dainty shoes, May crossed the barriers and descended a side staircase. An iron gate had been ripped from its hinges, and a charred door hung open as she entered a garden apartment, into what had originally been the kitchen. She listened for the hum and sizzle of fairy fire. There was none. She smelled the dust, which was fine for Alice but did almost nothing for her. *A pleasant little buzz, but I can take it or leave it.* That's not what caused her to salivate. *Where are you?*

Dust. Please, hurry.

Fine. With efficiency of movement, she dipped below fallen beams and came to the heart of devastation. *I did this.*

Hurry.

Fine… dust heads, all the same. Realizing she'd need a large and steady supply of dust to keep her haffling host silent, she knelt and ran a hand over a patch of glittery white resin. It stuck to her fingers. She rolled a bit into a ball the size of an M&M and popped it into her mouth.

Goody! Alice squealed, sighed, and then went silent.

"This could get annoying. I should have grabbed a purse." Still crouched, May rolled several dust bunnies, the term used by dust heads in the Unsee. Careful to not ruin her dress, she ran her fingernail into the hem, made a slight opening, and taking advantage of the dust's natural stickiness, she tucked them away. *How long will she sleep? Alice, are you there? Alice…. Perfect. Now my turn.* She stood and felt the air caress her bare skin. She gently closed the back of her throat and rasped up breath from deep inside. She smelled the smoke of fairy fire as it passed without burn through her lips. A stream of cookie-flavored smoke left her mouth, and like the directional arrow on a compass, she followed it. *Come out, come out, wherever you are.* It led her up debris-strewn stairs to the main level. The wisp turned, unconcerned about the devastation of the once-lovely building with its ruined stained-glass windows and charred oak balusters. Up it went, with May gliding in its path. *This is how it was meant to be.* Each passing moment in the See, telling her, reassuring her, *this time you got it right. I have magic here. I have all my magic…. And I want more.* She glided across gaping spans of flooring that had ignited like birthday candles. She hovered in midair and looked down to where she'd stopped and rolled dust bunnies. *I will rule here. And there, and everywhere.* The trail of smoke through her lips pulled her forward. She flew to the room's edge, its plaster walls reduced to dust and jagged slats. Her feet skimmed over ruined carpet as she followed the smoke. *And there you are.*

The creature, curled up in death, appeared human. He wasn't. Her fingertips brushed back his soft auburn locks and played across the tips of surgically altered ears. She examined his face. *Do I know this one? He is a Fall.* Something about him was familiar but like all the others who'd fled from her rule. *Traitor, you had this coming.* She held her hand before her face, and with forefinger pointed, willed the nail into a razor-sharp talon. Placing it in the notch of the dead creature's neck, she pressed down, and like a knife in butter, slit him open. Her mouth watered as she reached in and ripped out first his heart and then the blood-engorged liver. Mindful of her dress, she softened the flesh at the corners of her mouth, unhinged her jaw, and enjoyed her first real meal since escaping the Mist.

Mm, mm, mm. Delicious. She couldn't recall the last time she'd devoured a creature so lovely, so toothsome. Her misty fare of trolls and ogres was now a thing of the past. *So good!* Blood and magic trickled down her throat and swirled in her gut. For the first time in years, she felt full. But just like Alice and her dust cravings, May knew the hunger would return. She licked her lips as her jaw hinged back to a human form. The aftertastes of the beautiful fey were rich with hints of berry and vanilla.

She floated away from the eviscerated fey. *Traitor you were... but delicious you are.* The enormity of what she'd accomplished gave her pause. *From inside the Mist, I did this. And now I have a body, and I have my magic. I will retake all that was mine.* All the doubt that nipped at her thoughts dissipated. *I can do this. I will do this.*

Memories of an ancient time, a time before the See, the Unsee, and the Mist were three. When there was a single world, and she and her sisters, Lizbeta and Katye, ruled the Fey. A time when May had been centuries young and fallen in love... with a human. Or rather a man who was mostly human, most of the time.

She grimaced and hissed, "This is your fault." The face of her redheaded lover, like the coals of human fire, still burned. "Your fault." That he'd betrayed her love stung. But what had never lessened and had fueled her hatred through centuries and millennia, was his deceit. *How dare you!* "But payback, it's a-coming, lover. All you have taken, all my sisters have kept from me, I'm taking back." The sound of her voice through Alice's lips delighted her. She played with the inflection, a lilt here, a bit firmer there, just as she'd made beautiful music come from out of her now dead brother. "It's time to tear down the walls between the worlds. There need not be three." She thought of her traitorous sisters. "The queen of all, she will be me."

Thirty-Three

LIAM, LIANNA, Frederick, seventeen fey who passed as human, and three, like Nimby, who were visible to only a few, marched beneath the Washington Square Arch, headed north. Each plume of fairy fire, like *X* marks the spot, revealed May's inhuman targets. Some had escaped the carnage. Others were dead, as were many humans.

As the band approached each blaze, hope surged, and a new member would join their ranks. But then they'd come upon a dead sprite or tiny little fey gasping its last. "She brings war," Liam stated, ever more certain of what needed to be done. *Kill the haffling Alice, then kill May.* But then he'd look up to the night sky and know in his gut. *She is too strong.*

He kept those thoughts to himself.

As they marched, he learned. "I'd not imagined so many of us were in the See."

With Lianna on his right and Frederick Flower on his left, they educated him on the life of sidhe expats.

"We stick to the cities," Lianna said. "Except for the trolls and ogres, of course. It's harder for them. They prefer farms and places with land and deer and game. But for us, it's not difficult to find work after the surgeries."

"Tell me of those," Liam asked, having wondered if the loss of his ears and carnivore teeth was a typical price of passing between worlds.

Frederick pulled back his thick auburn hair to reveal two perfect human ears. "There are surgeons. The one most of us use is sidhe. Even the human ones ask few questions in return for cash. We say it's birth defects, and they ask us questions and wonder why our brains aren't addled. Apparently there are genetic conditions that can give a human pointed ears. Though when I learned of that, my thought was these could be hafflings. But no, it seems that humans born with pointed ears have terrible problems. So they take our money, and we get the *cut and shave*."

Lianna snorted. "Quite a lot of money, but it is necessary. Though humans tend to see what they want. So even before we get the ear cut and tooth shave, few notice… and a hat can hide a lot. As for the teeth, some humans have theirs filed to look like ours, a kind of vampire chic, so it's not hard…."

"In cities like New York, San Francisco, London, Cape Town, we blend in best," Frederick explained.

"We are that many," Liam stated.

"We number a few thousand worldwide," Lianna said. "But still…."

"Don't," Liam said, reading her emotions, as palpable as a shard of ice. "I will not be ruled by fear."

"Good. Then we will tell all that we know." She swallowed and met his gaze. "I'd know how the passage affected you."

"It took most of my magic, and it gave me the shave and cut and turned my skin and hair darker."

"I'd wondered," Frederick said. "No surgeries."

"No. I came through but two days ago. She was trapped in the Mist by her sister Lizbeta, who knew she could not hold her. She was right. So tell me more. Tell me everything."

The banter helped hold back the terror, the howl of sirens, and the wail of banshees.

"Cities are best," Lianna continued as the next plume of smoke appeared. As one, they headed down Eighth Street, where two fire engines pumped water into the basement of a building with a party supply store on the first floor and apartments in the six stories above.

"Frederick and I, many of the others, we find work as models. It pays well and suits our abilities. We age much slower than they do, and so we pretend for a while that it's healthy living and occasional plastic surgery. But if we stay too long in the public eye, they notice. We build second and then third lives. I'm going to school to become a lawyer…." She pointed to the smoking building. "I know this place."

Liam heard murmurs from the band of sidhe. "This is Norman's store."

"She got Norman's store."

They halted twenty feet behind the plastic barriers. This fire was like a repeat of the last several. The flames had been put out by the men in black with reflective yellow bands. But the smoke, thick and delicious, spilled up from the basement and through holes pierced in the roof.

"Wait!" Something shivered down Liam's spine. The fine hairs on the back of his neck and arms prickled. He stopped and put his hands on Lianna and Frederick's shoulders to keep them from moving forward. "She's here!" he whispered, as seventeen humanoid sidhe and three who fluttered on stolen butterfly wings followed his gaze.

He was not mistaken. They watched a pretty blonde teen, dressed for a ball in blue satin and lace, step across the barricades.

"She glows with power," Lianna whispered.

"She has fed… a lot," Liam replied.

"Tell us," Frederick said.

"She feeds on us, on humans as well, perhaps. Though of that I'm less certain."

"She didn't see us," Lianna said as they watched the beautiful young woman glamour a firefighter. She took his arm, and he escorted her down the stairwell and into the basement of the smoldering building. On either side of them, a thick hose pulsed with pressurized water.

The firefighter stumbled. "She's doing something to him," Liam said. *That could be Charlie.* Caution fled. *She's draining him.*

"Liam, no!" Lianna, Frederick, and others shouted as he broke ranks.

Not heeding their cries, he ran to the barricades.

A police officer approached. "Sir, no one can go in."

Liam met the man's gaze. He smiled and nudged his glamour across the distance between them.

A spark lit in the officer's eye.

"I must go in," Liam said.

"Of course…." The cop shook his head. "What am I saying? It's not safe. You can't…."

"It's okay." Liam stepped past the barrier, and the dazed policeman, who'd never once found another man attractive, could not look away.

"I'll come with you."

"No. You mustn't. Stay here," Liam said, aware of the danger. He looked from the policeman back to the band of sidhe, all eyes on him. He shook his head no. "No one is to follow me," he said to the officer. "Do not let them follow me."

He nodded and clung to the connection with the beautiful violet-eyed man.

"Thank you." And Liam followed May's footsteps down to the basement.

At the bottom of the metal steps, he came upon the firefighter, who clung to life by a thread. He looked into the man's wizened face. *She's stolen decades from him.* "I'm so sorry." *It's not Charlie… but it could be.*

He peered through the dense smoke for the pretty girl in her party dress. "You have to get out of here," he whispered to the dying firefighter.

"I must stay," he answered in a dull voice. "She told me to stay."

Liam swallowed as fear trickled through his veins. *She is too powerful. She has drained him and cast a glamour far greater than anything I possess. I have no chance.* Old thoughts fueled his fear. *I have to get out of here. I have to run. No… I will not run.* He fixed Charlie in his mind. The first time he saw him, he thought he was an ogre assassin, and when he took off his helmet…. *I started to love him then. A man who runs into a house on fire. I need that. I will be him. He will hate me for this, but I have no choice. I will be hard. I will be cruel.*

A movement up ahead, and he glimpsed her legs skipping up the stairs into the store.

His eyes teared from the smoke as he passed the source of the blaze, a two-foot crater that glittered with a thick sugar-white coat of fairy dust, with parallel streaks, like finger tracks. Aware of dust's narcotic and addictive properties, he knew she'd rolled dust bunnies. *Odd.* In all the time he'd been at her court, he'd never once seen her dusted. *Why is she rolling bunnies? Has she become a dust head?*

He stared up the charred stairwell and looked for a weapon. *What would Charlie do?* He went back to the aged firefighter.

"I need your ax."

"Take it. Why can't I move?"

"Because she glamoured you," Liam said as he gently unbuckled the ax. The man's bones, even through the thick material of his turnout coat, felt like matchsticks.

"I'm going to die, aren't I?"

"I hope not," Liam said. "I'm going after her." Without another word, he hefted the six-pound weapon with its steel pick on one side and blade on the other. He headed up.

In the garishly decorated store above, with rows of melted rubber masks and shelves filled with fun-making party stuff, he found May. She crouched over the body of a man with flame-red hair.

He raised the ax above his head as she ran a razor-sharp talon down the dead man's sternum and sliced him open.

Ax aloft, he inched closer as she scooped into the dead sidhe's chest and tore out first his heart and then his liver. Without turning from her meal, she spoke. "You betrayed me once, Liam Summer. You will not again."

He froze. His breath caught in his throat. He had lost the element of surprise, and the distance was too great for a frontal assault. *This is it.* He dropped the ax, knowing he would have a single chance and that all depended on her believing him. In that instant he turned back into the thing he loathed.

He dropped on bended knee. "No, my queen." A lifetime as her whore had given him a front-row seat to all her machinations. *If anyone knows you, it is I.* "I am your servant and your slave. I am yours to command or to kill. Do with me as you will."

She rose from her blood feast and faced him. In her right hand dripped the sidhe's stilled heart, and in her left, a large red-brown liver, still aquiver with life. With her jaw unhinged, she slurped them down, like oysters at a raw bar. She dabbed the corners of her mouth, pulled Alice's face back into its original form, and eyed Liam.

He felt the power of her magic as it washed across the distance between them. Alice's luminous blue eyes shone on him. She pursed her lips and blew out a thin stream of smoke.

Liam saw it coming. *She's casting a glamour.* Frightened as he was, he remembered a lesson his mother had taught him. It had not saved her and his father but was one of magic's most basic maneuvers—deflection. *She's too strong. It won't work. Shut up and try!* He imagined a thick wall of glass protecting him from her spell and reflected it back like a mirror. *What you send to me, back at you, times three. What you send to me, back at you, times three.*

WITH HER mouth filled with the savory and salt of a traitorous sprite's liver, May stared at her pretty Summer fey, still lovely but far more human than sidhe. "You are not to be trusted. Though 'tis a shame to rip you apart as I did your parents. Tasty as they were. And tasty as I'm certain you will be."

"I never lied to you. I am true fey, and we do not lie," he said on bended knee.

"You aided the Nevus boy. That was not what I'd ordered. You were to glamour him, seduce and enslave him, and then bring him to me. You did none of that." *Let's see if you can be of use.* She blew the glamour onto his silken head.

"I brought him to you, my queen. I kept him safe so that you could possess his body."

May pondered as the smoky glamour wrapped around him. *There is truth in his words.... He cannot be trusted.* She studied his movements. "Look at me," she ordered.

He raised his head. Their eyes met.

He is devious... but lovely. "The trip between worlds seems not to have broken you. If anything...."

"Yes, my queen," he said with the hint of an eyebrow raise.

"Your human form pleases me. It will please others. But you cannot be trusted." *See how he looks at me. My magic is strong. He will love and obey me. It's in his eyes. I cannot trust this lovely thing, but I trust my magic.*

"I am yours. I am yours alone. Do with me what you will. I will not resist. I am yours. I will do all you ask." All the time he chanted in his head: *What you send to me, back at you, times three. What you send to me, back at you, times three.* He felt the strength of her magic as it sought to penetrate through his eyes, his nostrils, every opening of his body and the pores of his skin. He pictured Charlie. *What you send to me, back at you, times three. What you send to me, back at you, times three.*

HIS WORDS touched a place deep inside May, a place she'd not felt since... the Hound. *So lovely, my Liam. I see it in your eyes. This is truth. You will rule by my side.* She weighed the obvious advantage of having her beautiful Liam to do her bidding. *But more. His face, his eyes, how they stare into me. He loves me. And I'd never realized I have feelings for him... for Liam.*

She spoke. "The trip to the See, it changed you…. I dreamed of you in the Mist. You could have been there."

"I was, and I saw. I am sorry that you suffered."

"As am I." She sniffed the air, and even through the smoke of fairy fire, she sensed it…. *He has magic.* "Tell me what powers you have here."

"Few," he admitted. "I have my glamour, but that is all." *What you send to me, back at you, times three. What you send to me, back at you, times three.*

"You will do everything I ask of you."

"Yes, my queen."

"And you will love me."

"With all my heart."

And you will share my bed…. "I require proof, Liam Summer. You must prove your fealty."

"Yes, my liege. Tell me what you will." Hope, albeit faint, rooted. *Her glamour failed.*

The police officer who'd tried to stop Liam from entering appeared in the door. "You two shouldn't be here. This building's not safe."

"Him," May said.

AT FIRST Liam heard whispers, like someone tapping on the door to his brain. But too concerned with the likelihood he was about to get his organs ripped out, he blocked them. Never dropping his reflective wall, he met her gaze and watched as her glamour, more powerful than any he had ever thrown, bounced back to her, its power magnified by his repel. *What you send to me, back at you, times three. What you send to me, back at you, times three.*

The whispers grew as her eyes sought out his. *I know that look.* He kept his expression warm and interested. His tongue spoke in honeyed tones. "Yes, my liege. Tell me what you will." The whispers, at first nothing more than hisses and random words, grew stronger. Whole sentences. *Her thoughts.* It surprised him, having concluded that while he still had the power of glamour, it was weaker and different in the See. *I cannot read Charlie's thoughts. I can read hers. She is glamoured.* Her gaze reflected back love and desire for him. Not dropping his deflection, he listened to her struggle.

Mustn't trust him… but so lovely. So…. Her musings of the two of them together, entwined in a lover's embrace.

It was the first time since coming to the See that he could read a glamour's thoughts, something that was a given in Fey. Her mind scrambled for a test of loyalty. He even sensed Alex's sister, not quite awake, but… *dusted. That's what the dust bunnies are for.*

His resolve to kill the haffling wavered. *There's no other way.* He felt May's attention shift to the patrolman as a single word crossed her lips. "Him."

"Yes, my queen." And rising from bended knee, he turned to the man who'd let him pass through the barriers.

"You," the officer sighed, still under Liam's thrall.

He looked at the man whose heart he was about to bind. He felt shame and hesitated.

"Do it!" May commanded.

He knew his next move would destroy the man's life. He would leave his wife and children and be bound to him. *There is no other way. She must not doubt my loyalty, and then, when she lets down her guard, I will kill the haffling, and then I will kill her.*

He approached the man, who stood frozen in the entry. "I'm sorry," he whispered as he placed his hands on either side of the policeman's face and moved in for the kiss. "I am so sorry."

As his lips neared the befuddled officer, Charlie, with Finn behind him, ran through the door. *"What the hell, Liam!"* Charlie roared.

Before the seal-the-deal kiss connected, Liam pulled back. *"No! Get out of here, Charlie! Run!"*

May shrieked. "You should be dead. Burned to a crisp. And that one. I know you!" Her mind scurried over related facts as she looked from Charlie to the redheaded Finn. "This means the Nevus boy is alive. Tell me! And you! Child of the Hound, how dare you!"

"Screw you." Charlie stared down the teen in her party dress and heels.

Liam pleaded. "Run, Charlie. Please…. *Get out of here!*"

A commotion sounded from within the building. Feet pounded up the basement stairs.

"Kill him!" May ordered. "If you don't, I will, and then you, my handsome traitor…."

Liam knew that, glamour or not, his plan was ruined. He either did as she commanded or died.

From the basement, Lianna, Frederick, and the others appeared.

"No," Liam cried. He turned from Charlie, who seemed more hurt by the near kiss than the fact they were going to die, to May. *Well, if this is it....* He met her gaze. "I will not kill Charlie Fitzgerald. I will not kill the man I love."

May's expression clouded. She stomped her heel on the floor. *"Then you die!"*

Liam felt her power as it crossed the room. Like the opening of a tunnel between worlds, time expanded. He strengthened his repel. *What you send to me, back at you, times three.* Over and over he repeated it in his head, just as he'd repeated it at his mother's side. While long dead, he felt her presence. *What you send to me, back at you, times three.* He expanded its mirrored surface and willed it over Charlie, Finn, and little Nimby, astride the redhead's shoulder.

What you send to me, back at you, times three.
What you send to me, back at you, times three.
What you send to me, back at you, times three.

Under the weight of her power, he felt and heard her thoughts. Far from anything fey or even human, but older, the hunger of a beast.

What you send to me, back at you, times three.
What you send to me, back at you, times three.
What you send to me, back at you, times three.

Her feet left the ground, and she floated toward him.

Liam panicked. *I can't move.* Her thoughts and her hunger clouded his mind. *She is too strong. Charlie, I have failed.*

She displayed a talon-sharp finger. Her smile broadened. "Such a pity."

He detected his glamour still in her eyes. *She loves me, and that is not enough. It will not stop her.* He gasped as the daggerlike nail tore the flesh at the notch of his neck.

"Such a pity." Her eyes fixed on his, torn between bloodlust and the other kind.

Time hung as blood trickled down his chest. Staring into her clear blue eyes, Liam heard another voice, Alice's.

"Help me."

It was faint, like a sleeper waking from a nightmare. With an inch between them, Liam pulled out his remaining trick. Putting everything he had into his voice, a lifetime of honing the art of seduction, he whispered, "If I am to die, my queen, let it be with your kiss on my lips."

Her smile brightened, and her paralytic magic faltered. Before she could gather her wits and reason why a kiss was not in her interest, he leaned in.

As their lips met, Liam felt the glamour's binding power surge. And for the first time, he felt no shame. While he didn't know if it would work, he'd done all he could. He did not break the contact. He thought of Charlie. *I have gone into the building on fire, Charlie. I have done it for you.... I have done it for me.*

Alice's voice flooded him. *Help me. Please, get her out of me!*

I don't know how.

Then kill me.

He felt the teen's body against his, her forefinger still lodged in his flesh.

Kill me! The teen's voice gained in strength as May was momentarily stunned by Liam's glamour.

Kill me! the teen pleaded.

It was what he'd intended. He could grab the ax and with a single swing separate her head from her body. It needed to happen. Expel May from the haffling. She would break in the See and be unable to rule.

Please kill me.

Another way. There is another way. With no time to reflect, he embraced the power that had caused him and those he'd turned it on inestimable heartache. *If she is glamoured, there is a chance.*

FOR THE second time that night, Charlie stood paralyzed. With Finn by his side and Nimby on his shoulder, the three stood like statues in the doorway of the burned-out store. Unable to move, he was tortured by what he'd seen. Liam about to kiss a patrolman... *at her bidding. Not like he didn't warn you. You thought what? One day with you would change what he said he was? What an idiot. The kiss has to do with his magic, the thing that sets it in stone.* But then Liam did the unexpected. He defied May's order.

What the hell. He just said he loved me. Then why was he gonna kiss that cop? Doesn't matter. It's magic. He has his reasons. He said he loves me. He loves me. His breath tightened as a possessed Alice Nevus, dressed in blue satin and lace, tore a gaping wound in Liam's neck with her finger. *No! Liam.... Stop!* He couldn't turn his head to look away or open his mouth to scream… to beg for her to stop. *Please, no!*

Nimby, on the other hand, could speak. Her tinny voice chattered with fright. "She is going to kill him. She is going to kill us. We are all going to die, die, die!"

Not helpful, Charlie thought. *I love him. He loves me.* Tears of rage and frustration tracked down his cheek as he realized the only man he'd ever loved not only loved him back but was willing to die for him. *Liam, run! Please run! What's he doing? He can still move.* Charlie watched as, rather than flee, Liam leaned in to the possessed teen as blood trickled down his throat and soaked the front of his shirt. *Run!*

Nimby whispered, "He's got a trick."

Charlie stared as Liam's mouth and beautiful lips landed on the girl's. He pulled her in tight.

May's spell broke. Like throwing a switch, Charlie, Finn, Nimby, and all those who'd come up the stairs unfroze.

Charlie raced to Liam's side, about to pull May off him.

Liam waved him back and clutched Alice tighter, his lips glued to hers.

Charlie replayed Liam's words from the dream after he'd kissed him. *"You should not have done that, Charlie Fitzgerald."* *It's his magic. It's how he binds people. Did he do that to me?* He snorted. In the midst of a night filled with horror and death, a night that was by no means at an end, he laughed.

"What is your problem?" Finn hissed.

"Him." They stared at Liam, in what seemed an endless kiss. "He thinks he put a love spell on me with a kiss. He didn't need to. I was lost the minute he made me wait in that death trap so he could save that dog."

"Naked Chihuahua Guy."

"Yup."

"Something's happening," Finn said.

A milk-white film clouded Alice's blue eyes. Her body shook as Liam eased her bloody finger from his throat.

"He's doing it." Nimby fluttered off Charlie's shoulder and flew to the ceiling for a better look. She was joined by the two other little fairies as the rest formed a wide circle around Liam and mad Queen May.

Smoke trickled and then poured from Alice's lips as Liam pulled back, his shirt drenched in blood. He cooed endearments. "My queen. My love… my only love."

What the hell? Charlie wondered but knew better than to break the connection. His focus shifted between the wound on Liam's neck and the way he held May in thrall.

"Sweetness," Liam whispered, but loud enough for all to hear. "Show me your splendor. Show me your power. Be with me."

Alice's eyes, now white as eggs, fluttered shut. Sparks flew out of her mouth and popped as they interacted with the air.

"Show me your glory." Liam held the teen by her shoulders. He didn't flinch as a spark caught his hair and singed his cheek before dying. "Be with me. Show me your truth. Show me, my queen, my love. My true love."

Alice's tremors coarsened. Her mouth opened wide… wider. Her jaw, like a snake about to feed, detached.

"It's happening," a tall blonde woman who'd come to stand behind Charlie whispered.

Before he could get clarification, Charlie witnessed the impossible. Alice Nevus's jaw unhinged. A white salamander with a broad flat head bigger than a man's peeked from between her jaws.

"My love." Liam gazed into two sparkling red eyes. "Be with me. Let me know your love." He stuck his head between Alice's gaping jaws and kissed the thing inside. He reached in and began to pull her out. "Come… be with me." His lips held those of the monster.

Sensing something was amiss, the salamander resisted and pulled back.

Liam redoubled his efforts. The muscles in his arms corded and strained. His voice filled with warmth, love, and promise. "Be with me."

"We have to help him," Lianna urged. "She'll pull him in."

Without pause, Charlie went to his side.

Liam pulled a hand from out of Alice's mouth and waved him back.

Charlie hesitated, sensing the worst thing would be to break the connection between Liam and the creature. It was agony to not be able to aid the man he loved… truly loved.

"By the arm!" Lianna said. "See if you can grab her arms."

Liam reached in deeper. His head, shoulders, and arms vanished inside Alice. His feet dug into the ground.

Charlie couldn't stand back. *She's going to swallow him.* He grabbed Liam around the middle, and like a fish too big for one man to land, he pulled with all he had.

"*Pull!*" Lianna ordered. "Get her out!"

She gripped Charlie, and like a fey tug-of-war, others added their strength, all depending on Liam's charm and his arms to not let go.

Inside Alice, Liam's lips stayed on May's, one hand on each of her front legs, as the talons raked the flesh of his hands and arms.

He pulled and twisted, feeling the muscular creature cling to Alice. His thoughts whispered inside May, giving her all the love, all the possibility of joy he'd been trained to cast. "I will be yours. You will be mine. Forever, my love. You will know peace. We will be happy. So happy. Delights you cannot imagine. Come to me. Come. Leave this sad body. Be with me. Taste what I have to serve."

The beast clung to the haffling, but Liam's kiss and the strength of her own magic mirrored back was too strong. She ached for him, for his kisses. The connection with dusty little Alice weakened. *You*, she thought. Words were impossible to describe the love, the hunger she felt. *You, you, you. Don't pull back. You, you, you. Love, love, love.*

"I won't leave you. Come to me. Be with me. Now… forever." He pulled and cajoled, feeling Charlie's strong arms like an anchor around his waist, his body pressed against his back. "Be with me. Now… forever." The words were whispered to May but meant for Charlie. "I will love you… just you."

Forever. You, you, you.

"Yes. Forever. Come…."

Inch by inch, it happened. A white salamander with a broad snout emerged from the five-foot-nine teen. Its long slick neck slipped through Alice's dislocated jaw as Liam, like birthing a calf, coaxed first one of its forelimbs and then the other.

"Come, be with me." His lips stayed on the creature's. His hands let go of the forelimbs as he urged her out of Alice, who would most likely die.

Others grabbed its head and its long, twisty neck. Two fey gripped Alice, and they gently pulled the girl back.

May's hind legs scrambled for purchase, her thoughts torn between the hunger and need for Liam and the mounting panic that something horrible was happening. *I can't think.*

No need to think. His lips pressed to her mouth, his thoughts in her head. *Just love.*

I could eat you.

No... be with me. Love me. He wrapped his arms around her, aware that she could easily devour him. He did not stop. His hands slid down as her body arched higher and higher, her mouth never leaving his. He reached into Alice's mouth for her back legs. *Be free with me. You and I, forever.*

Forever.

With a final tug between those grabbing Alice and Liam—with Charlie and others behind him pulling at the beast—May's tail slipped from the girl's lips.

"Get her away!" Lianna shouted to those who held Alice. The salamander flopped onto the floor. She convulsed and sparked as she hit the ground. The connection between her and Liam broke as he landed against Charlie and the others.

Lianna barked, "Get the haffling away! Get her out!"

The beast twisted on the ground. Its red eyes filled with rage and hunger. She looked back at her haffling host. She could not tell if she was dead or alive. But then she spotted Liam. *You, you, you.* With mouth agape, she lunged for him. *You, you, you.*

Charlie sprang to his feet. He circled behind the salamander and jumped onto the creature's back. Finn retrieved the ax from the floor and came to his aid.

With a flick of her tail and arch of her back, she hurled Charlie into the air. Her armored tail pounded the ground around him. Her gaze fixed on Liam. *You, you, you. Love you. Eat you. Love you up. Eat you up.*

Liam scrambled back toward the door.

"Why is she after you?" Charlie shouted as he tried to put himself between the beast and Liam.

Liam, his face slick from May's kiss, his hair singed, felt a freedom he'd never known. In that moment, death did not matter. *I have done this thing.* "She is glamoured by her own magic. She loves me." His feet shuffled back toward the door. "Know this, Charlie Fitzgerald. I do not know if I glamoured you or not. But it's you, Charlie. It's you I love."

Without another word, he bolted from the store.

The beast howled, raised up on its small hind limbs, and like a puppy after a red rubber ball, she gave chase. *You, you, you. Love you. Eat you. Love you more. Eat you more.*

Thirty-Four

LIAM RACED through the late-night streets of Manhattan, pursued by a lovestruck monster. The creature, which measured ten feet from the tip of its scaly tale to the rounded snout of its head, was visible to all.

Residents who'd fled their homes in the night of 132 fires turned, gawked, shot videos, and uploaded them to Facebook, Instagram, and Twitter.

Where they crowded in the streets, Liam screamed, "Out of the way!" as he raced toward the only destination he could think of. But from all his outings with the map the man in green had given him, he knew that to get from where he'd glamoured Queen May on Eighth Street, to Fort Tryon Park and the weeping tree where he'd left the Mist, was many miles north. He ran and shouted and wouldn't look back at the fire-spitting creature that hungered for him in all senses of the word.

He spotted a subway opening on the corner of Fourteenth and Seventh. He pictured the diagram on the map. *No, she'll follow. She'll kill, and not just me.*

His feet, clad in borrowed red sneakers, pounded the asphalt. *Faster, faster.*

While not the quickest of beasts, the salamander was engorged with magic, fairy fire, and love. She easily kept pace, her thoughts, like her mouth, not far behind. He tried to shut out her primitive pleas for him to stop, to turn, to be loved, to be eaten. *Love you, love you. Eat you. Eat you. Liam, Liam. Yummy, yummy in my tummy.*

Liam had not considered his body's incapacity to run for miles at a sprint. He'd never had to. In the Unsee he flew on the wind, and here there were subways, buses, and Charlie's red Ford. His legs burned, and blisters rubbed and popped on the balls of his feet and the back of his heels. He gasped as his lungs burned. *I must be strong.* He pictured Charlie breaking through that door, lifting him over his back, and waiting as he glamoured the little dog to jump through fire. Charlie on the beach, their hands joined. Tears clouded his vision as the beast's fiery breath nipped at his heels.

She's too close. At Twenty-Third Street, he zagged to the left, the location of the weeping mulberry like a beacon in his head.

Her thoughts, even over the sirens, pounded him.

Love you. Love you. Eat you. Eat you. Liam, Liam. Yummy, yummy in my tummy. Yummy, yummy, tummy, tummy.

Fear of failure, fueled by his body's growing exhaustion, tortured him. *At least I told him I loved him. He knows it was not a glamour. I love you, Charlie Fitzgerald.*

"*Liam!*"

Not stopping, he heard Charlie's voice shout at him. *I'm sorry, Charlie. I failed you. I failed... us.*

"*Liam, behind you!*"

He dropped his pace, and bouncing on the balls of his shoes, he turned and saw two things—salvation and death. To the left, coming fast, was the gamboling beast with the light of love in her flaming eyes. But passing her on the right was Charlie in his red Ford, with Finn at his side and Nimby fluttering in the windshield.

The truck drew past him. Finn opened the front and rear doors of the double-row supercab.

"Get in!"

They slowed, and Finn held out his hand. "Come on, Liam."

Liam grabbed Finn's wrist. He stumbled. The redhead gripped him tight and pulled hard. Liam jumped and was hoisted into the backseat, winded but alive.

At seeing her love and her prey disappear into the truck, the creature howled, reared back, and hurled herself at the Ford. Her jaw clamped onto the rear bumper. Her front legs dug vicious holes into the sides of the metal bed as her rear limbs clawed asphalt.

Charlie floored the accelerator. The tires spun. The air filled with the smells of fairy fire and burned rubber.

Liam stared at Charlie from the back. The firefighter's jaw was tight as he gunned the motor. Their eyes connected in the mirror.

"She's too strong."

"But she's stupid," Liam said. "She's broken. You're smarter, Charlie. You can do this."

Charlie nodded. "Buckle up! Now!"

Liam and Finn strapped in as Charlie slammed on the brakes.

The creature didn't let go but wasn't expecting that or what came next.

Charlie threw the truck into reverse. The heavy vehicle smashed back into the love-starved salamander.

Reflexively, its jaw unhinged and clamped hard onto the flatbed. Steel crunched and plastic cracked.

"Crap!" Changing directions, Charlie gunned the engine, and with a giant white salamander devouring his truck like a python chowing down on a rat, he flew down Twenty-Third Street. His rear tires *whomp*ed and *thump*ed as she bent the axle.

"Where we going?" he shouted.

"North," Liam gasped, his lungs not trained for multimile sprints. "Fort Tryon Park. There's a tree with leaves that scrape the ground. It's where I came back."

"Okay." He turned up Eighth. With one eye on the road and the other on Liam in the mirror, he asked. "You hurt?"

"No. You?"

"Right as rain. Finn?"

"Ducky," the redhead deadpanned. He twisted in his seat, his attention on the creature devouring the back of Charlie's truck. "Can you shake her?"

Before Charlie could respond, the right rear tire blew. The truck lurched and bounced as the rubber tore free from the rim.

Charlie gritted his teeth, and not slowing, he swerved left onto Forty-Fourth. The pickup fishtailed with the salamander stuck tight, her jaws working their way through steel and plastic. The left rear tire blew.

With his eyes on the road, he spoke. "Back there, when she told you to kill me. You said you loved me."

Liam looked into the rearview mirror. "Yes, Charlie. I do. I love you, and I'm sorry."

"Stop it! This is not your fault. If we get out alive, it's because of you and what you did. I love you, Liam. And here's the deal. I don't care if you worked some magic on me or are even still doing it."

Bare metal sparked as Charlie ran the red and took a hard right onto the Joe DiMaggio Highway. "Before Saturday, I didn't think I'd ever love anybody. And then you saved a little dog. And… it's not how you look, and yeah, you're hot, and so far out my league. But here it is, Liam Summer. I love you because you're smart and funny and stupid and crazy brave. And Finn, stop smirking."

"No smirking here, Charlie boy. Just praying this wreck holds out till we get to… crap, I can't even deal. But go on. You were declaring your love… and if I wasn't scared shitless, this is the most beautiful thing I've ever heard."

"Right. Liam, I love you. End of story. Or beginning of story, if we don't get killed." Charlie floored the accelerator. The rear axle dropped dangerously close to the road.

The salamander's unhinged jaw spewed smoke as it worked its way down the flatbed, separating the truck's body from the chassis.

In the backseat, Liam watched, horrified and fascinated, as the creature drew closer to the cabin's rear window. Down her gullet he saw fairy fire tear through and melt the metal. He heard her thoughts. *Love you. Love you. Eat you. Eat you.* Dangerous ideas floated to mind. *If I give myself to her now, would she leave them alone?* He reached for the latch on the rear window, which separated the cab from the flatbed.

"Don't!" Charlie said. "Finn, stop him!"

"How could you know what is in my head?" Liam asked, his hand on the plastic latch.

Charlie grew frantic. "Please. Stop! I know you, Liam Summer. I love you. And we're both going to make it through or go down together. I will not lose you. Do you understand? Do not run from me."

"Yes," he said, set to release the latch, push the glass aside, and hurl himself down her fiery throat. *Would that stop her? Would she let them go? Would she let Charlie live?*

Charlie tore his eyes from the road and saw what Liam intended. "Finn! For the love of God, stop him!"

Finn unbuckled, climbed over the back of the seat, and grabbed fast to Liam's middle. "Don't do it, guy."

The two of them startled as the creature's rasping tongue licked the glass of the rear window. Flames sparked from its forked tongue as it *tap-tap-tap*ped and cracked the pane as they passed under the George Washington Bridge.

"Hang on!" Charlie shouted as he swerved across three lanes and shot up the entrance to Fort Tryon Park.

Centrifugal force pulled the creature back, but not for long.

As the partially devoured truck struggled up the steep hill to the Cloisters, she was back at the glass.

"Which way?" Charlie shouted.

Liam pulled back, aware that somehow Charlie and his wonderful truck had done the impossible. *I know this place.* He spotted the bike path and imagined where it connected to the tiny deer trail that led to the weeping tree. Now it was up to him. *I am going to die, but maybe, just maybe....* "Stop the truck!"

Charlie slammed on the brakes, and before either he or Finn realized what was happening, Liam yanked open the rear door and raced into the night.

WITH ONLY moonlight to guide his steps, he ran up the bike path, his eyes glued to the dense foliage, his ears attuned to the beast as she abandoned her tasty truck and gave chase.

Love you. Love you. Eat you. Eat you.

His heart sank as he ran and ran. *Did I miss it? Is it somewhere else? Where is it?* In the silvered light, he caught a deeper dark in the hedge. He shot for it, and with branches catching in his hair and tearing at his arms, he hurtled through the thicket, the toes of his shoes catching in roots. He stumbled and clutched branches to keep from falling. *Please, please, please.*

Behind him, the love-hungry beast smashed through the undergrowth. *Love you. Love you. Eat you. Eat you.*

But there were other sounds, above the distant sirens and the ravenous thoughts of the broken queen. He heard Charlie and Finn... and frogs. Thousands of frogs and crickets and birds. Like a symphony in front of him, leading him forward. The sounds of another world fanned the dangerous whiff of hope. He barreled over the last twenty yards of the dirt path and emerged in the clearing. The moon flooded down onto the massive mulberry. *It's here!*

He screamed into the night as he raced across the clearing, the white salamander in pursuit. "Charlie Fitzgerald, I love you. Do not follow me. If you truly love me, do not!" He heard music from within the tree and the pounding of the beast inches behind him.

It nipped, hot and wet, at his ankle. With all he had left, he dove into the tangle of limbs.

"I love you, Charlie Fitzgerald."

As the crazed beast leaped after him, her mouth, with its razor-sharp teeth, clamped around his ankle.

Love you. Love you. Eat you. Eat you.

The pain, more than anything he'd experienced in his life as the bones in his leg cracked, did not lessen his moment of exaltation. *I have done what was asked of me. She is alive, and she is broken. I have known love. I am ready to die.*

Thirty-Five

LIAM AWOKE on his back in the roiling blue-gray splendor of the Mist. He heard and felt the howl of the beast and the rattle of chains. He scrambled onto his elbows. "I am not dead."

Charlie, in T-shirt and black pants with the bumblebee stripes, lay unmoving and curled at his side. For a horrible few moments, he thought the worst.

"No, we're not dead." Charlie sat up, faced Liam, and ran a hand through his hair. Unbidden, he kissed him.

"I am dead," Liam said, his breath hot between them. "I am, and this is heaven."

Charlie pressed his forehead against Liam's. "Not heaven, but close. You're alive. You have all your pieces, thanks to Lizbeta. Though know that I'd love you in any form."

"The creature had my leg." His hands played over his knee and down to the ankle. He pulled up his pant leg and remembered the pain. "Tell me, Charlie…." There was an angry red stripe around his shin, the imprints of her teeth like a dotted line around the limb.

Charlie's words choked. "I tried to pry her off. We both got sucked in here. We've been here before," he stated. His fingers entwined in Liam's hair.

Reality crashed down, his curiosity about his salvaged limb suddenly unimportant. *No!* His hand played over the sides of Charlie's face. Like a doctor inspecting a patient, he sought for subtle, or not so subtle, breaks. Did he gain a pair of horns? His ears still looked human. He stroked the stubble of his cheeks and ran a finger between Charlie's beautiful lips, fuller from the kissing. "Your teeth haven't changed."

"I'm not broken, Liam." And he returned the favor. Less about looking for defects and more about needing to feel every inch of him.

Liam nestled into the embrace. "You might be mad."

"True. But no crazier than before I met you…. No, that's not true. I am crazy. I see fairies, and I'm in love with the bravest, most beautiful man in three realms." He inhaled the smell of Liam, his strength, the singe in his hair and on his clothes. He whispered into his ear, feeling his stubble against his cheek. "I love you."

The white salamander howled from the Mist. Its feet hammered the ground as sparks lit the Mist in lightning flashes of orange, blue, and white.

Liam scanned in her direction, expecting her to emerge and come after him. For once fully glamoured, the results were irreversible… save for death.

"Lizbeta," Charlie whispered.

Liam's head swiveled from the direction of the white beast to Lizbeta in a gown that sparkled and mirrored the Mist. She looked upon the two men fused in their embrace.

"You did not break your lover, Liam Summer. As to your leg, I used the magic you brought to make it right."

"I don't understand. I lost my magic when I first passed through. Most of it, at any rate."

"To every rule there must be an exception. You know this, and you know why. It's part of what balances the worlds. Think…. Your lover, your Charlie came through before, and he was not changed."

"That was a dream. There must have been an exception because it wasn't real."

Charlie interjected, "Liam, we had the same dream. And I kissed you, and you told me that I shouldn't. Even I know why I'm not changed and why you haven't changed this time around. I think I even know what magic you—we—brought in here."

"But I glamoured you."

Charlie's expression darkened. "Liam Summer, I, Charlie Fitzgerald, love you with all of my being. And because magic, while it may be twisty, does not lie, you must accept the truth. Our love, yours and mine, is not the product of deception. I don't know what more proof you want. But the only protection in the travel between realms is unconditional and reciprocated love. It protected me, and it protected you… and that was before the kiss."

The beast roared as Liam realized what Charlie and Lizbeta said was truth. He, Liam Summer, cat's-paw and whore to the queen, was loved… and not through a trick of magic.

A world with a future opened before his eyes as he rested in Charlie's arms. They'd live in his wonderful garage apartment on Staten Island. "You'll show me how to do flooring and siding. Apparently I can make money wearing expensive clothes and having people take my picture."

Charlie let Liam's words wash through him. "Liam…."

"Charlie."

"You got to stop running from me."

"I'm done running. We'll be together. We'll rebuild Mike and Katie Fitzgerald's home. We could get a dog… not a cat. Unless that's what you want."

Lizbeta listened. She cleared her throat. "It sounds wonderful, and yet… you two are needed. My sister is clever, and she is strong. You have defeated, truly defeated, but half of May. Liam, you were tasked with bringing back the information we need to end this. Tell me what you've learned."

"Of course." And they spelled out all that had been discovered from Gran's exploration of Katye's texts and from Alex, Jerod, and Nimby.

Lizbeta listened and nodded. "This is our story. A war that lasted a thousand years. May was our general, and she fell in love with theirs."

"The Hound," Charlie said. He looked at Liam. "That's what she called Finn."

"Tell me," Lizbeta commanded.

"My friend Finn. She had frozen us with some kind of spell. And she pointed and shouted, '*Hound.*' In the grand hoo-ha of things gone weird, it was low down on the list of what we just went through."

Lizbeta pondered. "The Hound broke my sister's heart. But more, she believes he robbed us… her, of our lands."

Liam spoke. "In one of the books was a drawing of the truce. May and the Hound, his hair as red as Finn's. Each signed a copy. That's where she was tricked."

"Not a trick. It was necessary," Lizbeta said. "Though May disagrees. After a thousand years of war, we knew that coexistence was impossible between fey and human. The treaty was essential, and it is binding. She means to undo it. Your redheaded friend, Finn. Tell me his full name."

"Hulain," Charlie said. "Finn Hulain."

Lizbeta stumbled. Her gown, which on closer inspection was lit by thousands of tiny fey, lost its shimmer. "It all comes full circle." She drew a deep breath and with nimble fingers wove an image in the Mist. The specter of a man with red hair and even features appeared. It smiled.

"That's kind of him," Charlie said. "Maybe a relative." He took in the much taller man with his flowing flame-red mane.

"Of course, though what his role in all of this can be, I do not know. But here's the way of magic, Charlie. Treaties, like spells, can only be undone by those who create them. Your friend Finn carries the blood of the Hound. My sister means to reunite the realms and rule over all, with magic and bloodshed beyond imagination. We have contained but half of her. To rule, she must be whole. To rule, she must destroy the treaty and the truce and make herself as one."

"What do you mean 'half of her'?" Charlie asked.

"Charlie Fitzgerald, you're new to our world, but careful with questions. They come at a cost. May split in two. It's how she slipped my collar. I should have been prepared. I am now. Half of her went to the See, and as we speak, the other half wreaks murder and havoc in the Unsee. She gains power as she gorges on the magic of her subjects. None are safe. It is a world in need of heroes. In need of you."

Held tight in Charlie's arms, Liam felt the weight of her words crush his dreams. "This is truth." He shivered and took comfort as Charlie's arms wrapped him tighter. "Tell me, Lizbeta, of Cedric, his Marilyn… their haffling son, Adam."

"In hiding. For yes, she means to take that child."

Charlie nodded. "It's what she did with Alex and then with his sister."

Liam watched the fantasies of a life with Charlie and his boisterous family vanish. "I will go," he said and tried to pull free from the strong arms that held him.

"No!" Charlie interjected. "Look at me, Liam. If you're going, I'm going. And while you might think that I run blind into burning buildings, I know what I'm doing. We got lucky this time. If she's been snacking on magic folk, what we're about to face needs a plan… and reinforcements."

He kissed Liam's temple. "A dead hero is no hero. We do this together." Not taking his eyes from Liam, he addressed Lizbeta. "We will help, but we need to gather strength. Alex and Jerod will come, and there may be others able to make the trip."

Lizbeta nodded. "Yes, return to the See. I will keep this door open and await your return. You have saved one realm this day. I wish it were enough. So take a week, but any longer will see her too powerful. Or worse, she will find Adam Nevus. In which case all of our efforts will have been for naught, as she will again cross into the See and devour all who would stop her. She will find the blood of the Hound. She will not stop until the treaty and the truce are dissolved."

Charlie took Liam's hand, and they stood. "Let's get out of here. I'm taking you home."

Liam knew he should be frightened; he wasn't. "Strange."

"Tell me," Charlie said.

"I'm not afraid."

"It'll come."

"It's not that…. I've lived with fear my entire life. I'm not brave like you, Charlie." He squeezed Charlie's hand, puzzled by the emotions in his heart and the lightness in his chest.

"You are brave." Charlie turned into him, their noses touching. "It's not about fear, Liam, but what you do with it. You faced yours, over and over again. You are brave, and you are mine, and for as long as you will have me, I am yours."

"Then I'll have you forever."

They kissed. And when the kiss was done, they were no longer in the Mist but in the bower of a weeping tree, serenaded by a symphony of frogs, birds, crickets… and sirens.

CALEB JAMES is an author, member of the Yale volunteer faculty, practicing psychiatrist, and clinical trainer. He writes both fiction and nonfiction and has published books in multiple genres and under different names. Writing as Charles Atkins, he has been a Lambda Literary finalist. He lives in Connecticut with his partner and four cats.

Website: charlesatkins.com
Blog: calebjamesblog.wordpress.com
Facebook: www.facebook.com/Caleb-James-536765356387453

The Haffling: Book One

All sixteen-year-old Alex Nevus wants is to be two years older and become his sister Alice's legal guardian. That, and he'd like his first kiss, preferably with Jerod Haynes, the straight boy with the beautiful girlfriend and the perfect life. Sadly, wanting something and getting it are very different. Strapped with a mentally ill mother, Alex fears for his own sanity. Having a fairy on his shoulder only he can see doesn't help, and his mom's schizophrenia places him and Alice in constant jeopardy of being carted back into foster care.

When Alex's mother goes missing, everything falls apart. Frantic, he tracks her to a remote corner of Manhattan and is transported to another dimension—the land of the Unsee, the realm of the Fey. There he finds his mother held captive by the power-mad Queen May and learns he is half-human and half-fey—a Haffling.

As Alex's human world is being destroyed, the Unsee is being devoured by a ravenous mist. Fey are vanishing, and May needs to cross into the human world. She needs something only Alex can provide, and she will stop at nothing to possess it… to possess him.

www.dsppublications.com

BOOK ONE IN THE DARK BLOOD SAGA

DARK BLOOD
CALEB JAMES

Dark Blood Saga: Book One

Handsome, brilliant, and surrounded by good friends, twenty-three-year-old medical student Miles Fox has a secret—and it's not that he's gay. Though he harbors a crush on his straight best friend, Luke. Miles, like his grandmother, Anna, possesses the healing gift, an ability she's made him swear never to use or divulge, lest horrible things befall those he loves. It happened to her when Nazis butchered her family.

But it all goes to hell when Miles heals a terminally ill man on a New Orleans cancer ward and wakes locked in the psych unit. Worse, news of the healing miracle spreads. For millennia, its carriers have been hunted by those who would steal it. Dr. Gerald Stangl and his teenage son, Calvin, know what Miles possesses. They, like their predecessors, will stop at nothing to take it, including kidnapping, torture, and murder. As the Stangls' noose tightens, Miles and Luke are trapped in a death match with stakes higher than they could ever imagine.

www.dsppublications.com

For more
great fiction
from

DSP PUBLICATIONS

visit us online.
WWW.DSPPUBLICATIONS.COM

Made in United States
Orlando, FL
22 March 2026

79557634R00134